CAT T

"If you've followed the adventures of Joe Grey and Dulcie through the years, you certainly won't want to miss this latest adventure. On the other hand, if you have never read any of these novels, isn't it about time you tried one?"
The Californian

"Cat lovers and fans of cozy mysteries will truly enjoy this whodunit."
Ventura County Star

AND PRAISE FOR THE OTHER
JOE GREY MYSTERIES BY NINE-TIME
WINNER OF THE CAT WRITERS'
ASSOCIATION MUSE MEDALLION

SHIRLEY ROUSSEAU MURPHY

"Joe Grey is a savvy, cool cat."
Albuquerque Journal

"An irresistible mix of riveting action and purr-fectly marvelous two- and four-footed characters."
Monterey County Herald

"Try the Joe Grey series.... It is entertaining to see cat behavior from the inside out."
Houston Chronicle

"Excellent . . . The combination of interesting human characters and cats with human characteristics ensures that these Joe Grey mysteries will stay popular for many years to come."
Tampa Tribune

"Delightful entertainment. It would be a true cat-tastrophe if you let it pass you by."
Todd David Schwartz, CBS Radio

PRAISE FOR
TELLING TALES

By Shirley Rousseau Murphy

SHIRLEY ROUSSEAU MURPHY

CAT BEARING GIFTS

A JOE GREY MYSTERY

AVON

An Imprint of HarperCollinsPublishers

AVON BOOKS
An Imprint of HarperCollins*Publishers*
10 East 53rd Street
New York, New York 10022-5299

Copyright © 2012 by Shirley Rousseau Murphy
ISBN 978-0-06-180724-4
www.harpercollins.com

First Avon Books mass market printing: September 2013
First William Morrow hardcover printing: December 2012

Avon Trademark Reg. U.S. Pat. Off. and in Other Countries, Marca Registrada, Hecho en U.S.A.
HarperCollins® is a registered trademark of HarperCollins Publishers.

Printed in the U.S.A.

10 9 8 7 6 5 4 3 2 1

*For the cats who remember
their previous lives
in centuries passed and gone*

There is a Celtic belief that cats' eyes are the windows through which human beings may explore an inner world. In examining the power that the cat has to raise our feelings and to stimulate our imagination we can hardly fail to learn more about human nature in the process . . . The cat has not only been thought of as wholly good or evil, but has also been recognized as forming a bridge between the two. [Cat] has the power deeply to enrich our lives if, instead of obsessively loving or hating [him], we adopt a realistic attitude towards its paradoxical nature, and allow it to communicate its wisdom.

— PATRICIA DALE-GREEN, *Cult of the Cat*

CAT BEARING
GIFTS

1

THE CONFUSING EVENTS that early fall in Molena Point began perhaps with the return of Kate Osborne, the beguiling blond divorcée arriving back in California richer than sin and with a story as strange as the melodies spun by a modern Pied Piper to mesmerize the unwary. Or maybe the strangeness started with the old, faded photograph of a child from a half century past and the memories she awakened in the yellow tomcat; maybe that was the beginning of the odd occurrences that stirred through the coastal village, setting the five cats off on new paths, propelling them into two forgotten worlds as exotic as the nightmares that jerk us awake in the small hours, frightened and amazed.

The village of Molena Point hugs the California coast a hundred and fifty miles below San Francisco harbor, its own smaller bay cutting into the land in a deep underwater abyss, its shore rising abruptly in a ragged cliff along which Highway One cuts as frail as a spider's thread. Maybe the tale commences here on the narrow two-lane that wanders twisting and uncertain high above the pounding waves.

It was growing dark when Lucinda and Pedric Greenlaw and their tortoiseshell cat left their favorite seafood restaurant north of Santa Cruz. Lucinda had carried Kit to their table hidden in her canvas tote, the smug and purring tortie curled up inside anticipating lobster and scallops slipped to her during their leisurely meal. Now the threesome, replete with a good dinner and comfortable in their new, only slightly used, Lincoln Town Car, continued on south where they had reservations at a motel that welcomed cats—an establishment that even accommodated dogs if they didn't chase the cats or pee on someone's sandals.

They'd departed San Francisco in late afternoon, Pedric driving, the setting sun in their eyes as it sank into the sea, its reflections glancing off the dark stone cliff that soon rose on their left, towering black above them. The Lincoln took the precipitous curves with a calm and steady assurance that eased Lucinda's thoughts of the hundred-foot drop below them into a cold and churning sea. In the seat behind the thin, older couple, tortoiseshell Kit sprawled atop a mountain of packages, her fluffy tail twitching as she looked far down at the boiling waves, and then looked up at the dark, wooded hills rising above the cliff against the orange-streaked sky. The trip home, for Kit, was bittersweet. She loved the city, she had loved going around to all the exclusive designer's shops, riding in Lucinda's big carryall like a spoiled lapdog, reaching out a curious paw to feel the rich upholstery fabrics and the sleekly finished furniture that Lucinda and Pedric had considered. She loved the city restaurants, the exotic foods, she had rumbled with purrs when they dined grandly at the beautiful old Mark Hopkins Hotel, had peered out from her canvas lair secretly amusing herself watching her fellow diners. Part of her little cat self hadn't wanted to leave San Francisco, yet part of her longed to be home, to be back in her own village with her feline pals and her human friends, to sleep at night high in her own tree house among her soft cushions with the stars bright around her and the sea wind riffling the branches of her oak tree. Most of all, she longed to be home with her true love.

It had been a stormy romance since the big red tomcat showed up in Molena Point nearly seven months earlier, when he and Kit had first discovered one another, on the cold, windy shore. Pan appeared in the village just two months after Christmas, right at the time of the amazing snowstorm, the likes of which hadn't been seen in Molena Point for forty years—but the likes of that handsome tomcat, Kit had never seen. Almost at once, she was smitten.

Oh, my, how Pan did purr for her, and how nicely he hunted with her, letting her take the lead, often easing back and letting her make the kill—but yet how bold he was when they argued, decisive and macho and completely enchanting. Even as much as she'd loved San Francisco, she felt lost and small when she was parted from him. *Why can't I be in two places at once, why can't I be at home with Pan and Joe Grey and Dulcie and Misto and our human friends,*

*and have all the pleasures of San Francisco, too, all together in
the same place? Why do you have to choose one instead of the
other?*

In the city, the Greenlaws had hit every decorators'
showroom of any consequence, thanks to their friend, interior designer Kate Osborne, who had unlimited access
to those exclusive venues. How fetching Kate had looked,
ushering them into the showrooms, her short, flyaway
blond hair catching the light, her green eyes laughing as
if life were a delicious joke, and always dressed in something creamy and silky, casual and elegant. Kate's scent of
sandalwood blended deliciously, too, with the showrooms'
aromas of teak and imported woods and fine fabrics.

Lucinda and Pedric had made wonderful purchases
toward refurbishing their Molena Point house. Ten new
dining chairs and five small, hand-carved tables were
being shipped down to the village, along with a carved
Brazilian coffee table, three hand-embossed chests of
drawers, and six lengths of upholstery fabric that were
far too beautiful for Kit to ever spoil with a careless rake
of her claws. The bundles of fabrics and boxes of small
accessories filled the Lincoln's ample trunk and wide
backseat, along with the Greenlaws' early Christmas
shopping, with gifts for all their friends; Kit rode along
atop a veritable treasure of purchases—to say nothing
of even greater riches hidden all around her, inside the
doors of the Lincoln where no one would ever find them.

They had stayed with Kate in her apartment with a
grand view of the bay where, lounging on the window-
sills, Kit could watch San Francisco's stealthy fog slip in
beneath the Golden Gate Bridge like a pale dragon glid-

ing between the delicate girders, or watch a foggy curtain obscure the bridge's graceful towers as delicately as a bridal veil. But best of all were their evenings before the fire, looking out at the lights of the city and listening to the stories of Kate's amazing journey: tales that filled Kit's dreams with a fierce longing for that land, which she would never dare approach. Kate's adventure was a journey any speaking cat would long to share and yet one that made Kit's paws sweat, made her want to back away, hissing.

In her wild, kitten days, she would have followed Kate there, down into the caverns of the earth, and she would have ignored the dangers. But now, all grown up, she had learned to be wary, she no longer had the nerve to race down into that mysterious land, overwhelmed by wonder. Now only her human friend was brave enough to breach that mythical world with a curiosity at least as powerful as Kit's own.

It was just last June that Kate had phoned her Molena Point friends to say she had quit her job in Seattle and moved back to San Francisco. But then, after that one round of calls, no one heard from her again. Their messages had gone unanswered until two weeks ago when, in early September, she resurfaced and called them all, and this time her voice bubbled with excitement. She spoke of a strange journey but left the details unclear, she talked about a gift or legacy, a sudden fortune, but she left the particulars vague and enticing.

Now, Kit, safe in the backseat as Pedric negotiated the big Lincoln down the narrow cliff road, idly watched the white froth of waves far below glowing in the gathering night. She sniffed the wind's rich scent of kelp and dead sea creatures and she thought about the wealth that Kate had brought back, treasures Kate insisted Lucinda and Pedric share—as if gold and jewels were as common as kitty treats or a box of chocolate creams to pass around among her friends.

Though Kate made sure the Greenlaws took some of that amazing fortune back with them to Molena Point, she had in fact already sold much of the jewelry, traveling from city to city—Seattle, Portland, Houston—taking care that she wasn't followed, telling the dealers the most plausible of stories about her many European visits where, she said, she'd acquired the strange and exotic pieces. Though the gold coins she'd insisted on giving to the Greenlaws were common enough, she'd had them all melted down and recast into the tender of this world, they could be sold anywhere without question. "No one has followed me," Kate said, "no one has a clue. If anyone did, don't you think they'd have come after me by now? Someone would have broken into my apartment weeks ago, or intercepted me on my way to a bank or getting off a plane. And now," she'd said with a little smile, "who would suspect a respectable couple like you of carrying a car full of jewels and Krugerrands?"

Kate and Pedric together had removed the Lincoln's door panels, using special tools, one that looked like a fat, ivory-colored tongue depressor, and a long metal gadget that might pass for a nail puller or a bottle opener. They had tucked twenty small boxes into the empty spaces, taping them securely in place so they wouldn't rattle or become entangled in the wires and mechanisms that ran through the inner workings of the car. Pedric was as skilled in these matters as any drug smuggler, though his lawless days were long past. Kate said the coins were theirs to use any way they chose, and Lucinda suggested the village's cat rescue project, which the cats' human friends had organized early in the year to care for the many pets that had been abandoned during the economic downturn, cats and dogs left behind when their families moved out of foreclosed homes. There was enough wealth hidden in the car to build a spacious animal shelter and still leave a nice buffer for the Greenlaws, too, against possible hard times to come.

"I've seen what can happen," Kate said, her green eyes sad, "when a whole economy fails. That land, that was so rich and amazing . . . all the magic is gone, there's nothing left but the ugliest side of their culture, all is fallen into chaos, the castles crumbled, the crops dead, the people starving. Everyone is drained of their will to live, not even the wealth I brought back was of use to them. What good is gold when there's nothing to buy, no food, nothing to trade for? People wandering the villages scavenging for scraps of food, but with no desire to plant and grow new crops, no ambition to begin new herds or bring any kind of order to their ruined world. All their richly layered culture has collapsed, they are people without hope, without any life left in them. Without," Kate said, "any sense of joy or of challenge. Only the dark has prevailed, and it feeds on their hopelessness."

Now, as night drew down, fog began to gather out over the sea, fingering in toward the cliff as if soon it would swallow the road, too. As they rounded the next curve, Kit could see, far below, the lights of a few cars winding on down the mountain—but when she looked back, headlights were coming toward them fast, truck lights higher and wider than any car, racing down the narrow road. Then a second set of lights flashed past that heavy vehicle, growing huge in their rearview mirror, then the big truck gained on the pickup again, accelerating at downhill speed, the two vehicles moving too fast, coming right at them, their lights blazing in through the back window, blinding her. The truck swerved into the oncoming lane, passing the pickup, its lights illuminating the rocky cliff—then everything happened at once. The truck and pickup both tried to crowd past them in the left-hand lane, forcing them too near the edge. The truck skidded and swung around, forcing the pickup against the cliff, their lights careening up the jagged stone. At the same instant the cliff seemed to explode. Pedric fought the wheel as an avalanche of dirt surged down at them. Kit didn't understand what was happening. Behind them great rocks came leaping down onto the truck and a skyful of flying stones skidded across their windshield. She thought the whole mountain was coming down, boulders bouncing off the pickup, too, and on down toward the sea. Pedric crashed through somehow, leaving the two vehicles behind them. The stones thundering against metal nearly deafened her, a roar that she knew was the last sound she'd ever hear in this life.

And then all was still; only the sound of the last pebbles falling, bouncing across their windshield and across their dented hood.

2

VICTOR AMSON'S OLD gray pickup raced too fast down the steep two-lane, its bare tires squealing around the curves, its headlights glancing off the stony cliff, following the taillights of a big produce truck, drawing close on its tail. The truck driver swerved onto a turnout at the sheer edge of the drop, impatient for him to go on past. As Vic swung into the oncoming lane, he could see the round-faced driver giving him the finger. Prickly bastard. Moving on around him, Vic smiled, grateful that nothing was coming up the hill; though the narrow, winding road didn't bother him. Beside him, his passenger was hunched way over to the center, his eyes squeezed shut with fear. Didn't take much to scare Birely.

Once Vic was free of the truck he sailed right on down the mountain, driving one-handed, his tall, wiry frame jammed in behind the wheel, his lined face catching light from the dash in a cobweb of wrinkles, a thin face, narrow nose, his pale brown eyes too close together. Worn jeans and ragged windbreaker, rough, callused hands. Long brown hair streaked with gray, hanging down, caught on the back of the seat, loosely tied with a leather band. He drove scowling, thinking about those three cops in their patrol cars watching him when he came out of that fence's place.

The damn fuzz might not have been on his case at all but they sure as hell made him cranky, their marked units parked there in front of the Laundromat that the fence used as a front. That had made Birely fidget, too. Birely'd wanted to ditch the truck to get the cops off their trail, steal another car on some backstreet and then hit the freeway, he said they both should have had haircuts, that shaggy hair always set a cop off. Suspicious bastards, he said, and he was right about that.

Having passed the truck, Vic was coming down on a big sedan, shiny black in the wash of his headlights, maybe a small limo, its red taillights winking on and off as it negotiated the winding road, its headlights sweeping along the ragged cliff. When his lights hit it right, he could see a lone couple in the front seat, and what looked like a small dog perched up in the back. On past it, farther down the steep grade, occasional taillights winked, gearing down the steep curves, maybe trucks hauling their loads to one of the small coastal towns that stood like warts down there along the marshy shore. The truck behind gained on him again. Birely went rigid as a fencepost, glancing back, trying not to look down over the steep drop, his faded brown eyes turned away, his bony hands nervously clutching at his worn-out leather jacket that he'd probably picked up at some rescue mission. They had, until they hit the mountain road, been passing the bottle of Old Crow back and forth, but now, when Vic offered the bottle, Birely shook his head, glancing sideways toward the hundred-foot drop and scooting over even tighter against the middle console, his fists tight whenever their old tires let out a squeal. Made Vic wonder why the hell he'd linked up with Birely again after all these years, the guy was a total wuss, always had been. Scared of his own shadow, clumsy, always out of sync with what was going on around him, a real screwup.

Years back, when they were younger and ran together some, any time Vic had something profitable going, Birely managed to screw it up. Every damn time. Make a mess of it, blow the plan, and they'd end up with nothing for their trouble but maybe a night or two in the slammer.

He'd finally dumped Birely, didn't see him for years. Until three months ago, he'd run into him again. That was just after he'd confiscated this current pickup truck from a ranch yard north of Salinas, slapped on different license plates courtesy of a roadside junkyard, bolted on an old rusted camper shell he found dumped back in the woods. As he headed over to the coast, it had started to rain when he ran into Birely outside a 7-Eleven when he stopped for beer. Birely sat huddled on a bench out in front, under the roof that sheltered the gas pumps, sat eating one of them dried-up package sandwiches, and you'd think they were long-lost brothers, the way Birely went on. Bastard was broke, and happy as hell to see him.

Birely said he was headed over to the coast because his sister had died, how he'd read it in the paper. He still had the clipping in his pants pocket, all wrinkled up. Going on about the house she'd left to some stranger instead of to him, when he was her only family, how it ought to be rightfully his. How he meant to confront this woman who'd supposedly inherited Sammie's worldly goods, and how Sammie'd had a stash of money hidden away somewhere, too, way more than just a few hundred bucks, and he wanted to know what had happened to that. Listening to Birely's tale, Vic decided he was glad to see the poor guy after all, decided he'd give his old friend a lift and maybe help him out some. He knew that area pretty well, Molena Point and back up the valley, he'd used to grow a little weed back up in the hills there, break into a few cars now and then, never anything big time, and never did get caught.

Birely'd told him Sammie'd been shot to death, if you could believe it, her body buried right there under her own house. That hurt Birely, but mostly it was the loss of an inheritance, the loss of Sammie's love and confidence, that she'd leave everything to a stranger, that made him mad at the whole damn world. He didn't seem so much mad at the killer as he was mad at Sammie for getting herself killed and for leaving him nothing.

Birely needn't fret that the cops wouldn't find Sammie's killer, they'd already done that, the guy was doing time right now up at Quentin, some local Realtor there in Molena Point killed her, and that was a long story, too.

Well, the house she'd lived in wasn't much, but more than Birely'd ever had or wanted, until now. Sammie's death seemed to change him—he was Sammie's only family, but look how she'd gone and done him, she'd even made a regular will, leaving the big lot with its two small houses to, "Some woman friend of hers," Birely'd whined. "I'm her own kin. Why would she do me like that, leave it all to this Emmylou Warren? I met that woman once or twice when I came that way up the coast, stopped to see Sammie, just some dried-up old woman, nothing special about her. Who could be so special, over Sammie's own brother?"

"Maybe Sammie thought you wouldn't want a house," Vic had said, "being a hobo and all. You always said you couldn't stand to live under a roof, to be fenced in, you always said that."

"Maybe. But there's more than the house, there's the damn money, I never said I wouldn't want the money, I just never thought about her dying. Well, the newspaper didn't say nothing about no money, just a will leaving the property. Maybe," he said, frowning, "maybe this Emmylou Warren don't know about that."

"Where'd your sister get money?" Vic had said, watching Birely as alertly as a rattler onto a mouse.

"Old uncle left Sammie a wad. Even after all these years, she still had half of it, she told me that's what she lived on. Except for those times she worked at some job, housecleaning, bagging groceries. She was real tight with money. Told me she still had over half of it hidden away different places, right there in the damned house. Old bills left over from the middle of the last century. She never did like banks. Our old uncle, he stole it but she never would tell me much about that. Well, hell, she was just a girl when the old guy sent it to her, mailed it to her in a box, for Christ's sake, from somewhere in Mexico."

It was such a wild story Vic wondered if Birely'd made it all up, a pie-in-the-sky daydream because he wanted there to be money and maybe because he wanted a reason to be mad at Sammie. That would be like him, mixed up sometimes between what was real and what he thought was real. But hell, whatever was in the poor guy's head, what could it hurt to take pity on him and go have a look.

They'd come on over to the coast, got to Sammie's place, got a glimpse of the old woman who'd inherited the property, living right there in Sammie's house. They'd watched her for a few days, while they lived in the truck, hidden back up in the woods or moving the old pickup around the winding village streets from one small neighborhood to another, sleeping at night in the rusty camper shell and, in the daytime, approaching the old woman's house on foot. They'd watched her for over a week, doing some kind of carpentry on the house during the day but she went to bed early, the lights would go out at eight or nine, and they never once saw her go up the hill through the woods, to the old stone cabin on the back of the property; she seemed to have no interest in the old abandoned two-story farm building that was on Sammie's land, shed underneath, one-room stone shack on top. Birely said Sammie hadn't had much use for it, either, just left it there overgrown with bushes. Said the land was plenty valuable, if she ever needed more money she could sell it but she never had.

Late one night they'd moved into the stone shack when Emmylou was sound asleep, house all dark, and they didn't make a sound, didn't use a flashlight. Vic had picked the old lock, and had jimmied the padlock on the shed, too, hid the truck in there, fixed the lock back so it looked untouched, still hanging rusty against the peeling paint of the old, swinging shed door.

The single stone room had maybe been workers' quarters back in the last century, when there were mostly little scraggy farms up here. At some time, rough planks had been fitted up against the bare stone walls, nailed onto two-by-fours, most likely for warmth. Stained toilet and old metal sink in one corner. Stone floor, cold as hell under their sleeping bags.

It was some days before Birely, lying in his sleeping bag staring at the plank walls, said, "Money could be up here, where no one'd think to look. Maybe Sammie didn't leave Emmylou *all* of it, maybe she left some for me to find, in case I wanted to come looking. Sure as hell she didn't put it in any bank, she got that from Uncle Lee, he *robbed* banks. He told her, never trust your money to a banker. As little as she was, maybe nine or ten when he left for Mexico, I guess she listened." Birely shrugged. "Sammie lived all her life that way, hiding what she earned and hiding what Uncle Lee sent her. Lived alone all her life, stayed to herself just like the old man did, never got cozy with strangers—until this Emmylou person."

There were no cupboards in the stone shed to search, no attic, no place to hide anything except maybe in those double walls. They'd started prying off one slab of wood and then another, putting each back as they worked. Used an old hammer they'd found in the truck, had muffled the sound with rags when they pulled the nails and tapped them back in real quiet, moving on to the next board, and the next. Underneath the boards, some of the stones were loose, too, the mortar crumbling around them—and sure as hell, the fifth stone they'd lifted out, behind it was a package wrapped in yellowed newspaper. Unwrapped it, and there it was: a sour-smelling packet of mildewed hundred-dollar bills. Birely'd let out a whoop that made Vic grab him and slap a hand over his mouth.

"Christ, Birely! You want that old woman up here with her flashlight, you want her calling the cops?" But nothing had happened, when they looked out the dirty little window no lights had come on down at the house below.

"Hell, Vic, there's a fortune here," Birely said, counting out the old, sour-smelling hundred-dollar bills.

Took them several days to examine all the walls. They'd found ten more packets, and made sure they didn't miss any. They came away with nearly nine thousand dollars. But even then, Birely said that originally there'd been maybe two hundred thousand in stolen bills, and he'd looked down meaningfully toward the larger house.

Over the next weeks, whenever they saw the old woman get in her old green Chevy and head off into the village, they'd go down through the woods and search the house, and that tickled Birely, that he still had his key to the place, that Sammie'd given him years back, in case he ever needed a place to hide out from the law or from his traveling buddies.

While they searched her three rooms they took turns watching the weedy driveway so the old woman wouldn't come home and surprise them. Emmylou Warren was her name. Tall, skinny. Sun-browned face and arms wrinkled as an old boot. Long brown hair streaked with gray. She had a couple of cats, maybe more, there were always cats around her overgrown yard and going in and out of the house.

They'd see her drive in, watch her unload lumber that was tied on top the Chevy, all the while, cats rubbing against her ankles. Birely said, "You think that's Sammie's money she's spending for all them building materials? Or," he said, his face creasing in a knowing smile, "or did Sammie only *tell* her about the money, tell her it was hid, and she's looking for it?

"Sammie would do that," he said. "Not put anything in writing to keep from paying inheritance. Sammie didn't like the gover'ment any better than she liked banks.

"*That's* why she's tearing up the walls," Birely said, scowling at the nerve of the woman. "Tearing them up just like we're doing, and it's rightfully my money."

"If she's *found* any," Vic said, "why's she driving that clunky old car? I'd get me a new car, first off. And if she *is* looking for the money, why would she have help coming in, those two carpenters that are here sometimes, and that woman carpenter? She wouldn't have no one else around. That dark-haired woman's a looker, I wouldn't mind getting to know her better." Slim woman, short, roughed-up hair. Fit her faded jeans real nice. He'd heard the old woman call her Ryan, she drove a big red king cab, her own logo on the side, Ryan Flannery Construction. Pretty damn fancy. Well, hell, Vic thought, she was likely too snooty to give him a second look.

He did meet a little gal down in the next block, though, and she wasn't too good for him. Debbie Kraft, flirty little gal with two small children, both girls, light-fingered woman not too good to steal, neither, he soon found out.

They burned no lights in the stone house at night, and

didn't cook none, or warm up their food. Just opened a can of cold beans, kept a loaf of bread handy and maybe doughnuts. He missed hot coffee. Even in the hobo camps they boiled coffee. And they didn't drive the truck, just left it hidden in the shed below and hoped she'd stay away from there. If they needed beer and food they'd walk up the hill through the woods and then down the next street to the village. Carried out their trash, too, dropped it in a village Dumpster, in one alley or another, always behind a different restaurant. Fancy place like Molena Point, even the Dumpsters were kept all neat and covered.

They'd kept on slipping down to the house whenever Emmylou went out, searching where she was starting a tear-out, fishing back between the studs, but then one night she came up the hill snooping around the stone house. They were inside sitting on their sleeping bags eating cold beans and crackers, they heard her come up the steps, saw her through the smeared window, and they eased down out of sight. They were sure she'd have a key, but she didn't come in. They'd stayed real still until they heard her leave again, her shoes scuffing on the steps, heard her rustling away down through the bushes, heard her door open and shut.

They'd waited a while after her lights went out, feeling real nervous. They'd opened the shed door real quiet, shoved some food and their sleeping bags in the pickup, with what money they'd found, hoping she wouldn't hear the pickup start. Had eased up the dirt lane and around through the woods, and moved on away from there. Had parked for the night way up at the edge of the village beside an overgrown canyon. Had waited until dawn, then had made a run back down near Emmylou's place, where Vic tended to a deal he'd made with Debbie Kraft. Had picked up some goods he'd told her he'd sell for her up in the city and some fancy, stolen clothes. A nice stroke of luck, when he'd seen Debbie and her older child shoplifting, and had got the goods on them. A nice little deal he'd set up with her: he'd make the sale and take his share, and not turn her in to the cops. He'd met with Debbie, picked up the goods, and then headed for the city. Let Emmylou think they were gone for good—if she ever *was* onto them living right there above her.

They were gone a week up the coast, boosting food from a mom-and-pop grocery or a 7-Eleven, and they'd gone on into San Francisco, where he'd made the business transaction. That turned out pretty good, except for the damn cops sitting out in front, there. Well, hell, the goons hadn't followed them, maybe it was just coincidence, maybe they were watching someone else.

He'd made a bit of cash off that, and who knew what other arrangements he might make with Debbie. Now, headed back down the coast to the stone shack, he hoped the old woman had settled down and they could finish looking for the money. Vic was daydreaming about what he'd do with that kind of cash, when the produce truck he'd passed came roaring down right on their tail, its lights so bright in his mirror he couldn't see the road ahead. Swearing, he eased over to let it pass. Truck hauled right down on them, riding their bumper. Let the bastard tailgate that big sedan up ahead, it was moving too damn slow anyway. That was what was holding him up, some rich-ass driver in that big Lincoln Town Car—one more curve, he was right on top of the Town Car, and the damn truck was climbing his tail. Swearing, he pulled over, pushing the big sedan closer to the edge. "Go on, you bastard!" Why the hell didn't the guy driving the Lincoln step on the gas, get on down the grade? Vic drew as close to the edge as he could to let the truck pass, tailgating the Town Car, then pulled toward the left lane. But the truck shot past him, rocking his truck, kicking up gravel, shaking the road with a hell of a rumble, and its headlights made the cliff look like it was moving—well, hell, the cliff *was* moving, rocks falling, bouncing across the road. He stood on his brakes but couldn't stop. The whole mountain was sliding down. The Town Car shot past, rocks thundering down across its tail. A whole piece of the mountain was falling. The big truck skidded, Vic smashed into its side and into the cliff. The front end of his pickup crumpled like paper, squashed against the bigger bumper. The passenger door bent in against Birely like you'd bend a beer can, Birely struggling and twisting between the bent door and the crumpled dashboard. Pebbles and rocks rained down around them. The produce truck lay turned over right in his face, one headlight striking off at an angle, catching the rising dust, its other light picking out the black Town Car on the far side of the rockfall, where it had plowed into the cliff. That light shone into the interior where the driver and passenger were slumped, and picked out through the back window the eerie green glow of a pair of eyes, he could see the animal's tail lashing, too, and realized it wasn't a dog, but a cat. Who would travel with a *cat*! A damn cat, its eyes reflecting the lights of the wrecked truck where it peered out, watching him.

3

 VIC COULDN'T OPEN the truck door, it was bent and jammed. The passenger side was pushed in, trapping Birely against the dash. Birely lay moaning, his face and neck covered with blood, reaching out blindly for help. The big delivery truck lay on its side among the fallen boulders, Vic's pickup crumpled in against the roof of the truck's cab, its right front fender jammed deep against its own wheel. Well, hell, the damn thing was totaled, was no use to him now.

But when he looked off across the rockfall at the Lincoln, it didn't look too bad. Looked like it had missed most of the slide, rocks and rubble thrown against it and scattered across the hood, but he could see no big dents in the fenders to jam the wheels, and the hood and front end weren't pushed in as if to damage the engine. The couple inside hadn't moved.

Reaching under the seat for the tire iron, he used

that to break out what remained of his shattered window. Knocking the glass away, he crawled out and swung to the ground. Stepping up onto the unsteady heap of rocks, trying not to start the whole damned mountain sliding again, he worked his way around to the other side of the pickup, to have a look.

Birely didn't look good, sprawled limp and bleeding across the dash. Poor Birely. So close to finding the rest of his sister's money, and now look at him. What kind of luck was that? Vic thought, smiling.

Vic's one working headlight shot into the big truck's cab, casting a grisly path onto the driver. He lay twisted over the wheel, his head and shoulders half out the broken window, his throat torn open by a spear of metal from the dashboard, his blood coursing down pooling into the window frame. Dark-haired guy, Hispanic maybe. No way he could be alive with his throat slit. Vic turned his attention again beyond the fall of rocks, to the black sedan nosed in against the cliff. As the door of the Town Car opened, he stepped back behind the turned-over truck, out of sight.

The driver's forehead was bleeding. Vic watched him ease out of the car, supporting himself against the open door. The minute his feet touched the ground his right leg gave way. He fell, pulled himself up, stood a moment, his weight on his left leg, then tried again, wincing. Tall old man, thin. White hair. Frail looking. Easing out of the car on his left leg, clinging to the door and then to the car itself, he moved painfully around to the back of the car, making his way on around to the far side, to the woman.

He stood beside her, reaching in, clinging to the roof of the car. She was as thin as the man, what Vic could see of her. She sat clutching the cat to her, mumbling something. The man reached past her into the glove compartment, found a flashlight and held it up, looking at her, and then looking at the cat, studying it all over, giving it more attention than he gave to the woman; but he was talking to the woman, mumbling something Vic couldn't hear over the crashing of the sea below. The man spoke to the cat, too, spoke right to it, the way someone'd speak to a pet dog. People made asses of themselves over their dogs. But a cat, for Christ's sake? He watched the old man flip open a cell phone. Speaking louder, now, the way people did into a phone, as if they had to throw their voices clear across the damn county. He was talking to a dispatcher, giving directions to the wreck. Hell, here he was, the truck no use to him, smashed too bad to get him out of there, and the damn cops on the way.

The old guy had turned, looking across the rock slide toward him, but Vic didn't think he could see him, there behind the truck. Guy told the dispatcher, "Nothing stirring over there. I'll have a look, see what I can do. Yes, I'll stay on the line."

He spoke to the woman again, dropped the phone in his pocket, and started limping across the rock slide. He turned back once, to the woman, his voice raised against the pounding of the surf. "You sure you're okay?" She nodded, then mumbled something as he moved on away. The old guy negotiated the rock pile half crawling, his white hair and tan sport coat caught brightly by the truck's one headlight. But Vic's attention was on the Town Car, on the big, heavy Lincoln. A car like that could take a lot of abuse. Even with deep dents and dings from the slide, it looked like it would move right on out and with plenty of power to spare.

Easing back around to the pickup, where the old guy crossing the rocks couldn't see him, Vic pulled the plastic bag of money out from under the seat and stuffed it inside his shirt. He didn't speak to his passenger; Birely was pretty much out of it, close to unconscious, gasping as if he wouldn't last too long. Vic watched the old man approach, balancing precariously, the pain showing in the twist of his long face. He moved on past Vic, never seeing him, and as he scrambled and slid down the unsteady boulders, Vic eased closer in behind the camper, hefting the weight of the tire iron. The old guy paused at the turned-over delivery truck, stood looking in at the dead driver. Shook his head and moved on, to the pickup. He still didn't see Vic until Vic stepped out into the truck's headlight, holding the tire iron low against his leg. The old man looked him over, took in the tire iron, and glanced into the cab of the pickup. "Your friend needs help."

"Best let him be," Vic said, "best not move him."

The old man nodded, watching him. "My wife's hurt. I called 911, ambulance is on its way. They'll both have help. I've got to get back to her, I think her arm is broken. You have any flares? I have two, I can set them down the road, at that end."

Vic didn't say anything. He nodded and stepped closer. The man was lean and, despite his look of frailty, Vic could see now that he was wiry, tightly muscled. He wore his white hair short, in a military cut, ice pale against his tan. The old guy was quick, he saw Vic's intention—the instant Vic swung the tire iron he lunged, grabbing for it despite the hurt leg.

But his timing was off, Vic stepped aside, hit him a glancing blow across the head. When he tried to break his fall, clutching at loose rocks, Vic kicked him hard. He went flat, didn't move again, lay bleeding onto the blacktop. Stepping around him, Vic saw Birely looking out at him, helpless and pleading.

He'd thought to leave Birely, the guy was already half dead, but some stupid softness touched him, he couldn't leave the dumb bastard. "Hoist yourself out of there, Birely." He didn't wait to see if Birely *could* get out, he headed on past the old man, who was bleeding bad now, past the turned-over truck and across the rockfall toward the Lincoln. He heard Birely struggling behind him, groaning as he tried to free himself. Hell, he wasn't jammed in there that tight, he could get out if he tried.

Approaching the driver's side of the Lincoln, Vic saw that the bumper was knocked loose on one end. It wasn't low enough yet to drag and make a racket, he'd find something to tie it in place. He didn't see much else wrong, he just hoped to hell the other side wasn't bashed in or that the other wheel wasn't bent. The passenger door hung open, the interior lights on. The woman sat holding her left arm, the damn cat still in her lap. He could see the keys in the ignition. He stood by the hood, watching her, holding the tire iron low and out of sight.

KIT WATCHED HIM approach, the thud of his steps timed to the rhythm of the breaking waves. He paused by the hood of the car, and frantically she nudged Lucinda, her nose against Lucinda's ear. "Get out," she whispered, "get away. Now, Lucinda! Move!"

Slowly Lucinda climbed out, unsteady on her feet, shaking her head as if to clear it, cradling her hurt arm.

"Hurry," Kit hissed.

"I can't, I can't move faster."

The man stood watching. *Can he hear me?* Kit thought. *So screw him.* "You can!" she hissed, her fur bristling. "*Run, Lucinda. Run!*" her voice more hiss than whisper.

He stepped to the car, blocking Lucinda. Lucinda grabbed Kit with her good hand, catching her breath with the pain. She twisted awkwardly, threw Kit as far as she could, out toward the rock slide. "Run, Kit! Run!" Kit landed on rubble, spun around and leaped atop the car. Lucinda had turned, reaching in. She backed out holding the big flashlight where he might not see it. When he grabbed for her, she swung.

But again he was faster, he snatched her hand, jerked the flashlight from her, shoved her down against the fallen rocks. Kit leaped on him, landed in his face clawing and raking him. Lucinda rose awkwardly, turned, kicked him in the shin then in the front of the knee. He swung the tire iron hard across her shoulder, shoved her down again as Kit rode his back, clawing. He grabbed her by the scruff of her neck, swinging her out away from him. When she bit down hard on his arm, he threw her against the car. She tried to run, but staggered dizzily. Sick and confused, she backed away among the fallen rocks. He was a hard-muscled man, his arms brown and knotted and tasted unwashed. Long hair hanging down his back, dishwater brown, a short scraggly beard oozing blood where her claws had raked. Ice-blue eyes, cold and pale. He had moved around the Lincoln to the driver's side when, across the slide, she heard a car door open.

The passenger in the pickup staggered out. A small man with short brown hair, his face and plaid shirt slick with blood, his nose running blood. He came slowly across the rock pile, stumbling uncertainly, breathing through his mouth, wiping at the blood that ran from his nose. The man with the tire iron got in the Lincoln. "Get a move on, Birely." He started the engine, gunned it, paying no attention to Lucinda sprawled so near the front wheels. His friend stumbled on across, falling on loose rocks, clutching at the larger boulders, stepping over Lucinda as if she were another rock. Edging around the Lincoln, he crawled awkwardly into the passenger seat. The driver pushed the engine to a roar. Kit ran to Lucinda, Lucinda grabbed her and rolled away as he backed around narrowly missing them. He took off in a shower of rocks, heading fast down the mountain on the twisting two-lane.

ALONE AMONG THE wreck with only a dead man to keep them company, Kit and Lucinda huddled together trembling with rage. Against the rhythm of the waves came the metallic ticks of the two wrecked trucks, settling more solidly into the highway. From higher up the mountain among the pine forest, a lone coyote began to yip.

"Cops will be here soon," Kit said, "and an ambulance."

"I'm fine," Lucinda told her. "Go to Pedric. Go and see to Pedric." Her color was gray. She held her left shoulder unnaturally, and her left arm hung limp. Kit pressed a soft paw against Lucinda's wrinkled cheek, pressed her face to Lucinda's jugular, listening. Lucinda's heartbeat was too rapid, faster even than Kit's own feline rhythm. She pawed into her housemate's jacket pocket, careful not to touch Lucinda's arm or shoulder, searching for Lucinda's phone. It seemed forever ago that Pedric had called 911, but she couldn't hear even the faintest sound of sirens down on the flatland, could see no flashing emergency lights below approaching up the two-lane, no one to help them. The shushing of the sea, with its eons-old assurance that all was well, that all of importance in the world would last forever, didn't comfort her much. She thought about a car coming down the mountain from above moving too fast as those trucks had done, the driver ignorant of the wreck ahead, not yet seeing the lone and disembodied headlight shooting up the rock slide. How far could such a light *be* seen, on that curving road? With no flares to mark the wreck, would an approaching car stop to help or would it crash into them? She found the phone, and before she raced to Pedric, she hit the key for 911.

She had no notion where central dispatch was located for these small coastal towns north of Molena Point, and she didn't know if they could track a cell phone. Some areas could, and some didn't have that equipment. When a woman dispatcher came on, Kit gave directions as best she could. She said Pedric had called earlier but that no one had come. She was so afraid of another car plowing into them that she was nearly yowling into the phone, her frightened words not much better than the scream of a common alley cat. "Hurry! Oh, *please hurry* . . . They've stolen our car, a black Lincoln Town Car, could you watch for it? Put out a BOL on it? Two men in it, one hurt bad." She described the men as best she could, all the while thinking about the treasure hidden in the doors of the Lincoln, wondering how soon the thieves would find that. The wealth was of no consequence, compared to her hurt housemates, but it enraged her to see it stolen. Clicking off, she stood looking down the highway wondering if, alone, she could drag Lucinda off the road and up among the boulders, safe from an oncoming car? Drag Pedric up, too, get them both higher up, away from further danger? When the dispatcher asked for her name, she said, "Lucinda Greenlaw. My husband's hurt, the man who took our car beat him." When the dispatcher told her to stay on the line, Kit laid the phone down, set her teeth firmly in Lucinda's jacket on her unhurt side, and began to pull. She *could* do this, she *had* to do this. Maybe the loose rocks beneath Lucinda would serve as a kind of rolling platform. Straining to get Lucinda up onto them, she fought as she had never fought, every muscle of her small cat body taut and stretched, crying out, her paws scrabbling for traction until her pads tore and became slick with blood that made her slip and slide. Lucinda tried to help, tried to roll with her, tried twice to get up but fell back, sweating with pain.

"Go to Pedric, Kit. You can't move me. Let me rest, then we'll try again. Maybe easier, once I've rested. Go help Pedric. Is he bleeding? Can you stop the blood?"

Kit licked Lucinda's face, her own face wet with tears, then headed fast across the rock slide, praying for the gift of strength, knowing that if she couldn't move Lucinda, she couldn't move Pedric, either, only knowing that she had to try, that she had to help them.

4

IF EVER KIT cursed her small size it was now as she raced across the slide to Pedric. Diving under the twisted delivery truck, its metal cab tilting over her, loose rocks shifting under her blood-slippery paws, she heard the coyote yodel again, high above her, and then go ominously still. Pedric lay in a pool of blood beside the crumpled pickup, his forehead running blood. Hesitantly she pressed her paw against the gash where it flowed hardest, telling herself that head wounds always bled a lot. Soon she was pressing with both paws, with all her weight, but still the blood pooled warm beneath her pads, mixed with her own blood. She tried not to think of the billions of cat germs she was sharing with Pedric, that might harm him, and about the gravel her paws had collected, that would become embedded now in his open wounds. He was conscious, but only barely, whispering vague little love words to her. The only other sounds in the empty night were the tick, tick of the settling vehicles, the voice of the waves far below, and the dripping of some liquid nearby that she prayed wasn't gasoline. Well, she didn't smell gas, so maybe it was oil or water.

Her paws grew numb with the pressure, but soon the bleeding did ease, and when the coyote yipped again she wondered if he smelled Pedric's blood on the rising sea wind. Pedric said, "Don't let me sleep, Kit, keep me awake. I need to stay awake." He talked vaguely about a concussion, then rambled on from one subject to another that had no connection to what was happening at that moment. When he went silent she nudged him and made him talk again. Once, as she shifted her weight over him, he startled and tried to rise, looking around fearfully as if expecting another blow from the tire iron.

"He's gone, those men are gone. Lie still."

"Lucinda? Where's Lucinda?" he said, pushing her aside, straining to get up.

"She's fine," Kit lied, trying to press him down. "She's only hurt a little, she . . ." She went still, listening, her heart quickening. She could hear, far down the mountain, the faintest echo of sirens whooping, she heard that thin ululation long before Pedric did. "They're coming," she said, "the cops, an ambulance." Rearing up, she could see lights flashing far down the mountain, red and blue lights disappearing around the curves and appearing again, accompanied by the approaching *whoop whoop* and scream of emergency vehicles that put the coyote's cries to shame. Now Pedric heard them, and he lay back, dragging her onto his chest, hugging and loving her.

But soon again he rose on one elbow looking past the

turned-over truck, searching for the reflection of the Lincoln's lights that had been angled up the cliff, lights that would mark the wreck on the other side, for the approaching cars to see. "Lucinda," he said, struggling up. "They won't see her. I left the lights on . . . Did she shut them off?" He rose further, looking. "Where . . . ? Kit, where's the Lincoln?"

She looked at him, puzzled. Hadn't he seen and heard the Lincoln drive away? "It's gone," she said softly. "They took our car, those men took it."

He struggled up, the blood gushed harder again. "*Lucinda. Where's Lucinda?*"

"She got out before they took the car, she's fine." She nuzzled him, but as the sirens drew near she spun and raced away again, under the cab of the big truck and across the rockfall. Surely they'd see Lucinda lying there. How could they help but see her? The sirens blared, approaching up the steep highway, soon their lights would blaze along the side of the cliff. But Lucinda seemed so small, lying there unprotected and alone. *In just a second they'll be here, the world will be filled with their bright, swinging lights, they'll see her, there'll be uniforms all over the place, they'll see Lucinda and help her and comfort her. They'll help Lucinda and Pedric, cops or sheriff's deputies or whoever come, they'll have spotlights, they—*

Oh, she thought, *but what will they do with me?*

Or try to do, if they could catch me?

They sure wouldn't take her in the ambulance, that was probably against the rules, to contaminate their germ-free rolling hospital with kitty fur and dander. Maybe they'd try to lock her in a squad car, drop her off at the nearest animal rescue to be kept "safe" in a locked cage until someone claimed her, like a piece of baggage lost at some lonely airport.

And, if no one claimed her soon enough, if no one thought to look for her there, what, then, would they do with her?

No way! No one's taking me *to the pound.*

She found Lucinda several feet higher up the rockfall than she'd left her, lying huddled into herself, the phone abandoned beside her, her face white with the effort it had taken to climb just that far. She licked Lucinda's cheek and nosed at her worriedly. She prayed to the human God or the great cat god or whoever might be listening, prayed for Lucinda, and then the cops were there, the flash of colored lights, the last whoop of the sirens, the powerful shafts of spotlights sweeping back and forth. Patrol cars skidded to a stop, cops spilled out, the flashing strobe lights blinded her, strafing the highway and the fallen rocks, picking out Lucinda and the two wrecked trucks. Lucinda clutched at her, attempting to hold her safe. Kit ducked beneath Lucinda's jacket, trying to decide what to do.

The thought of strangers' hands on her, even the kindest of cops, the thought of barred cages that she might not be able to open, of being locked in some shelter all alone, the thought of possible clerical mistakes where she'd be put up for adoption before anyone could come to fetch her, or consigned to a far worse fate, was all too much. Cops knew how to care for needful humans, but that might not extend to a terrified cat. Snatching up Lucinda's phone between her gripping teeth, she scrambled out from under the jacket and ran.

"Oh, Kit, don't . . ."

She didn't look back, she fled straight up the cliff, dodging between rivers of sweeping light, gripping the heavy phone; it nearly overbalanced her as she scrambled up the sheer wall of stone. Only tiny outcroppings offered a claw hold until, higher up, an occasional weed or stunted bush kept her from falling. The phone grew heavier still, forcing her head away from the cliff. Twice she nearly fell. Scrambling in panic, she veered over into the rock slide where she had more paw hold, though the rocks were wobbly and unsteady. Moving up over the loose stones and boulders, she was afraid the whole thing would shift and go tumbling again, hitting her and raining down on Lucinda, who lay now far below her. Higher and higher she climbed, dodging away whenever a slab shifted, breathing raggedly around the phone through her open mouth, her heart pounding so hard that at last she had to stop.

High up on the lip of the slide, she laid the phone down on a stone outcropping. Below her, portable spotlights blazed down on Lucinda and two medics in dark uniforms knelt over her. Two more medics, one carrying a stretcher, the other carrying a dark bag that would be filled with life-saving medical equipment, were headed across the slide to Pedric. Young men, strong and efficient looking. The very sight of them eased her pounding heart.

Where will they take them? What hospital? I have to tell Ryan and Clyde, but what do I tell them? A hospital somewhere in Santa Cruz, that's where we were headed. They'll know the hospitals, they'll call CHP to find out, Ryan and Clyde will know where to come, and they'll come to get me, too, she thought, comforting herself. *But how soon? Soon enough, before those coyotes up there find me, soon enough to save my little cat neck?*

Maybe she should go back down, slip into the medics' van while they were busy, and the cops were all working the crash scene. She watched another set of headlights coming down the mountain on the other side of the slide, watched a lone sheriff's car park beyond the wrecked truck. A lone officer got out and started across to join the others. The back doors of the white van stood open. In a flash she could be down the cliff and inside, hiding among the metal cabinets and oxygen tanks and all that tangle of medical equipment. *I could hide in there close to Lucinda and Pedric and, at the hospital—a strange hospital, a strange town—I could hide in the bushes outside and watch the door and wait for Ryan and Clyde or maybe for Charlie to come, and then . . .*

Oh, right. And if those medics spot me in their van trying to catch a ride, they'll try to corner me in that tight space. If they shut the doors, and surround me, and I can't get out and one of them grabs me, what then? They'll lock me up somewhere, to keep me safe? One of the cops will shut me in his squad car? No, she was too upset and uncertain to go back. Taking the phone in her mouth again, she moved from the top of the slide on up into the bushes that stretched away to the edge of the dense pine woods, damp and dark and chill. There she laid the phone down among dead leaves and pine needles and pawed in the single digit for the Damens' house phone. Crouched there listening to it ring, she watched the lighted road below as the medics slid Pedric into their van, working over him, attaching him to an oxygen tank. Lucinda sat on a gurney as the other two medics splinted and taped her shoulder and arm. The phone rang seven times, eight. On the twelfth ring, she hung up. Why didn't the tape kick in? The Damens' answering machine, which stood upstairs on Clyde's desk, was so incredibly ancient it still used tape, but Clyde wouldn't get a new one, he said it worked just fine, you simply had to understand its temperament. *Right*, Kit thought, with a little hiss.

She tried Wilma Getz, but she got only the machine. Where was everyone? She left a garbled message, she said there'd been an accident, that she had Lucinda's cell phone, that it was on vibrate so the cops wouldn't hear it ring. She hung up, disappointed by the failure of the electronic world to help her, and worrying about Lucinda and Pedric. What might happen to them on their way to the hospital, some delayed reaction that would be even beyond the medics' control? Or what might happen *in* the hospital? If ever a cat's prayers should be heard, if ever a strong hand were to reach down in intervention for a little cat's loved ones, that hand should come reaching now. This was *not* Lucinda's or Pedric's time to move on to some other life, she wouldn't let it be that time. Punching in the Damens' number again, she was crouched with her ear to the phone when she realized that, down on the road, Lucinda had awakened and was arguing with the medics, her voice raised in anger. Kit broke off the call, and listened.

"You can't leave her, you must find her. If I call her, she'll come to me. I won't go with you, neither of us will, unless you bring her with us."

The two medics just looked at her, more puzzled than reluctant. The taller one said, "You can't find a runaway cat, in the dark of night, it'll be scared to death, panicked. No cat would—"

The dark-haired medic said, "We'll send someone, the local shelter . . ."

"No," Lucinda said fiercely. "I want her with us. You can't take us by force unless you want a lawsuit."

Oh, don't, Kit thought, *don't argue. Let them take care of you.* But then she realized that Lucinda, in her anger, sounded so much stronger that Kit had to smile.

But stronger or not, Lucinda didn't prevail. Kit didn't know what the medic said to her, speaking so quietly, but soon she went silent and lay back again on the gurney, as if she had given up, yet Kit knew she wouldn't do that. *She knows I'll call Clyde and Ryan,* Kit thought. *She knows I can take care of myself.* She watched them wheel Lucinda to the van, her tall, thin housemate straining up against the safety straps, trying to look up the cliff. Lucinda was so upset that Kit thought to race back down and into the van after all, but before she could try, before she knew what *was* best to do, they had shut the doors, two medics inside with Pedric and Lucinda, and the other two in the cab. The engine started, the van turned around slowly on the narrow and perilous road, and moved away down the mountain, heading for a strange hospital where no one knew Lucinda and Pedric, where there was no one to speak for them.

Two black-and-whites followed them. The other two sheriff's deputies remained behind, one car parked on either side of the rockfall. Kit watched them walk the road in both directions, setting out flares, and maybe waiting to meet the wrecking crew that would haul away the truck and pickup, maybe to wait for the tractors and heavy equipment that would arrive to clear away the tons of fallen rock from the highway.

When those earthmovers start to work, when they start grabbing up boulders with those great, reaching pincers—like the claws of space monsters in some old movie—I'm out of here. Again she punched in the Damens' number. *Come on, Clyde, come on, Ryan, will you please, please answer!* Crouched in the night alone, she looked behind her where the forest of pines stood tar-black against the stars. The coyotes were at it again, two of them away among the trees yipping to each other. *When the machines come to move the wrecked trucks and clear the road, I'll have to go higher up in the woods away from the sliding earth, I'll have to go in among the trees, where those night runners are hunting.* She looked up at the pines towering black and tall above her, and she didn't relish climbing those mothers. The great round cylinders of their trunks had no low branches for a cat to grab onto, only that loose, slithery bark that would break off under her claws. And what if she did climb to escape a coyote, only to be picked off by something in the sky, by a great horned owl or swooping barn owl? This was their territory and this was their hour to hunt. She thought of great horned owls pulling squirrels from their nests, snatching out baby birds with those scissor-sharp beaks. The world, tonight, seemed perilous on every side.

She called the Damens seven more times before Clyde answered. "We just got in. I guess the tape ran out."

A temperamental machine was one thing. A run-out tape was quite another. Now, on the phone, Kit didn't say her name, none of the cats ever committed their name to an electronic device. They might use man-made machines, but they weren't fool enough to trust them. Anyway, Clyde knew her voice. She pictured him in his study, his short brown hair tousled, wearing something old and comfortable, a frayed T-shirt and jeans, worn-out jogging shoes. She started out coherent enough, "Lucinda and Pedric are hurt," but suddenly she was mewling into the phone, a high, shrill cry this time, in spite of herself, a terrible, distressed yowl that she couldn't seem to stop.

"I'll get Ryan," he said with a note of panic. She heard him call out, and then Ryan came on, maybe on her studio extension. Kit imagined them upstairs in the master suite, Rock and the white cat perhaps disturbed from a nap on the love seat.

"What?" Ryan said. "Tell me slowly. What happened? Where are they? Where are you? *Slowly, please!*"

Swallowing, Kit found her sensible voice. She tried to go slowly, to explain carefully about the wreck and to explain where that was. But try as she might, it all came out in a tangle, the kind of rush that made her human friends shout, made Joe and Dulcie lay back their ears and lash their tails until she slowed, but she never *could* slow down. ". . . boulders coming down the mountain straight at us and I thought we'd be buried but Pedric hit the gas pedal and the Lincoln shot through and the whole mountain came thundering down behind us and when the slide stopped the road was covered with boulders and rocks and there was a pickup on the other side crashed into the mountain and into a big delivery truck lying on its side and the driver was dead and . . ."

"*Slow down*," Clyde and Ryan shouted together. Ryan said, "Tell us exactly where you are. Did you call 911? How badly are they hurt? *Did* you call the CHP? Where . . . ?"

"I called," Kit said. "They took Lucinda and Pedric

away and Pedric's head was bleeding and Lucinda was conscious sometimes but then she'd fade and I think her shoulder is broken and the medics took them in the ambulance and I was afraid to hide in there because if they found me they'd take me to the pound and take the phone away and I could never call you to say where I was and if I couldn't work the lock on the cage . . ."

"*Stop!*" they both yelled. "Where?" Ryan said patiently. "Where are you, Kit?"

"Somewhere north of Santa Cruz but south of Mindy's Seafood where we had dinner. When the tractor gets here and starts moving the boulders . . ." She wanted to say, I won't be able to yowl and cry out to you, there are coyotes up here and owls who can hear everything. She wanted to say, When I'm up in the woods I'll be scared to make a sound. She said, "Can you bring Rock? To track me? Joe can find me, but Rock's bigger and . . . and there are coyotes and I love you both but humans are no good at scenting . . ." And she prayed that, this one time, no one was listening in on her call.

"We'll bring Rock," Clyde said. "We're leaving now. Be there in an hour or less, with luck. Please, my dear, keep safe."

Kit hit the end button, feeling small and helpless. She wasn't a skittish cat, she'd spent plenty of black nights prowling the dark hills above Molena Point and farther away than that, hunting and slaughtering her own hapless prey, but tonight the wreck and her fear for her injured housemates, and then the hungry cry of the coyotes, had taken the starch right out of her. She thought about her big red tomcat traveling all alone down this very coast, making his way from Oregon down into central California, *Pan traveled all that way and he wasn't scared, so why should I be?* But she was. Tonight she was afraid.

Pan had come to Molena Point following little Tessa Kraft, nearly a year after Tessa's father threw the red tomcat out of the house. Tessa's mother didn't want him, either, she didn't like cats. Pan hadn't returned, but he had watched the household. He knew when Debbie Kraft moved to Molena Point, and he followed the family, tracking his little girl and, as well, looking for his own father.

He could only guess that Misto, when he vanished from Eugene in his old age, might have returned to the shore of his kittenhood where he'd grown up among a feral band of ordinary cats; no other speaking cat among them, that Pan knew of, but the place was Misto's kittenhood home. And Pan had been right, he had found the old yellow tomcat there, and he had found Tessa. *And he found me*, Kit thought. *That's where we found each other.*

Where is Pan now, right this minute? Could he be thinking of me and know I'm scared, the way he senses me when we're hunting, the way he knows where I am even when he can't see me? Or is he crouched in Tessa's dark bedroom, as he so often is, whispering to her, ready to vanish if her mother comes in?

Pan isn't scared of Debbie, but if she catches him there'll be trouble for Tessa. Probably right now he's whispering away and laughing to himself because Debbie doesn't have a clue that he's anywhere near Molena Point. But no matter how Kit tried to distract herself, thinking of Pan, all she could really think about was that she was all alone and scared clear down to her poor, bloodied paws.

5

 **IN THE LITTLE** wooded neighborhood below Emmylou Warren's house, the red tomcat was indeed crouched on Tessa's windowsill looking into the dark bedroom where she and her big sister slept head to foot in the one twin bed. The other bed was unoccupied. A light shone under the closed bedroom door, from the kitchen. When, approaching Debbie's ragged cottage, he'd looked in through the kitchen window, Debbie sat at the table sipping a cup of coffee, the dark-haired, sullen-faced young woman sorting through a stack of new purses and sweaters with the tags still dangling from them, items that he knew she hadn't paid for, beautiful clothes and gaudy ones laid out across the oilcloth as she clipped the tags from them.

At the bedroom window he reached a silent paw in, through a hole he'd made in the screen months before. Silently he flipped the latch and pulled the dusty screen open. Sliding in under it, he pushed the window casing up with infinite care and finesse so as not to make even the smallest sound and wake twelve-year-old Vinnie. Tattle-tale Vinnie, who would let her mother know at once that he had followed and found them.

Not even Tessa herself knew that he had arrived in Molena Point against all odds, like a cat in some newspaper story traveling across the country to follow his family. Pausing on the sill, at the head of the bed, he watched the two sleeping girls, listening for sounds from the kitchen. When he was sure that both children slept soundly, and that Debbie remained occupied sorting through her stolen bounty, he eased down onto Tessa's pillow, the tip of his red striped tail barely twitching.

He sat quietly watching her, the flicker of her dark lashes against her smooth cheeks, her pale hair tousled across the pillow. And softly, as she dreamed, he pressed his nose close to her small ear and began to whisper, to send gentle but bold words into the child's dreams, painting strong visions for her.

Tessa was only five, hardly more than a baby, and a silent one, at that, a timid little girl who seemed always fearful, never eager for life, a drawn-away, wary child. Perhaps only Pan knew how watchful she was beneath the shyness, how aware of what occurred around her. Few grown-ups ever saw Tessa smile or saw her reach out to embrace the bright details of life that so fill a normal child's world, few ever saw her pluck a flower from the garden, snatch a cookie from the plate and run, laughing, or tumble eagerly across a playground screaming and shouting. Tessa Kraft clung to the shadows, bowing her head at her moth-

er's voice, backing away from the overbearing tirades of
her sister. Her father wasn't there to stand by her, not that
it had ever occurred to him, even when he was home, that
Tessa might have feelings that he should nurture, fears
that he might have soothed and healed. Tessa's mother
didn't bother to explain about her pa going to prison, or
to help with her daughter's loss. Eric Kraft's final absence
from their home, which had begun long before his ar-
rest and sentence for murder, had left a deep hollowness
within the child that, Pan thought, nothing in her future
could ever erase. But he meant to try.

Since Tessa and her family had arrived in the village,
and then Pan had followed them there, the other four
speaking cats had come to know the child, too, and to
care about her, as had their human friends. Maybe only
they saw Tessa's hidden joy in life, saw the secret pleasures
that she so carefully concealed from the dominance of her
mother and sister. They watched and waited. They stood
by Tessa when they could, hindered by a tangle of legali-
ties specific to the human world, rules that no cat would
pay attention to.

But Pan, with his own goal clearly in mind, sought
to lead Tessa with his whispered suggestions, to slowly
strengthen and transform the silent little Cinderella into
a bold young princess. "Don't let their talk hurt you," he
told her over and over as she slept. "Inside yourself, you
can laugh at them. You are stronger than they are, that's
your secret. You are your own strong person, and you
never need to be afraid.

"You can be quiet and secret in your thoughts, but all
the while you can see the world clearly. You can be wary of

others but strong in yourself, and you will grow up stronger than they are. One day, you will pity their stubborn ignorance.

"You're little now, Tessa. But you grow bigger every day and already, on the inside, you're bigger than they are. You're stronger than they are, you have a wall of strength inside you that no one's meanness can hurt. Your mother and sister can't hurt you, they can't touch the part of you that's whole and bright and that loves the world around you."

As Pan whispered, reaching deep into Tessa's sleeping mind, he thought about his pa, too, and about that other little girl so long ago. That child far back in time who had also needed a special friend, the little girl Misto remembered from an earlier life among his nine cat lives.

How strange, Pan thought, the mirroring of father's and son's connections with the two little girls from two different times. Tessa here in this time. Misto's friend, Sammie, from sixty years past and from the other side of the continent.

How strange that Sammie, now dead, lay buried right here in this village, a continent away from where Misto had known her. Sammie Miller, found shot to death right there beneath her own house, that she had willed to Emmylou Warren. What a strange tale it was and a convoluted one, a saga of three generations, Sammie's part of it ending here, in this village.

It had been young Sammie Miller's photograph that had stirred Misto's memory of his earlier life, a picture that the yellow tomcat discovered when he visited Emmylou, a childhood picture that had drawn him back again and again to look at little Sammie, his visits generating a comfortable friendship with the old woman though he never spoke to her, he never breached the cats' secret.

The grown-up Sammie Miller, having no family but her wandering brother who could never stay in one place, had willed her cottage and the old stone building in the woods above to Emmylou. She told Emmylou more than once that Birely had no use for a house, that he preferred to travel footloose and free. Nice euphemisms, Pan thought, for a man with no ambition, for a drifter who let the world do with him as it would.

In the warm bed beside him, Tessa stirred suddenly and Pan drew back, crouching on the pillow. But the child only whimpered and turned over, dreaming. Often Kit came with him on his nighttime visits, she was his lookout, watching Debbie through the kitchen window, ready to hiss a warning if the woman rose and headed for the bedroom. But this night Kit was off up the coast with her humans, visiting the city. Or maybe they were already on their way home, after a week of shopping in what Kit said were "elegant stores that *smell* so good." How long it seemed, and how he missed her.

He had loved Kit since that first day he arrived in Molena Point, hitching the last leg of his journey on a tour bus, and then making his way through the small village to the sea cliff. Pushing through the tall, blowing grass above the sea, he'd seen the tortoiseshell hiding, watching him, her yellow eyes so bright with curiosity that even in that instant he knew that he loved her. Now he not only loved her and missed her but, as he crouched beside the sleeping child, his thoughts left Tessa suddenly and uneasily, the fur down his back stood stiff, his thoughts suddenly all on Kit. What was this shivering fear he felt, what was happening?

His ears caught no sound save Tessa's soft breathing, yet he heard Kit's silent cry. His fear made him abandon the child, sent him flying out the window knowing that Kit was in trouble, that she was afraid and alone. He sensed her crouched shivering in the black night and he was filled with her terror, he wanted to run to her but she was far away, she was in danger and far away and he had no way to find her or help her.

But maybe the disaster had already happened, he thought sensibly. Maybe he was feeling her fear from a moment already gone, maybe now she was safe. Maybe she and Lucinda and Pedric had already returned to the village, maybe he was feeling her residual fear telegraphed between them. Maybe if he raced up across the rooftops to her tree house he'd find her already there, safe and dreaming among her pillows. Willing this to be so, Pan scrambled to the roof and took off fast, racing through the night across the peaks and shingles, praying Kit was home and safe—but knowing, deep down, that she was not, that Kit was still in danger.

6

CROUCHED HIGH UP the rocky slide, having crept into a dark cavity between two jutting boulders, Kit shifted from paw to paw listening to the coyotes yipping back among the woods, and they sounded more focused now and intent. Nervously she watched the road below for the first glimpse of Clyde and Ryan's red king cab. Flares glowed along the narrow highway, those nearest to the slide reflecting sparks of light against the wrecked trucks. How lonely the night was, now that the medics had taken Lucinda and Pedric away. Who would look out for them and sign papers at the hospital, if Lucinda fainted from the pain of her shoulder, if Pedric passed out from the concussion? Who would make phone calls to their own doctor and to their friends, who would make sure that everything possible was being done to help them?

Ryan and Clyde will, she thought, trying to ease her worries. Down below her on the highway, even the two

CHP cars looked lonely, one parked to the north of the rock slide, one to the south. She could hear their police radios' static mumbling and could smell coffee from their thermoses, each man cosseted in his small electronic realm, maybe talking back and forth on their cell phones as they waited for the wreckers and then the earthmovers to come and clear the highway.

She thought about their nice new Lincoln—a used one, but new to them and the first car Lucinda and Pedric had bought in ten years. The Lincoln gone, with all their beautiful purchases for their home and for Christmas. And Kate's treasure gone. Those men had a fortune hidden in the door panels, but they didn't know that. Maybe they wouldn't discover what they'd stolen, she thought hopefully.

Or do they know? Somehow, in San Francisco, did they find out what Kate had, did they spy on her, and then follow us here, follow us down Highway One?

Not likely, she thought. *I'm letting my imagination run. But*, she thought, *will they, for some reason of their own, remove the door panels anyway, and find Kate's treasure there?*

Whatever they did, they were sure to root around in the glove compartment, find the car registration with Lucinda and Pedric's address, and they already had the house key, right there on the chain with the car keys.

But why would they go to Molena Point? They were probably headed miles away in the stolen Lincoln, maybe away from the coast where the cops might not be looking for them yet. Above her, the coyotes had eased nearer, through the trees, muttering among themselves. At a faint yip she crouched lower. They'd soon catch her scent, if they hadn't already, and come snuffling down among the rocks, hungry and tracking her.

If the beasts attacked, those two cops down there wouldn't help her. Why would they? A cat screaming in the night, they'd think it a wild cat, maybe hunting or mating, all a part of nature. All part of a world in which they had no call to interfere. How long before help *would* come, before she saw the lights of Clyde and Ryan's truck approaching up the road? It seemed forever since she'd called them. Hunkering down between the rocks, she stared up at the vast night sky, stared until the wheeling stars turned her dizzy, and made her feel so incredibly small. Tracing their endless sweep, she couldn't conceive of anything so huge that it went on forever.

What was *she*, then, in this vastness? Forgetting the innate cat creed that made each individual cat *know* that he was the center of all else, Kit thought, at that moment, that she was less than nothing, a speck of dust, a pinprick.

Except, I have nine lives to live, and that is not nothing.

And to a hungry coyote I'm something. I might be nothing in the vastness of time and space, but I'm something to those hungry mothers.

But then she was ashamed of her fear. *What if, right now, no one knew I was here, no one in all the world was coming to help me? What would I do, then? I've rambled all over on my own, I grew up alone without humans to help me, and ignored by the other clowder cats. I made out all right, then. I always outsmarted the coyotes, I didn't cower, then, shivering like a silly rabbit. So what's the big deal, now? I'll just hunker down here between the boulders where they can't reach me, and damn well bloody them if they try.*

But then she thought, *Maybe I have more to lose now. More than I did when I was a harebrained youngster wandering alone. Now I have Lucinda and Pedric, I have all my friends, cat and human, I'm part of the human world now, as I never dreamed could happen. And best of all, I have Pan. I can't die now in the mouth of some slavering predator, and lose what we have together.*

From the moment she'd spied Pan up on the cliffs, heading for the windy shore searching for his father, she'd never doubted they were meant for each other, never doubted it even if, sometimes, their arguing grew volatile. *We always make up*, she thought with a little cat smile, and making up was so nice. *No*, she thought, *I don't mean to check out of this world now, in the jaws of some slobbering coyote. Screw the damn coyotes.*

Listening with renewed disdain to the beasts' yodeling, she backed deeper down between the rocks where she could lash out in safety, where they, if they tried to reach her, would meet only slashing claws. Curling up in a little ball, she deliberately made herself purr, and in a more sensible feline mind-set she imagined herself, as was proper to a cat, the very center of the vast universe. *She* was the center of all time and all space, one small and perfect cat, the universe whirling around her in endless veneration. This was cat-think, even nonspeaking cats knew in their hearts this assurance, and it made her feel infinitely better. Soon she felt whole again. Sheltered deep down among the rocks, too deep for a prying nose or reaching paw, Kit smiled to herself, and she slept.

BUT TO **P**AN, tonight, the universe seemed unruly and fierce as he hurried from the last roof down a pine tree, and across the Greenlaws' dark yard. Scrambling up Kit's oak tree to her tree house, clawing up over the edge, he already knew she wasn't there, her scent was old, mixed with the aged smell of feathers from a bird she had consumed weeks ago. The high-roofed aerie was empty, its cedar pillars pale against the night, Kit's tangle of cushions abandoned, crumpled together and half hidden by browning oak leaves.

Looking back along the oak branches to the big house, he saw no light in any window. There was no sound, and no lingering whiff of supper. No faintest scent of exhaust from the empty driveway as if the Greenlaws had only now returned and perhaps already gone to bed, as if maybe Kit would be tucked up under the covers between them.

Maybe they're on their way. Maybe they stopped for supper along the coast, and will be here soon. Sand dabs and abalone, and Kit's making a pig of herself. Trying to reassure himself, he crept at last onto Kit's cushions. Burrowing among the leaves and pillows, he lay on his belly watching the street below, his whole body rigid with waiting and with his lingering sense of danger. He was so tense he couldn't rest; soon he rose again and began to pace, his heart filled with Kit's fear, his belly churning with her uncertainty and loneliness. He was pacing and fussing when the sound of leaves crumpled in the yard below by approaching paws brought his fur up, sent him peering over the edge, swallowing back a growl.

EARLIER THAT EVENING, two blocks up the hill from where Pan would spin his whispered magic for little Tessa Kraft, Joe Grey and Dulcie had slipped down through Emmylou's ragged yard, departing the stone shack. Over the past weeks, whenever they found its two scruffy occupants absent, they had searched the fusty room, pawing behind whatever boards the men had loosened, sniffing the old stone wall so long concealed there. Early on, when the men first moved secretly into the stone shack, the cats, spying through the dirty window, had watched them searching and had pressed their noses to the glass wondering what could be of such interest, wondering why two tramps would tear the siding from the walls, removing it board by board and digging into the concrete behind, lifting out loose stones. What were they looking for?

What the cats had found was the oily smell of money, old paper bills, sour with mildew, but no money was there now in those spidery recesses. From the size and shape of the concentrated scent, they were certain thick packets of old bills had lain there. Hidden away for how long? Looked like the men hadn't finished searching, one whole wall was still boarded over. The cats took turns, tabby Dulcie crouched on the windowsill watching the woods and the weedy driveway below, while Joe Grey sniffed and poked behind the loose boards, where rocks were loose or missing. Was this Sammie's money, that had been hidden here? Did Emmylou know about it? In the six months since she'd inherited the place and moved in, they'd never once seen her near the stone hut.

It was Dulcie who first discovered the men slipping down through the woods and into the stone house carrying two grocery bags, a loaf of bread sticking out. She had been sunning herself on Emmylou's roof, deeply absorbed in composing a poem, when their stealthy approach made her fur go rigid.

"They've broken in," she'd said to Joe later. "Emmylou can't know they're there, she doesn't go up there, she's said nothing to Ryan though Ryan has been helping her with the lumber for her renovation." They were about to pass the word, see that it got back to Emmylou through human channels, when Joe saw the men as he was hunting rats in the yard below. From the looks of the smaller man, and from descriptions he'd heard, he thought that was Sammie's brother.

"Why would he be so secretive?" Dulcie said. "Why wouldn't Emmylou welcome him, Sammie's own brother?"

"Let's wait a while, and watch them."

"But . . ."

"Emmylou's perfectly capable of taking care of herself," Joe said. "You've seen her swing that sledgehammer, breaking up those concrete steps." Emmylou was tall, well muscled, despite her slim build and gray hair. "Besides, when she talked about Birely she made him out a timid soul, easygoing. Not like someone who'd make trouble."

"Humans don't always see others truly," Dulcie said with suspicion. They'd waited and watched, and of course the minute the men went out, they'd tossed the place.

Not much to toss, in the one room. An overflowing trash bag, half a loaf of stale bread, seven cans of red beans, dirty clothes thrown in the corner beside a pair of sleeping bags that were deeply stained and overripe with human odor, the few boards that had not yet been nailed back against the rock wall, and five loosened stones lying beside them. But tonight, something was off, tonight the room seemed abandoned. The sleeping bags were in the same exact position as when they'd last come in, but the two greasy pillows and the extra blankets had been taken away, and when they prowled the room there was no fresh scent of the men, even their ripe smell was old and fading. The canned beans were gone, too, the only food was three slices of bread gone blue with mold in the package. Dulcie said, "Is their old truck still down in the shed?"

There was no way to tell except by smell, no way to see into the shed, not the tiniest crack in or under its solid door, which fit snugly into its molding. When they trotted down the steps to investigate, there was no recent scent of exhaust. Any trace of tire marks in the gravelly dirt had been scuffed clean by the wind.

"Maybe they're having a little vacation," Joe said, "hitting the homeless jungles for a change of scene. But why did they leave their sleeping bags?"

"I would have left them, too," Dulcie said with disgust.

Trotting down through Emmylou's weedy yard, they'd scrambled up to the roofs of the small old cottages in the neighborhood below. Leaping from house to house, trotting across curled and broken shingles, they'd moved on down the hill until Dulcie, quiet and preoccupied, left Joe, heading away home to her own hearth. To her white-haired housemate and, Joe suspected, to Wilma's computer. Watching her gallop away, her tabby-striped tail lashing, Joe knew well where Dulcie's mind was. The minute she sailed through her cat door she'd head for the lighted screen, where she'd be lost the rest of the night, caught up in the new and amazing world she'd discovered, in the secret world of the poet.

7

It was earlier in the year, during that unusual February that brought snow to the village, when Joe found Dulcie in the nighttime library sitting on Wilma's desk, the pale light of Wilma's work computer glowing around her. When Dulcie turned to look down at him, the expression on her face was incredibly mysterious and embarrassed. How shy she had been, telling him she was composing a poem; only at long last had she allowed him to read it, to see what she'd written.

The poem made him laugh, as it was meant to do, and within the next weeks Dulcie produced a whole sheaf of poems, some happy, some uncomfortably sad, and the occasional funny one that made Joe smile. His tabby lady had discovered a whole new dimension to her life, to her already amazing world. That's where she would be now, sitting before the computer caught up in that magical realm where Joe could only look on, where he was sure he could never follow. Where he could only be glad for her, and try not to mourn his loss, of that part of his tabby lady.

To Joe Grey, words and language were for gathering information and passing it along—and for making certain your humans knew when to serve up the caviar. But Dulcie used language as a painter used color, and the concept was nearly beyond him, the inner fire of such expression quite beyond his solid tomcat nature. How many speaking cats *were* there in the world, living their own secret lives? And how many of *them* had found their souls filled suddenly with the music of words, with a new kind of voice that Joe himself could hardly fathom? Contemplating such wonders of the mind and heart left him feeling strange and unsettled, like trotting along a narrow plank high aboveground and suddenly losing his balance, swaying out over empty space not knowing how to take the next step, a devastating feeling to the likes of any cat.

Joe took a long route home, thinking about Dulcie and trying not to feel left out from this new aspect to her life; but soon again his thoughts returned to the two tramps, to questions that as yet had no answers, and to the paper money they were surely finding, money old and rank with mildew. Who had hidden it there?

How long had it lain within those damp walls? That stone building was more than a hundred years old, it had stood there since the early nineteen hundreds, when it was an outbuilding for the dairy farm that had once occupied that knoll of land. Ryan and Clyde had spent hours in the history section of the Molena Point library perusing old books and photographs of the area, when they bought the little remodel just two blocks down from Emmylou, where Debbie Kraft and her girls were now living. Had the money been secreted there since the place was built, or had a subsequent owner, Sammie or someone before her, stashed it away in those old walls?

Emmylou might not know about that hidden stash, but he didn't understand how she could fail to know that two freeloaders were camping on her property, not fifty feet from her. Yet she didn't seem to have a clue. Misto visited her often, he was sure she thought the old place as empty as a clean-licked tuna can.

It was strange, Jesse thought, that when he talked about the missing money, Misto grew silent and withdrawn and a curious look shone in his yellow eyes. As if he knew something, or almost knew but couldn't quite put a paw on what was needling him. As if some long-lost memory had surfaced but wouldn't come clear, leaving the old yellow tom puzzled and uncertain. Strange, too, that Misto spent so much time with Emmylou, visiting her and prowling her house, almost as if he felt a tie to the property.

Or maybe a connection to the dead woman who had owned it? If there were memories here, if there was a story here, either Misto wasn't ready to share it or he didn't remember enough to share, maybe could recall only tattered fragments. But this, too, unsettled Joe. Fragments of memory from when? Sometimes Misto talked about past lives, and Joe didn't like that, he didn't buy into that stuff. Even if they *did* have nine lives, which no one had ever proven, what made a cat think he could remember them, that he could recall those faraway connections?

As he crossed a high, shingled peak, the scudding wind

hit him, thrusting sharp fingers into his short gray fur. Below him, the dark residential streets were black beneath the pine and cypress trees, only a few cottage windows showed lights, the soft glow of a reading lamp, the flicker of a TV. He was crossing a tiled ridge near Kit's house, just a block over, when he stopped and reared up, looking.

The windows of the Greenlaw house were all dark, with Lucinda and Pedric and Kit still in the city. There should be no one about, certainly there should be no creature prowling Kit's tree house among the oak branches, but there against the starry sky moved the silhouette of a cat pacing fretfully back and forth across the high platform, an impatient figure, an interloper prowling Kit's territory where no strange animal was welcome. Joe sniffed the air for scent but the sea wind was to his back, heavy with iodine and the smell of a rotting fish somewhere. Heading across the interceding rooftops, he slipped silently down to the Greenlaws' garden and then up again, up the oak tree to Kit's high, roofed platform, his fur prickling with challenge.

LIGHTS WERE ON at the Damens' house, upstairs in the master suite, lights silhouetting hurrying shadows against the shades, the commotion stirred by Kit's phone call as Ryan and Clyde hastily pulled on jeans, sweatshirts, and jackets, grabbed up backpacks, stuffing in flashlights, cat food and water, and the first-aid kit. Rock, the big silver Weimaraner, was off the love seat and pacing; he knew they were going on a mission and he couldn't be still.

The upstairs lights went off again, the stair light came on, then the porch light blazed as the three of them headed out for the king cab, Ryan locking the door behind them. Rock bounded past Clyde into the backseat, lunging from one side window to the other with such enthusiasm he rocked the heavy vehicle like a rowboat, staring out into the night looking hopefully for the first hint of his quarry and then poking his nose in Ryan's ear or against Clyde's cheek, urging them to hurry, demanding to be out on the trail tracking the bad guys. The sleek silver dog had no clue that tonight his target would not be an escaped convict armed and dangerous, but one small cat, frightened and alone, a quarry who, if at last he found her, would snuggle up to him purring mightily.

But even to find one small cat, a tracking dog needs a sample of his mark's scent, a clear and identifiable smell to follow among the millions of odors he'd encounter along the high cliff. "Pillows," Ryan said. "Stop by the Greenlaws."

"Pillows?" Clyde looked over at her, frowning.

"Kit's tree house. Her pillows. I brought a clean plastic bag."

"You're going to climb the oak tree?"

"Ladder," she said, glancing up at the cab roof where, above it, her long construction ladder rode securely tethered on the overhead rack. "Just take a minute, we'll have a nice, fur-matted pillow for Rock to sniff."

"If we had Joe, he'd put Rock on the trail. Where the hell—"

"Even with Joe," she said, "I'd want a scent article, as you're supposed to have, so as not to spoil Rock's training."

"The one time Joe might be of help," Clyde said, ignoring her logic, "he's off hunting. Or off with Pan whispering in that little kid's ear. Talk about an exercise in futility."

"If Pan can help that little girl, we ought to cheer him on. Scared of her mother, bullied by her sister. Besides, Joe might not even be with Pan. He and Dulcie have been hanging around Emmylou Warren's all week, around that stone building up behind, whatever that's about."

"I don't want to know what that's about. More trouble, one way or another."

Ryan just looked at him.

"Name one time Joe went off on some crazy round of surveillance that he didn't stir a carload of trouble."

"Name one time Joe wasn't leaps ahead of the cops," she said. "That he didn't drop valuable information in Max Harper's lap, a lead that Max was grateful for, even if he didn't know where it came from." She sat scowling at him. "Don't be so hard on Joe, we're blessed to know him, and all you do is rag him."

Clyde grinned. "He loves it. Rags me right back."

"You don't realize how lucky you are just to share bed and supper with Joe, just to know those five cats. But," she said, "there is something strange going on at Emmylou's that Joe doesn't want to talk about. I guess, in time, he'll tell us," she said. "In his own good time."

JOE SLIPPED UP the oak tree and onto Kit's tree house ready to fight the intruder, his ears and whiskers flat. Only when the pacing cat turned, startled, and approached him stiff-legged, did Joe laugh and relax. Pan paused, too, tail twitching, his ears going back and up, edgy and questioning.

"What?" Joe said. "What's wrong?"

"I don't know." The big tom lowered his ears uncertainly. "Kit's in trouble, I can feel her fear, she's scared and alone somewhere out in the night."

Joe took a step back. "She's miles away, up the coast. You can't know what she's feeling, what she's doing." This kind of talk made his paws sweat.

Pan drew his lips back. "She's in some kind of trouble."

"Nightmare," Joe said. "You fell asleep and dreamed of trouble." Generally the red tom was a steady fellow, macho and straightforward—until he got off on this perception nonsense beyond all logic and reason.

But Pan's amber eyes blazed, he growled deep in his throat and spun around and was gone along an oak branch and in through the dining room window, through the cat door. "The Greenlaws, their cell phone . . ." he said over his shoulder. "Help me find the number."

Joe sighed. He was crouched to follow, knowing they'd sound like fools to the Greenlaws with such a call, when car lights came down the street below. They slowed, and Ryan's red king cab turned into the drive, headlights sweeping the front of the house and up through the oak branches, blazing in Joe's face. Squinting, he peered over, breathing exhaust as the engine died.

Ryan emerged from the passenger side, stepped around to the rear bumper and up onto it, reaching up to the overhead rack where the extension ladder was secured. He watched Clyde swing out the driver's door and move to help her. Why did they need a ladder? They *had* a key to the house, all the Greenlaws' close friends had keys. From the dining room, Pan shouted, "*You* picked up! Say something. Pedric? *Is this Pedric?*" Silence, then, "*Pedric, are you all right? Where's Lucinda?*" Another silence, then, "*Who is this? If this isn't Pedric, who are you? Why do you have Pedric's phone? Where's Lucinda? Speak up or I call the cops, they'll put a trace on you!*"

Joe smiled. He didn't think MPPD was set up to trace the immediate location of a cell phone but it sounded good. He watched Ryan open the extension ladder, lean it against the edge of the tree house, and climb nimbly up. Joe waited until his housemate had swung up onto the platform and switched on her flashlight, then stepped out into its beam. The eerie nightglow of his eyes made her catch her breath.

"Did you have to do that, sneak up like that?" she asked shakily.

"*I'm* sneaking? What are *you* doing climbing up here in the middle of the night like some—"

"Like some cat burglar?" she said, laughing. She knelt and grabbed him up and hugged him. Her hugs always embarrassed him, but they made him purr, too.

Putting him down again, she fished a plastic bag from her pocket and reached across him to snag one of Kit's well-used pillows from the untidy pile. He watched her drop it into the plastic bag and seal it up with a twisty. He looked over the edge at the king cab where Rock was hanging out the open window, whining softly. He looked toward the house where Pan was on the phone, and looked again at Ryan. Now there was silence from the house. Joe watched Pan emerge through the cat door, ears back, tail lashing, his tabby forehead creased with worry, unsettled by that distraught phone conversation.

"Come on, Pan," Ryan said, swinging onto the ladder and down, frowning up at Pan there above her. "Come on, we're headed up the coast." She looked worriedly at the red tom. "It's Kit," she said softly. "She . . . We're going to look for Kit."

Pan leaped from the oak to the ground, sinking deep in the leafy mulch, fled to the king cab and up through the window past Rock. Joe followed, as Ryan descended the ladder clutching Kit's pillow. Inside the pickup, Pan was crouched on the back of the driver's seat, tail lashing. Joe, unsettled by the red tom's unnatural perception, hopped sedately up into the front seat beside Clyde, and snuggled close. Pan might indulge in these wild flights of fancy, but he could count on Clyde for a soothing dose of hardheaded commonsense.

8

Vic pulled down off the highway into the village, easing the Town Car away from the main street and through the darkest neighborhoods, the narrow lanes as black as the Lincoln itself. Molena Point streets were not lighted, and here among the crowded cottages only weak lampglow shone through a few curtained windows, vaguely illuminating the nearest tree trunks. Heading a roundabout way for the stone house, the big car slid through the inky streets nearly invisible except for its low beams picking out parked cars and an occasional cat racing across. In the passenger seat Birely huddled, his arms around himself, moaning at every bump and there were plenty of those on these backstreets, potholes, and warped blacktop where tree roots pushed up, jolting even the easy-riding Lincoln. The trip down Highway One had been tense, watching for cops. There hadn't been much traffic and the Town Car stood out too clearly, making him jumpy as hell.

Leaving the scene of the wreck and moving on down the winding two-lane, they'd barely hit the flats, the highway straight and flat along the shore, when they'd heard sirens ahead. He'd turned off into a clump of eucalyptus trees, onto a narrow road that led away to a distant farmhouse. Pasture fences, faint lights way off up the hill. Waiting there on the dark dirt road for the cops and ambulance to pass, he'd done what he could for Birely, had cleaned the blood off his face with bottled water and an old rag. Birely's nose wouldn't stop bleeding, and he couldn't bear anything pressed against it. He couldn't hardly breathe, as it was. And the way he was holding his belly, whimpering, he was hurt more than a bandage could fix. When they'd left the wrecked pickup Vic had cleared out the glove compartment, had left most of the junk from the previous owner that he'd stole it from, but had pocketed a beer opener, an old pocketknife, and an out-of-date bottle of codeine prescribed in the name of the truck's owner. He'd given Birely two of those, had left the wreck trying to figure out what to do with him when they got back to Molena Point. He sure couldn't show up at a hospital emergency room driving the Lincoln; by this time, there'd be a BOL out. First thing was to get the Town Car out of sight, then decide what to do.

Waiting on the side road, he'd felt the inner pockets of his windbreaker, patting the one pack of bills he'd kept on him. Most of the money they'd found, that he'd been carrying, he'd stashed in the Lincoln itself. Rooting behind the stacked packages in the backseat, he'd pulled down the armrest and found a space lined with a plastic tray, the old folks had a couple of them little water bottles in there. Pulling the bottles out, he'd stuffed the packs of bills in, ten stacks of hundreds, all bound up in their little paper sleeves. One sleeve tore, spilling its contents, but he gathered it all, slipped the torn wrapper back on, and sandwiched it between the other packets. The hiding place, when it was covered up with packages again, would be easy enough to get to in a hurry. He still couldn't figure out if the woman Sammie'd left the place to, that Emmy-lou Warren, knew about Sammie's stash.

Had to, he thought, with all that carpentry work she was doing down there. Sure as hell she was going to find the money. Sammie'd told Birely, long ago, that she'd split the cash up, that she hadn't hid it all in one place. Sammie must have wanted Birely to have it, to tell him that— maybe wanted him to know about it, but not know too much, in case he turned greedy before she passed on, and came looking, nosing around maybe egged on by some "friend" he'd met on the road, Vic thought with a smile. Birely never was one to see he was being used. If she'd wanted Birely to have the money, but not while *she* was still around, she must've meant him to have the house, too. But something made her change her mind, and she wrote that will to the Warren woman instead. It didn't make sense, but people seldom made sense. He was just pulling off the street onto the dirt lane that led back through the woods to the stone building when the cell phone rang, the phone he'd taken off that old guy. It began to gong like a church bell. Birely sat up rigid, groaning with pain, staring around him like he thought he was about to receive the last rites.

He came fully awake and grabbed up the phone.

"Don't answer it," Vic snapped. "Don't *answer* the damn thing." But Birely, groping, must have hit the speaker button.

"I didn't *answer* it," he said. "I just . . ." A man's voice came on, soft and quiet. "Pedric? Pedric, is that you?"

"I told you not to answer."

"I didn't, I only picked it up. What . . . ?"

"You punched something. Hang up." Vic grabbed the phone from him.

"You picked up!" the caller shouted. *"Say something. Pedric? Is this Pedric?"*

Vic stopped the car among the trees, couldn't figure out how to turn the damn phone off.

"Where's Pedric?" the voice shouted. *"Pedric, are you all right? If this isn't Pedric, who are you? Where's Lucinda?"* Vic started punching buttons. The screen came to life rolling through all kinds of commands, but the voice kept on. *"Who is this? Why do you have Pedric's phone? Where's Lucinda? Speak up or I call the cops, they'll put a trace on you!"*

"Sure it's me," Vic said. "Who did you expect?"

There was a short silence. *"This* isn't Pedric. I want to talk to Pedric."

Holding the phone, he wondered if the cops *could* use it to trace their location. Maybe some departments had the equipment to do that, he didn't know. But this little burg? Not likely. He tried to recall the soft, raspy voice of the man he had hit with the tire iron. Uptight-looking old guy, neatly dressed, tan sport coat, white hair in a short, military cut, white shirt and proper tie. Lowering his voice, he tried to use proper English, like the old guy would. "Of course this is Pedric, who else would have my phone? Could you tell me who is calling? We seem to have a bad connection."

There was a long silence at the other end. The caller said no more. Vic heard him click off.

The encounter left him nervous as hell, made his stomach churn. An unidentified call, coming over a stolen phone like the damn thing had ghosts in it. Birely had curled into himself again, as if the pain were worse. His smashed nose was bleeding harder, his breath sour, breathing through his mouth. Where his face wasn't smeared with blood, he was white as milk. Vic knew, even if he stashed the Lincoln out of sight, got some other wheels and hauled Birely to an emergency room, they'd start asking questions and who knew what Birely'd say? The little wimp wasn't too swift, at best, and in the hospital, drugged up for the pain, he might tell the cops any damned thing.

It had started out as a lark, when they'd first headed over to the coast to find that wad of money that Birely swore Sammie'd stashed away, a simple trip to retrieve Birely's own rightful legacy, and the whole damn thing had gone sour. It was that run up to the city that did it, their pickup totaled, and now the cops would be after them because they'd taken the damn Lincoln. But what else could he do? He didn't *have* no other way to get Birely to a doctor, he'd tell them that, with Birely hurt so bad, and all. And that truck driver dead, which would sure as hell send the cops after them, too. They'd be all over him for that, claiming you weren't supposed to leave an accident victim. Hell, the guy was dead, it wasn't like he could have helped him none. With Birely bad hurt, what could he do but take the one working vehicle to go for help? *He* didn't kill the truck driver, the rock slide killed him.

But the old man and his skinny wife, that was another matter. If one of *them* died he'd sure be charged with murder even if he didn't hit either of them very hard, not hard enough to kill them. If they died from shock or something, was that *his* fault? And there again he'd had no choice, had to get them off his back so he could help Birely. The law never took into account extenuating circumstances, they had no feel for a person when you were really up against it. Sure as hell those two people could identify him—and would swear he'd attacked them. And now, once he'd hidden the Lincoln, what was he going to do with Birely?

It was after they'd turned back on the highway, after the cops and ambulance went by, that was when Birely had started to talk. Rambled on as they skirted the little cheap towns along the peninsula, when the codeine took hold and loosened up his tongue. Talked about how strange Sammie was when she was a child, rambled on about their old uncle, the old train robber who was close to Sammie when she was small. All so long ago that Birely wasn't even born yet. He'd heard the stories from Sammie, how the old man had robbed some government office of big bucks, hid the money and got away clean, and the feds could never pin anything on him. Back to prison on other charges, and then a year later made a prison break and took off with the money, down into Mexico.

And then, some years later, maybe with a guilty conscience, he'd shipped a big share of it back to Sammie. Birely'd grown up knowing only those parts of the story that Sammie chose to tell him, he wasn't much good at filling in the spaces between.

Easing the Lincoln on down through the woods, Vic was about to pull around to the front of the stone shed, hoping to hell he could squeeze the Lincoln into that little space that had probably been built for cows or farm machinery, when he saw a light in the yard down below, saw Emmylou Warren descending the hill, heading down from the stone house. He killed the engine, watched to see if she'd heard the car. She made no indication, didn't pause or glance back. Had she been poking around inside there? Had she seen them before they left, knew they were staying in there? That would tear it. Was she looking for the rest of the money, maybe had found some down at her place, decided when she saw them that they were looking for it, too? Birely said the original theft was two hundred thousand, a big haul, back in those days.

But maybe Emmylou Warren didn't know nothing, was just out in the yard maybe feeding those cats that hung around her. Useless creatures, what were they good for? In the light from her porch he watched her poking around down in her yard and she didn't once look his way. Dark as hell up behind the pines and heavy bushes. He watched her head up the steps to her back door, that big yellow cat walking along beside her, following her like a dog, old woman talking to it, crazy as hell, walking around in her yard in the middle of the night gabbing away to a cat, talking as if the damn thing would answer her.

9

MISTO GLANCED UP twice toward the woods as he followed Emmylou up the back stairs and inside. He was quite aware of the black car that had pulled in among the trees high above the stone house, though Emmylou was not. He could smell the fumes of its exhaust drifting down, cutting through the scent of the pines, and on the riffling breath of the night he caught a whiff of blood that tweaked his curiosity. Accompanying Emmylou inside, he leaped to the sill where he could look back up the hill, studying the denser blackness among the night woods where the big car stood. Pretty nice car to be jammed in among the trees that way. He'd like to tell Emmylou to turn the porch light off so he could see better but he never spoke to her, she didn't share his secret, she was not among the few who knew the truth about the speaking cats, she was simply a kind and comfortable friend. Misto had, in fact, a number of secrets he didn't share with

Emmylou Warren—though it was she who had, unwittingly, opened a new door to Misto. Had, by accident or by strange circumstance, pulled aside a curtain into the tomcat's ancient memory, had let cracks of light into a life he'd lived long before this present existence.

Maybe the memories began with the smell of the mildewed money there in Emmylou's house, often it was a smell of some sort that stirred a lost vision. The sour stink of those three packets of old bills she'd found had nudged him as if a hand had reached up from his past, poking at him, bringing back scenes from a life nearly forgotten. Or maybe it was the grainy photograph in a tin frame that had awakened those long-ago moments, the picture of a child who had, by now, already grown up, grown old, and died. Maybe that little girl's eager smile had stirred alive that lost time.

Back in February, when the cops found Sammie's body, Misto had no idea who the dead woman was but he knew her name, it stuck in his thoughts and wouldn't go away. He hadn't put it together until later, that *this* Sammie was the little child from his own past, from a life lived many cat generations before this one.

Emmylou usually left the back door open while she was working inside, replacing Sheetrock and sawing and hammering. Hearing her work, he'd slip in for a visit with the stringy, leathery woman. With his own humans away for the week, Dr. John Firetti and his wife, Mary, off at a veterinarian conference, he'd been up here every day. He was staying with Joe Grey and the Damens, which suited him just fine: sleeping on the love seat with the big Weimaraner and little Snowball, or up in the tower with

Joe. But Ryan and Clyde were busy folks, Clyde with his upscale automotive business and Ryan with her construction firm. And Joe was off at all hours with his tabby lady, following their lust for crime, hanging out with the cops at MPPD, waiting eagerly for some scuzzy human to be nailed and jailed. Sometimes, then, Misto would slip up to visit this homey and comfortable woman, to stretch out on her windowsill as she went about her work. He liked to watch her tear out cabinets and finish the walls with new Sheetrock, and Emmylou was good company. That was how he came on the picture of the child, she had moved it back onto the dresser after shifting the furniture around. He'd hopped up there to be petted, and there it was, the picture of a child that so shocked him he let out a strange, gargling mewl.

"That's Sammie," Emmylou had said, looking down at him. "Sammie when she was little, so many years ago. My goodness, cat, you look frightened. How could an old picture scare you?"

The photo was sepia toned, and grainy. The child was dressed in an old-fashioned pinafore, crisply ironed, and little patent-leather shoes with a strap across the instep, over short white socks. He had known this child, he remembered her running through the grass beside a white picket fence, he could see her bouncing on her little bed with the pink ruffled spread, he could hear her laughing. Those moments from another life crowded in at him in much the same way he remembered fragments from a long-ago medieval village, scenes so clear and sudden he could smell offal in the streets and the stink of boiled cabbage and the rain-sodden rot of thatched rooftops.

Here in Emmylou's house, the time of Sammie's childhood grew so real he could smell the bruised grass on her little shoes, could feel her warmth when he curled up close to her, the softness of her baby skin, the smell of little girl and hot cocoa and peppermints, the sticky feel of peanut butter on her small fingers. How strange to think about that lost time. How clearly he remembered the humid Southern summers, the buzz of cicadas at night, the days as hot as hell itself, and so muggy your fur was never really dry. How had he been drawn here to this place where, so many long years later, the grown-up Sammie had lived and died?

Soon he wasn't going off with Joe Grey at all, or even with his son, Pan, but heading up alone to see Emmylou and revisit those memories that so stirred him, to sit on the dresser looking at little Sammie while Emmylou hammered and sawed and talked away, and all the while it was Sammie's young voice he wished he could hear.

He wasn't sure how many of his nine cat lives he had spent, and he wasn't sure what came after. Some of his lives were only vague sparks, bright moments or ugly, a scene, a few words spoken, and then gone again. Only his life with Sammie was so insistent. As each new memory nudged him, another piece of that life fell into place, toward whatever revelation he was meant to see, another moment teasing his sharp curiosity.

But tonight, crouched on Emmylou's windowsill, a different kind of curiosity gripped Misto, too. He waited patiently until he saw the black car move on again down through the woods, following the lane that led to the old, narrow shed beneath the stone house. Misto guessed, with its wide, hinged doors, it was a kind of garage, maybe built for farm tractors or a Model A. Did the driver expect to fit that big car in there? Not likely, not that long, sleek vehicle. Though in the reflection of light from Emmylou's back porch he could see dents and scrapes in the fenders, too, and a loose front bumper. The driver stepped out, left the motor running, the taller of the two men he'd seen coming up there before, shaggy brown ponytail hanging down the back of his dark windbreaker.

He opened the heavy swinging doors, got back in and, amazingly, he pulled the car on inside. It was a tight fit, barely enough room for him to help his companion out, the shorter man stumbling, and that's where the smell of blood came from. Blood smeared down his face, soaking into the rag he held to his nose. Moving up the stone steps to the room above, he bore much of his weight on the wooden rail. The taller man closed the shed doors, replaced the padlock, and followed him up. Watched him struggle into the house but didn't help him. The door closed behind them. Misto heard the lock snap home.

No lights came on inside, except the faintest glow as if they had an electric lantern up there. Wanting to see more, Misto dropped from Emmylou's windowsill to the floor and trotted out through the old cat door that was cut in the back door. Emmylou's own three cats used it, wild creatures he thought might have been feral, who came and went as they chose. Galloping up the hill and up the stone stairs, through the men's scent, he leaped to the stone sill beside the door, peered in through the dirty glass.

10

HEAVY FOG HUGGED the coastal highway, slowing the king cab as Clyde negotiated the blind lanes following the dim taillights of the sheriff's car that led them, both drivers watching for unexpected obstructions in the heavy mist. He and Ryan and the two tomcats were all fidgeting, thinking about Kit alone somewhere on the cliff ahead, her little tortoiseshell face peering out from some stony crevice that could hardly protect her from larger predators, waiting for help to come rescue her. Kit might act brash and brave with her friends but tonight her voice on the phone had been shaky, scared, and uncertain.

"Good thing we have friends in the department," Joe said, rearing up on the backseat peering out the side window into the rolling mist. "*Someone* to get us through the roadblock back there. I wouldn't have wanted to climb up this damnable, fog-blind road ducking falling boulders you can't even see coming down at you."

"The rocks have quit falling," Clyde said. "Ryan and I will be climbing, carrying you and Pan."

Max Harper had called the Santa Cruz County Sheriff, who had, in turn, alerted his deputies to let them through the barrier down at the foot of the mountain. "Deputy will meet you," Max had said, "lead you on up." Now as they climbed above the flatland on the narrow, rising curves, the fog blew and shifted, arms of whiteness blinding and then revealing, playing with their senses, with their perception of place and balance. The streaming wisps made even the two cats giddy. Joe was glad they had the heavy king cab with its reliable four-wheel drive to keep them grounded. The only unsteadiness about the truck was Rock lunging nervously from one side of the backseat to the other, his eager weight rocking the heavy vehicle and, at each lunge, shouldering Joe and Pan aside.

"Settle down," Ryan told him, "you'll wear yourself out before you ever start to search." Rock gave her a sullen look, but he lay down, sighing dramatically, sprawling across the wide seat. Ryan had, long ago, filled the leg space of the backseat with empty boxes, and laid a thin pad over both boxes and seat to make a solid platform, preventing the big dog from losing his balance on the narrow bench. The resultant bed would have accommodated all three animals nicely if Rock wasn't hogging it all. Joe watched the deputy's disembodied taillights leading them up through the shifting blanket of white, watched the blurred reflection of their two sets of headlights move along the black cliff in their ethereal, half-blind world. The deputy leading them, plump and baby faced, had told them the wind was stirring higher up the mountain, "Maybe the night'll clear, make your tracking easier," but his tone had implied that this venture was nonsense, to bring a tracking dog all the way up here in this weather to find some lost cat. Maybe the fog *would* clear, Joe thought, but right now they couldn't even see the edge of the road where it dropped away to the sea; the muffled sound of the waves from far below seemed stealthy and threatening.

But central coast fog was notional, slipping along the base of Molena Point's coastal hills one moment, rising the next to leave the lowland clear and enfold only the tallest peaks. Many afternoons the cats, hunting across the high meadows, would watch a thin, white scarf of fog creep in from the sea just above the Molena River, down below the hills that rose bright green and clear. And the next time they looked, the fog had expanded to cover all the hills and the sun, hiding the world around them.

Now suddenly Rock leaped up to pace again, and so did the red tomcat, the two shouldering past each other peering out one window and then Joe, too, caught a whiff of coyote mixed with the smell of the sea and of the pine forest. Pan's ears twitched back and forth, his striped tail lashing as he fretted over Kit, his every movement urging them to hurry. The red tom had traveled this coast, one small cat alone following Highway One from Oregon to Molena Point, he knew the bold beasts that hunted these coastal mountains, he knew the way coyotes tear their prey, and that was not a pleasant picture. He was aware of the bobcats and owls, too, the silent night hunters, and he was frantic for Kit.

Even as Clyde had backed the king cab out of their drive, Max had called them back to tell them that Lucinda and Pedric were safe in the ER, in Santa Cruz, but that both were driving the staff crazy, fussing about their cat. "They've refused to have the X-rays and MRIs that were ordered," he said crossly, "until they know someone's gone to fetch the damn cat." Max wasn't big on cats—though he had grown unusually fond of Joe Grey, brightening at Joe's presence on his desk or in his bookcase, and not a clue to the cat-sized detective lounging across his reports; to Max Harper the five cats were no more than housecats. "Why the hell did they take that cat with them? Try to control a cat, in a car? Why can't they have a nice little lap dog that they can keep on a leash?"

Joe imagined the tall, lean chief and Charlie, his red-headed wife, disturbed from an evening at home, tucked up before a warm fire in their hilltop living room maybe with an after-dinner toddy, maybe watching an old movie. The chief didn't get that many leisurely nights off without some emergency or another breaking in, too often taking him out again into the small hours. Max said, "You think Rock *will* track that cat?"

"Of course he will," Ryan said indignantly, "he's primed for the hunt."

"Charlie's making noises like she wants to head for the hospital. We may see you there, or she will," and he'd clicked off.

They were high up the mountain when, around the next sharp bend, a line of sputtering orange flares broke the thinning fog. The deputy parked beside two more black-and-whites. The landslide loomed beyond, a ragged hill of fallen boulders blocking the highway, the tons of rock lit like a movie set by three spotlights fixed to tall tripods, their blaze picking out broken glass and twisted metal, too, where the wrecked truck and pickup lay tangled together in a deathly heap. Clyde parked beside the patrol car that had led them, both cars backing around so their rear bumpers were against the cliff. The deputy got out of his unit and stepped over to talk with them, his round face pulled into a frown. "Town Car was on this side. It barely slid through, or they'd be dead. Strange what some people will think of, time like that. Worried about a *cat*."

He didn't like bringing civilians up to a crash scene, he didn't like them tramping around the scene of a wreck, and didn't like the idea of these people going up the slide area with their dog, didn't like that at all. Most likely they'd get in trouble, fall down the cliff, and that would complicate matters, but orders were orders. "Well, at least the fog's lifted," he said dourly. "There's a hiking path on up the road another quarter mile. That'll put you up to the tree line, and bring you back there, right above us. I want you to stay in the woods. You're not to go down on the slide. Can you control your dog?" He looked doubtfully at Rock, who was huffing at the air, sucking in scent and staring up the tall, rocky cliff. "That cat could have taken off for anywhere. You ever try to catch a scared cat?" he said, backing away from Ryan's door so she could get out of the truck.

"We'll find her," Clyde said mildly. He reached over the seat for his backpack as Ryan strapped on her own heavy pack. Neither Joe nor Pan was in sight. The deputy looked at Rock, and reached a hand for the Weimaraner to sniff. "Nice hound. Trouble is, when that cat sees this big beast it'll take off like a bat in a windstorm, you never will find it."

"Dog and cat are friends," Clyde said, his voice slow and measured. "They eat out of the same supper bowl. Cat'll be happy to see him."

The deputy shrugged, unconvinced. "Wreckers and earthmovers'll be here at daylight. If the wind dies and more fog rolls in, you won't be able to see your own feet."

Not until he had moved away did Ryan make a rude face, and she and Clyde grinned at each other. Joe peered out of Clyde's pack, watching the pudgy officer depart, and from Ryan's pack Pan uttered a low, angry growl.

Climbing gingerly over the rock pile toward the upper road and the trail, they left the key in the king cab in case the deputies needed to move it. Negotiating the unsteady boulders, they tested every step, moving with infinite care despite Rock's eager pulling on his lead. Coming down onto the solid macadam again on the other side, past the wrecked trucks, they headed up the two-lane, passing two more sheriff's cars that had come down from the north. Rock pulled Ryan up the steep grade, straining on his leash. He wasn't expected to heel, he was working now, heeling and city manners weren't part of this program. In her left hand Ryan carried the plastic bag with Kit's scent. Once they'd left the rock slide, they didn't talk. Clyde swept his beam along the road ahead, lighting their way, while Ryan shone her light up the cliff, cutting back and forth through dried-up vegetation and ragged outcroppings, all of them hoping to see a pair of bright eyes reflecting back from the stony drop. Joe, half smothered in Clyde's backpack, didn't like the silence, he didn't like that there was no distant sound of coyotes yipping to one another, silent coyotes were bad news. Kit had *said* there were coyotes, he *smelled* coyotes, and their silence meant they were watching, well aware of them. But worse still, there was no sound from Kit, not the faintest mewl to tell them where she was.

Not likely she'd mewl with the coyotes so close, but I sure wish she would, wish she'd yowl like a banshee. Her silence made him shiver with dread.

11

THE HARSH RING of the phone woke
Kate Osborne, but when she reached
for the phone in the dark room, trying to sit up, tangled in the covers, she
couldn't find the damn thing. Feeling
around her, she realized she wasn't in
bed; her bare legs were tangled in fur,
making her shiver. She gingerly touched the animal feel
of it, realized she was stroking the fur throw that she kept
on the couch, that she'd gone to sleep in the living room.
The phone was still ringing. Last night, she hadn't bothered to turn on the answering machine. She used it when
she went out, if she thought of it, but since she'd returned
to San Francisco from her long, dark journey, she'd found
even that innocuous electronic gadget annoying. This
change in her life, leaving her cozy and successful designer's position in Seattle, opting for unfettered freedom
back in California with no obligations, taking the small
apartment in the city, and then the amazing events that

led her down through the cavernous tunnels into that terrifying other world, all of it had left her nervously intolerant of anything nonhuman speaking up for her. She found the phone on the ninth ring. Snatching it up, she pushed her pale hair out of her eyes, found the lamp, and switched it on. Her watch said ten o'clock, but it felt like way after midnight. "What?" she said. "If this is a sales pitch—"

"Kate, it's Charlie Harper."

She sat up, shivering in the cold room, pulled the heavy throw around her, shoved another pillow behind her. Beyond the open draperies the great, lighted span of the Golden Gate thrust its curves against the night.

"Wilma and I are in Santa Cruz, at Dominican Hospital. There's been a wreck. Lucinda and Pedric aren't hurt too bad, but—"

Kate came fully awake. "What happened? Are they all right? Where's Kit? *Charlie, is Kit all right?*" A wreck at night on that narrow, winding two-lane. "*Where's Kit?*" she shouted, imagining Kit thrown out of the car or running from the crash, terrified.

Charlie said nothing.

"*Where is she?*" She pictured Kit hurt, the confusion of cops and EMTs crowding in at her, Kit running from them in terror and confusion, the little cat who was more than cat but who, under stress, could revert to her basic feline instincts, running mindlessly, hiding even from the people she loved best, just as an ordinary cat might do.

"Ryan and Clyde have gone to look for her. She ran, but she's all right. She called," Charlie said, "called on Lucinda's cell phone. She's all right, Kate. They're taking Rock, he'll find her."

Kate kicked the fur cover to the floor. Carrying the headset listening to Charlie, she made for the bedroom. "Where's the wreck? Where *exactly* . . . ?"

"You can't do anything, Kate. They'll find her. I only thought you'd want to know—"

"I'm coming. Kit's all alone—"

"She's not, she . . . Rock will be there soon, Rock and Joe and Pan, they'll find her. You'd only . . . If you took Highway One, you couldn't get past the slide, you wouldn't be able to drive on down to the hospital. You'd have to leave your car there, walk across, and ride with someone."

"I'm coming. On my way. I'll take 280 . . ."

"Come to Dominican, then. In Santa Cruz, we'll meet there. I know a vet there, I've already called him, just in case. But she'll be fine, Kate, trust me. Kit's a resourceful little soul."

In the bedroom, pulling off her robe, she thought about getting a car in a hurry. She'd been taking cabs and cable cars since she'd returned to the city, didn't want to bother with a car, had rented one when she needed to. She thought about how Kit had loved the city, how only yesterday Kit had been right here shopping with them, the little tortoiseshell whispering secretly in her ear, letting no salesclerk see her, but so filled with joy at the wonders of the elegant stores and restaurants, and now she was lost, frightened and lost and maybe hurt. Oh, God, she couldn't be hurt.

Standing naked in the bedroom she called 411, got the number for the Avis office just down the block, made arrangements to have a car brought around. Pulling on panties and jeans and boots and a dirty red sweatshirt, she snatched up her purse and headed for the door. Whatever she needed, toothbrush, change of clothes, she'd buy somewhere. She stopped at her desk long enough to lock her safe. She checked the balcony glass doors, locked her front door behind her, and headed for the elevator.

The driver was at the curb, a tall, thin redheaded man, his long hair tied back beneath a chauffeur's cap. Kate drove him back to the Avis office over streets slick with fog, waited in the car for him to run her credit card, and then headed south, the city's narrow streets reflecting passing car lights and colored neon from the small cafés and shops. She pictured the city as a friend had described it from sixty years ago when Kate's grandfather was alive, her mother's father, Kate's link to her amazing journey. It was a friendlier city then, without the stark, tall buildings whose lighted offices thrust up into the night around her now like tethered rocket ships, dwarfing the cozy neighborhoods of an earlier day. A city that had somehow soured with the spoils of modern greed and degradation. A gentler San Francisco then, where you could walk the streets in the small hours unmolested, laughing and acting silly but never in danger; and where so many true artists had come together, living in the lofts and in the Sausalito houseboats, their work singing with the passion of life, Kate's own father among them. She had only recently visited his paintings again, in the San Francisco museums—but only his earlier works. Braden West, too, had gone down into the Netherworld, had lived there a long life with her mother.

She knew, now, that they had returned at least once, bringing their youngest child back with them, had made that last journey up to the city to put Kate herself into the care of a San Francisco orphanage. They'd had no choice. Even then the Netherworld was crumbling, they had wanted her away from its inevitable fall, wanted her to grow up in a city that would offer her some future, in a country brighter with promise than that decaying land.

As the tires of the rented Toyota sang along the wet macadam of the Embarcadero, she debated taking Highway One despite Charlie's advice. She moved on past the entrance to the AT&T Park. The traffic seemed light for this time of evening. Accelerating up onto the 280, she merged into fast traffic heading south between the clustered lights of the bedroom cities that ran one into the next, San Mateo, Palo Alto, the smaller communities separated like islands by short realms of black and empty night. The east hills rose invisible in the darkness, marked only by their scattered lights high up like gathered fireflies in the night sky. She'd be in Santa Cruz in less than two hours. She knew Charlie was right, that she could do nothing for Kit but get in the way of the searchers, slowing and causing them added trouble. But she prayed for Kit, her own kind of prayer that had little to do with churches, she prayed for Kit and was filled with an aching fear for her, for one small and special cat shivering and alone among the vast, wild cliffs.

KIT LOST HER nerve when the coyotes drew too close. Crouched among the jutting rocks, she shot out of the dark niche at the last minute, scrambled back down the crumbling cliff where she hoped the beasts wouldn't venture. She still carried the phone, reluctant to leave her only link to the world of humans, but its weight was a hindrance, and put her off balance. Halfway down, sliding and clinging to the scruffy clumps, she heard the rush of the beasts above her, and when she looked up their shadows were too close, coming down the boulders. She scrabbled away across the face of the cliff, lost her balance and nearly fell, and it was then she dropped the phone. She froze, listened to it clunk end over end down the mountain.

When she looked up again a coyote stood just above her, peering over the top of the slide, his pale eyes narrow and hungry. She looked past him to the trees and knew she couldn't make that long run. He stank of spoiled meat, his smell made her flehmen, pulling back her lips with disgust.

He padded casually along just above her, easily keeping pace as she worked her way along the cliff's face, moving more easily now without the weight of the phone. She kept moving, seeking some fissure or shelter, until at last, ahead and below her, the black scar of a narrow crevice cut down into the earth. Zigzagging toward it, nearly falling, she slipped down into the four-inch crack. There was barely room for a cat, no room for the larger predator. The rough sides of the cleft was perfumed with the old, faint scent of skunk. She followed it deep, smug in her escape but terrified of being trapped in there if the earth should shift again. Above her, the coyote clawed at the stone, and she edged deeper down until she could go no further, until the rock closed beneath her hind paws. Above her the coyote's eyes shone in, reflecting light from the floods on the road below. He began to dig.

Watching his frantic, shifting silhouette, listening to the beast's scrabbling paws and smelling his rank breath, she longed to bloody that toothy muzzle. If ever the great cat god reached down with a helping paw, she needed him to do that now. Soon the coyote was joined by another and then a third, the beasts edging cleverly down the unsteady rocks and digging at the narrow crevice, panting and slavering, hungry with the smell of her. The night sky was milky, fog settling in again as the wind died, the thick mist easing down like a pale quilt over the shaggy beasts. She didn't know how long she cringed there wanting to leap out and attack and knowing she'd lose the battle. She was shivering with cold when the coyotes suddenly stopped digging.

Turning, they stood looking down toward the road; they shifted nervously, the faint hush of paws on stone. A new, moving light reflected up against the roof of fog and she heard a car's engine, heard tires crunching on the fallen gravel. Not one car, but two. She could hear voices muffled by the fog and the surf. The coyotes moved away and then back again, began to dig again. Still she heard voices, she listened for some time and then the talking stopped and she could hear someone walking up the road, two sets of boots tapping softly along uphill. Only then did the coyotes shift away, their shadows gone above her, but still she sensed them there, maybe crouched and waiting. She started up to look, scrambling up the narrow rift, straining, pulling herself up until she was at the top of the fissure again and could peer out.

Fog was thickening across the road below but she could see a long pickup. Ryan's king cab? Or maybe only the first of the cleanup crew, come to disentangle the wrecked trucks, preparing to haul them away? Looking along the cliff, she saw the coyotes crouched in fog at the edge, their backs to her, looking down the steep drop, too bold to back away, too familiar with the human world to fear the approaching hikers. Disdainful of mankind but still tensed to run, their ears moving nervously. Could she run now, while they were distracted? Streak away, and up that nearest tree that stood tall and ghostlike at the edge of the misty woods? Could she reach it before they were on her?

She was crouched on the lip of the cleft, poised to spring away, when one of the beasts turned, glancing back at her. She vanished down the hole again, scrambled down as deep as she could go. Now the beast blocked the hole, digging, his breath as rank as soured garbage. His frantic seeking stopped when a glare of light shone behind him, picking out his shaggy coat. She heard a roar—Rock's snarling roar, heard humans running, heard Rock's barking attack, and a cat yowled with rage, and another cat, the night rang with snarls and cat screams, she heard the thunder of boots on stone. Ryan screamed, "Hold, Rock. Back off!" Rock's roar was like a great wolf above her, a coyote screamed in pain, and she heard Pan's yowl of challenge.

Clyde shouted, "Not there, the cats . . ."

A gunshot thundered down the cleft, deafening her, accompanied by a pained yip. Another shot, another cry of pain, cut short. Running paws scrambling away across the stony escarpment.

Then, silence.

She peered up to the mouth of the cleft. Pan looked over, backlighted by the beam of a flashlight behind him. Joe Grey and Rock looked over. Ryan and Clyde crowded to peer down behind them.

"Come out," Pan said. "One of the beasts is dead, the rest ran off. Come out, Kit." The light swept away, out of her eyes, and she could see again. She scrambled out, bolted into Pan yowling and crying and talking all at once.

A dead coyote lay beside the cleft. Ryan held Rock away from it, the big Weimaraner fighting to get at the animal, but then he strained up toward the woods, too, where the others had vanished. He huffed and pulled at his lead, torn between the two prey, but held in check by Ryan. Kit backed away from the mangled coyote, its face torn and bleeding. She glanced at Ryan's revolver.

"I fired point-blank," Ryan said, "away from you, away from everyone." But Kit was hardly paying attention. Pan was licking her face, and she preened against him.

Ryan picked Joe up and held him in her arms, cuddling him, and she pulled Rock close, admiring them both, praising them both for their tracking, telling them they were the finest of SWAT teams. Joe Grey tried to look modest—not easy when he could still taste coyote blood, could still feel his claws in its rough coat, and felt more fierce than modest.

It was Clyde who had pulled Joe off the beast, forcing him away, and had grabbed Pan and somehow got hold of Rock's collar, too, and dragged them away so Ryan could fire and keep them from being bitten. Joe allowed Ryan to admire him until he heard someone coming up the hiking trail.

"The sheriff's deputy," he said softly, peering down the cliff where the trail angled up toward them, watching the law approach to see what the shooting was about. "You two better get your story together," he murmured. He wasn't sure whether shooting an attacking coyote, in California, like shooting any wild animal in the state, was a major crime, whether such an act was punishable by unrealistic fines and extreme jail time.

"He attacked me," Ryan said, "and he attacked Rock. Get in my pack, Joe. You, too, Pan. We don't need any extra cats on the scene."

Joe dropped from her shoulder into the pack, silent and obedient. Clyde scooped Pan up and deposited him unceremoniously in his own pack, then picked Kit up and cuddled her.

Settling down inside Ryan's pack, Joe thought about rabies, and about the red tape and bureaucratic confusion that was going to follow this little event, maybe even quarantine for all of them while the carcass was examined and rabies was ruled out. *Or not ruled out*, he thought glumly. Looking down at the dead coyote, he hoped this one was clean. Looking out through the netting in the side of the pack, he watched the baby-faced trooper step smartly up the trail, his hand poised lightly over his holstered weapon.

12

Vᴵᴄ ɢᴏᴛ Bɪʀᴇʟʏ into his sleeping bag, kneeling uncomfortably on the hard stone floor wishing to hell they had a couple of cots. The only light in the room, the only light they ever had, was the dinky emergency lamp with its six-volt battery, its glow so faint that from outside it didn't show at all. Even so he kept it under the sink to fully block it from the window.

"Can you pull the bag up higher, Vic? It's so cold."

Vic hauled the edges of the sleeping bag up around Birely's neck, immediately soaking it in blood. Guy must have lost a bucketful of blood, and it wasn't just his nose that got smashed. Every time he touched Birely, the little turd groaned and clutched his belly. When Birely began to retch, Vic snatched an empty fried chicken tub from the overflowing trash and shoved it under his face to catch the throw-up. That made Birely heave harder, maybe at the rancid smell. Dry heaves, but all he coughed up was blood.

Christ, what had the damn fool done to himself? The way he'd been thrown across the dashboard, Vic guessed the dash had gouged some kind of wound in his belly. When Birely started begging for water, Vic found a paper cup that smelled of stale coffee, filled it from the tap at the sink. Water always ran rusty, there. He rooted through Birely's pack, found a neatly rolled-up pair of Jockey shorts that *looked* clean, used it to wipe the blood off Birely's face. Found a shirt to tie around his face, to soak up the blood that was still gushing. Bleeding would stop for a while but if Birely moved at all or talked too much, it'd start again. Vic left his mouth clear so he could breathe, that was the only way he could get air in. Once the blood stopped for good, he'd be all right.

Vic's own hurts from the wreck were mostly bruises, but he sure as hell was sore. Probably bruised all over, if he'd bothered to pull down his pants, pull up his shirt, and have a look. He knew there'd be a gash down his leg where blood was seeping through his jeans. He wasn't a bleeder, never had been, he expected it would stop in a while. Birely asked for water again, he was lucky the water was working. That had been a plus, when they first broke in. Turned the tap on expecting they'd get nothing. Vic thought maybe the indoor and outside water were all on one cutoff, maybe Emmylou had left it on so she could water the half-dead flowers down in her scruffy yard. When Birely began to moan again, Vic gave him another codeine. He kept whining that his belly hurt, but Birely'd always been a whiner.

"What're we gonna do, Vic, now the truck's wrecked? I need you to take me to a doctor," as if he'd forgotten they had the Lincoln. Though Vic sure didn't want to be driving it around, under the noses of the local cops.

"It's okay," Vic said, "don't worry about it. If you get worse I'll take you to somewhere, Doctors on Duty, one of them twenty-four-hour walk-in places." He got up from the floor rubbing his knees, waiting for Birely's codeine to kick in, so he'd drift off. Digging into one of the paper bags on the kitchen table, he pulled out a can of red beans, opened it with the rusty can opener, found the Tabasco and dumped some in. They hadn't eaten since Denny's on the outskirts of San Francisco, way early this morning, hours before they headed south. He stood scooping beans out with a plastic spoon, wolfing them down, filling his belly.

They'd spent the morning, in the city, looking up the fence he'd been touted on, taking care of business with him. Old man working out of a Laundromat. Guy had given him a fair deal, though. Birely'd been edgy about going in there, but hell, *they* hadn't stolen the stuff. That little chippie, Debbie, that was her haul. He wasn't sure why he'd helped her out. Maybe because she worked so damned hard at conning him. Well, hell, he'd take his thirty percent like he'd told her, give over the rest. Maybe something would come of it. Young, dark eyed, and feisty, she wasn't a bad looker.

Scraping the last of the beans from the can, he watched Birely drifting off, sucking air through his open mouth, the blood still running down staining his teeth red. Good thing they had the codeine, put him out of his pain for a while. But what if he got worse? And what would happen if he died? That would complicate matters.

The way things stood, he figured Birely had some kind of legal claim to this property and to the cash, too. He *was* Sammie's only relative, so he said. Maybe a claim they could make stick. All they had to do was find some softhearted defense group, a two-bit lawyer providing free legal help for the needy, making his money from some kind of federal grant. Guy like that, he went into court, he could get anything.

But if Birely died, what? In a way, that would free things up. He could just take off with the money, get the hell out of there, and who would know? Forget about the property that he'd thought Birely could sell, move on out with the cash, and the cops'd never think about any hidden money, how could they know? Sure as hell Emmylou wouldn't tell them, if she'd found any of it for herself. Not unless she could prove it was hers, which he doubted. Say she did tell the cops there was hidden cash, but couldn't prove she had some legal claim. Cops got in the act, she'd never see those packs of bills again, they'd vanish like spit in a windstorm.

Picking up the keys to the Lincoln where he'd laid them on the edge of the stained sink, he stood looking at the other five keys on the ring. Had to be a house key on there, and who knew what else? Little fat key that might fit a padlock or a safe. Moving to the far wall, he removed the last few planks they'd left loose, removed the loose stone behind them. Reached down into the disintegrating pocket of old concrete, fished out the last two packs of musty hundred-dollar bills they'd left stashed there. Turning toward the door, he saw Birely was awake.

"What you doing, Vic?" Little bastard had raised up

on one elbow, groaning watching him, his breath wheezing in his throat.

"Going to hide this in the Lincoln with the rest," Vic said easily. "Maybe pull off one of the door panels. If that Emmylou comes snooping, spots us in here and maybe calls the cops, we'll need to take off fast. I want the money stashed where they can't find it, ready to roll."

Birely retched and coughed and reached for the cup of water that Vic had set on the floor beside him. "What if the cops get their hands on the car, what then? We'll never see that car again, and there goes my money, every damn bit of it." Birely always put the worst spin on things, he never could see the positive side.

"I'll muddy up the license plates until I can steal some. Maybe I'll dirty up the whole car." Vic smiled. "A bucket of garden dirt, a little water. Don't look like the cops have a BOL out on the Lincoln yet, we passed three CHP units on the highway and two sheriff's cars, and not one of 'em even turned to look. Maybe that old couple didn't think to report the car stolen, maybe they were too far gone."

But Birely wasn't paying attention, he was real white. "I need a doctor, Vic. Otherwise I'm gonna die. You got to take me somewhere, to an emergency room."

"Codeine should have kicked in by now," Vic said. "I'll give you another pill, then you'll rest easy."

Birely was hugging his belly and wheezing for air, and Vic felt his temper rise. Birely was going to slow him down, was going to get in his way, going to give the cops time to start looking for the Lincoln, and maybe time to find it.

As Vic stood pondering what to do, Birely began to talk as he had earlier, as he'd been muttering on and off ever since the accident, snatches of his childhood, some of them repeated over and over, useless memories of his sister and their old uncle, that old train robber that he guessed was famous in his day. "It was our uncle, Lee Fontana, sent the money to her," Birely said now, "and Sammie only a kid, twenty-some, that old man sending her money like that, what was that about? He didn't send me none."

"Why didn't she put it in a bank?" Vic said. If Birely kept on talking he'd wear himself out and go to sleep again.

"Maybe she hid it all that time because it was stolen," Birely said, "afraid the feds had the serial numbers and would trace them if the money went in the bank, maybe thought the feds would want to know where she'd got it. Well, anyway she hated banks. Uncle Lee hated banks, she got that from him. I'm not so fond of banks, neither. Never have done business with one, all my life long." That made Vic smile. Birely'd never had no money to *put* in a bank.

Some of what Birely muttered about was things before he was born, that Sammie'd told him. Some man following their mother, coming to the house when her daddy was off in the war. World War II, and that was some long time ago. Birely'd said Sammie was about seven. This stuff Sammie'd told him years later, it got stuck in his memory and he'd keep repeating it, stories about the man following and beating their mom, and the cops wouldn't do anything, garbled stories warped by time and distance. Birely started whimpering again, as if the codeine hadn't ever taken hold. Vic didn't know how much codeine he could give him before he checked out for good, and he was torn about that. You had a dog this sick, hadn't eaten and couldn't eat, dog hurt like that, you'd put it out of its pain.

Sick man, dying man, what use did he have for two hundred thousand in musty bills? Nor did Emmylou, neither. What was she going to do with that kind of money? All she ever did was work away at her so-called remodeling project, and clump around in her scraggly yard talking to that mangy yellow cat. That in itself showed she didn't have good sense. Sure as hell she was seeking out the money little by little, down there, as she tore out the walls. What a waste, what would she use it for?

OUTSIDE, EVEN AS Vic headed over to open the door, the yellow tom dropped down from the window and was gone. He'd watched from among the trees as the man stared around into the night searching for a prowler he'd never find. He'd heard enough through the window to know that Birely *was* Sammie's brother, and to remember more clearly that moment from his earlier life. To remember that ex-con following Sammie's mother and beating her. The other guy was a classmate from her high school. Sammie's daddy off in the Pacific fighting in the war that was meant, once again, to end all wars, and this scum comes onto his young wife. Now, listening to Birely, that distant time came clear, the rooms of their tiny cottage in that small Southern town, the polished floors and handmade rag rugs, a gold-colored cross hanging over the bed; and then the old gas station and garage that Sammie's daddy bought when he did get home from the war, bought to make a living for the three of them. Birely's words woke in him sharp fragments of memory, each scene filtered through the eyes of the young and careless tomcat that he had been in that earlier life.

13

LUCINDA GREENLAW'S GLASS-FRONTED cubicle in the Santa Cruz ER was so tiny that Kate had to slide in sideways, pushing back the canvas curtain, joining Charlie Harper and Charlie's aunt, Wilma. The two women stood crowded against the wall between the water basin, the hazardous-waste receptacle, and Lucinda's hospital bed. But Lucinda was even more constricted, bound to her bed by a tangle of tubes and wires, as captive as a bird caught in a net, this active older woman whom everyone admired for her youthful outlook and vigorous lifestyle. Now, she slept, she was hardly a bump beneath the thin white blanket, so fragile, her breathing steadied by the oxygen that whispered through her mask. She wore a cast on her lower left arm, and a heavy white bandage around her left shoulder.

Charlie gave Kate a hug. "Sorry I brought you out in the night." Her unruly red hair shone bright in the overhead light, tied back crookedly with an old brass clip, caught across one shoulder of her brown sweatshirt, which she'd pulled on over what looked like a pajama top, pale blue with little white stars.

"I'd have been mad if you hadn't," Kate said. Her questioning look at Charlie brought a shake of the head. There was no word, yet, of Kit, then. Wilma took Kate's hand, trying to look hopeful. She wore a red fleece jacket over jeans and a navy sweater, had pinned her gray hair hastily back into a knot. Her canvas carryall stood on the floor beside her booted feet, looking so suspiciously lumpy that Kate knelt and peered in.

Dulcie looked up at her, the expression in her green eyes worried for Kit. Above them in the narrow bed, Lucinda stirred a little, muttered then was silent again.

"Still sedated," Charlie said. "They set the arm right away, and slipped her dislocated shoulder back into place. Thank God it wasn't broken. She's bruised all over, and scraped down her left side, where he jerked her out of the car. The nurse said she was still mad as hell, too," Charlie said. In the bright fluorescent light, Lucinda's skin seemed as thin as crumpled tissue, the veins of her wrists dark above the adhesive that held the invasive needles. She barely resembled, now, the slim, robust woman who walked the Molena Point hills several miles a day with Pedric, their Kit racing joyfully ahead leading them to the wildest paths and up the steepest climbs.

"She was able to describe what happened, then?" Kate asked, still kneeling and stroking Dulcie.

"Clearly," Charlie said. "We talked a few minutes, while they were preparing her for surgery. It's Pedric who doesn't remember much, and that's worrisome. Some moments come clear, but then he can't fill in the spaces between. That should come with time," she said. "Even so, he remembers enough to be raging mad, too. When they're awake and lucid, they're both impatient to talk to the CHP, to the county sheriff up there, and most of all, to Max." Max Harper, Charlie's husband and Molena Point chief of police, would most likely coordinate the Greenlaws' statements for the other law enforcement agencies. "He'll bring it all together," she said, "that will help ease Lucinda and Pedric from so many interviews. Multiple interviews are necessary, but it will wear them out."

Charlie watched Lucinda, sleeping so quietly. "You won't get these two down for long," she said hopefully. She filled Kate in on the wreck and the attack, repeating what Lucinda had told them. "There's a BOL out for the Lincoln. If those two men are picked up, they'd better be *locked* up, away from me."

"Away from all of us," Kate said, looking into Dulcie's own angry eyes. "By now, who knows how far away they've gotten. Headed where? Arizona? Oregon? Mexico?"

"Lucinda told us what's in the car," Charlie said. "If they dump the car or sell it, will they trash all those lovely purchases? But maybe," she said, "maybe they won't find the rest.

"At least Kit wasn't in the car," she said, thinking of what Kit might have tried to do, trapped in the Lincoln with those two men, and what they might have done to her.

"Have Ryan and Clyde called?" Kate asked. "Can you call them?"

"They called once," Wilma said, "when they parked up at the slide. They were just setting out to search." She touched Kate's shoulder, where she knelt beside the carry-all. "Kit's tough, Kate. She's smart and quick—and she has Lucinda's phone. When she sees the Damens' truck, sees them start up the cliff, don't you think she'll use the phone or else call out to them, lead them right to her?"

"If she's not afraid to lead something else to her," Kate said. She wished she were there, she couldn't shake her fear for Kit, she felt as weak with fright as if she herself, in cat form, crouched small and lost up there in the black night, with only her claws and little cat teeth to protect her against whatever prowled, hungry and listening.

"Their house keys are on the ring with the car keys," Wilma said. "Ryan said that first thing in the morning she'll get her lock man out. I'll put holds on the credit cards. They have some blocks on them and on their bank accounts, but better to be safe.

"Pedric gave the hospital their insurance information, he still had his billfold, the guy missed that, too busy harassing Lucinda and stealing the Lincoln. When we got here, Lucinda's focus was all on Pedric and on Kit, she couldn't rest at all. She wouldn't let them take the X-rays until we assured her the Damens had gone after Kit, she just kept begging for Kit, fussing and trying to get out of bed. She made such a rumpus she disrupted the whole floor, the nurses had a time with her. We got here, talked for only a few minutes, told her Rock was tracking Kit. Finally they took her to X-ray, gave her a shot, and in less than an hour she was off to surgery."

The three women watched Lucinda and watched the

lighted monitor above her bed with its moving graphs and numbers that mapped Lucinda's life processes, oxygen level and blood pressure and the slow steadiness of her heartbeat. "Once we've taken care of the credit cards and changed the locks," Charlie said, "we need to make arrangements for when they come home. Maybe they won't have to go into rehab, if we take turns staying at the house, have nurses come if they're needed. We *could* put someone in their downstairs apartment if . . ."

She shook her head. "I'd even thought of Debbie Kraft," she said with a wry smile. "She needs the job, and the Damens' would be thrilled to get her out of their cottage. But it would take more effort to ride herd on Debbie than to move in ourselves. To say nothing of the torment that older girl would dish out. There'd be no peace, with Vinnie in the house."

"I can stay," Kate said. "I'd planned to be with them for a while. I could stay, and you all could run the errands, pick up the meds and groceries. Would that work?" She wanted to be there, in part to watch over Kit, whose wild but vulnerable nature was so like Kate's own temperament. She longed to hold the little tortoiseshell safe, keep her close and safe. No one said, If Pedric comes home, if he heals from the concussion, and can come home. No one said, If Kit comes home, if Ryan and Clyde can find her. Wilma took Kate's hand and Charlie's, as if by touching, by all of them willing it, they could help to heal the older couple and could bring them home, and bring Kit home. It was in that quiet moment that tabby Dulcie crept out from Wilma's carryall and slipped up onto Lucinda's bed. Stepping delicately among the snaking tubes, she padded up beside Lucinda, on her unhurt side, slipped under the covers, laid her head on Lucinda's shoulder, and softly began to purr. Maybe Lucinda, deep in dreams, would imagine she held Kit in her arms, snuggling close, maybe that thought would help to heal her.

LEAVING BIRELY HALF asleep, Vic headed out the door and down the stairs along the side of the stone building carrying a couple of rusty screwdrivers he'd found in the stone shack, an empty old bucket and a dirt-crusted spade he'd found in the yard, and a paper bag with four bottles of water, eight cans of beans, the rusty can opener, and the two packs of hundred-dollar bills he'd had on him. Maybe he'd find something useful among all that junk in the Lincoln, maybe a couple of blankets. The rest of the stuff he'd dump somewhere, all them fancy packages from the San Francisco stores. He should have had all this when he linked up with the fence, it'd be worth something. He didn't know much about upholstery material, if that's what those bolts of cloth were, but the fancy pictures and lamps had to be worth something—that old couple were big spenders. Had to be, driving a Town Car and all. Maybe when he headed out he'd swing through Frisco again and see what he could get for the lot.

Standing in shadow at the bottom of the stairs, he watched the house below. The old Chevy was parked off to the side on the dirt drive where that stringy old woman kept it. There was no light in the kitchen window, no reflection of lights from anywhere in the house, shining out against the pine trees. Moving around to the shed door, he removed the lock, eased the door back so it wouldn't squawk, and slipped inside.

He deposited the paper bag among the packages in the backseat, then carried the bucket outside again. Kneeling close against the stairs, he began scooping up loose garden dirt with the spade and with his hands. Filling the bucket, he turned back inside, poured in a bottle of water, and stirred the mess with the spade, into a thick mud. Earlier, leaving the wreck, he'd hidden the cash behind the back console. Maybe he could do better than that before he took off, maybe find a hiding place the cops wouldn't think to poke into with just a casual stop, a stop he might talk his way out of. If he changed his looks, got a haircut, cleaned up in different clothes, maybe he could slip by.

He thought how drug dealers pry off the door panels of a car to secure their stash, he'd watched a guy do that, once. Took special tools, which he didn't have. He sure didn't want to bend or crack the panel, not be able to put it back right. But he didn't want the money on him, neither. And if he decided to stay put here for a while, he didn't want to hide it again in the stone room. He had an uneasy feeling about Birely up there whining and carrying on. If that old woman heard him and came nosing around, who knew what she'd poke into that was none of her business?

Pulling down the armrest, he removed the packs of hundreds. The little metal tray beneath was screwed in place, with a small square hole in the front, along with two small connections where, he thought, people could charge their cell phones. When he poked the screwdriver down in the hole he could feel a space beneath, about an inch deep. Using the Phillips, he removed the screws and lifted the tray out.

The space beneath was big enough to stash most of the packs of bills. He stuffed the rest in his pocket, screwed the black plastic tray back in place, then got to work on the outside of the car. Stirring up the bucket of dirt and water, and using a wadded-up shirt from Birely's pack, he began to spread the mud on. First the license plates, and then the outside of the car, dirtying up the shiny black paint and the dents, just enough, not to overdo it. Working away humming to himself, he thought about a better place to hide the car, away from that old woman poking around. One thing, he'd have to lift a new set of plates, maybe from the far side of the village. But the car itself he wanted nearby where he could keep an eye on it.

There were plenty of empty houses down the hill, abandoned places, no one ever around, no furniture when he'd looked in through the dirty windows. Skuzzy neighborhood, foreclosures, empty rentals, the grass grown tall and brown, FOR RENT signs tipped crooked or lying on the ground. Their narrow, one-car garages, the ones he could see into, were empty. Stash the Lincoln for a few hours, steal himself another set of wheels or borrow them.

That little tart Debbie Kraft, she owed him one, the good sale he'd made for her. Maybe he'd use her old station wagon. Take the money he'd got from the fence down to her, and make nice. He'd sold everything she'd stole. When he handed over near three thousand in cash, that should make those dark eyes sparkle. Hell, she couldn't refuse the loan of her car, not when she knew he could finger her for stealing, tip the cops that she was boosting the local stores. She sure wouldn't want the cops to know she was using her daughter Vinnie as a distraction and, sometimes, setting the kid up to heist small items herself, silk bras and panties, a few pieces of costume jewelry, while Debbie kept the clerks busy.

Judiciously Vic went on spreading mud, not too much, keeping it to the lower parts of the car, the wheels and fenders and bumpers. Spreading the slop, watching it splash onto the shed's dirt floor, he smiled. It was all coming together, his running into Birely like that, south of Salinas, the story Birely'd told that turned out to be true, the money in hand now, everything going real smooth. He had only a few more moves and he'd be out of there. Sell the Lincoln, get some shiny new wheels, not like Debbie's old heap, and head north out of California, maybe way north, up into Canada. Get lost up in Canada for a while and then off again, he could go anywhere he wanted now, with this kind of money.

14

 THEY'RE SURE TO stop us," Ryan told Clyde as they entered the hospital from the covered walkway. She avoided looking directly at the two guards in dark uniforms who watched them from within, through the wide glass doors. "We look like a couple of tramps, with our dirty backpacks, look like we're up to no good." Their wrinkled, stained clothes smelled of sweat and of dog, of gunpowder and maybe of coyote, too, to a discerning nose, maybe even the scent of animal blood. "And my mop looks like a Brillo pad," she said, pushing back her dark hair where it clung, frizzled into tight curls from their night in the fog. "Not to mention how your backpack is bulging. Be still, Kit," she muttered, leaning close to the pack, afraid the guards would see it move and want to investigate, would paw through the pack and find Kit staring up at them or scrambling to bolt away.

But no one bothered them, they received only a bored glance from the two uniformed men who were deep in conversation, totally uninterested in what they might be carrying inside with them. Maybe they looked too tired and limp to be bringing in a bomb, to be smuggling in anything that would take much effort. Or maybe Santa Cruz Dominican hadn't had any problems yet with bomb threats or petty vandalism, as the bigger city hospitals were experiencing.

But when they reached the emergency room, down an open flight of stairs, that area was more secure. The ER's doors were locked, they had to give a nurse their names, and provide Lucinda's and Pedric's names, and wait for another nurse to lead them in through the heavy double doors. The short, pillow-shaped woman in green scrubs escorted them past the inner nurses' station and on past rows of small, glass-walled rooms not much larger than a walk-in closet, some with the curtains closed, some open so they glimpsed patients within, sleeping or looking forlornly back at them. Lucinda's glass doors stood open, the canvas curtain drawn halfway across, the lights dimmed down to only a soft glow. Wilma Getz and a lean, dark-haired nurse in scrubs stood one at each side of her bed, frowning as if they'd been arguing. Lucinda lay awake, scowling, but she seemed groggy, too. She smiled vaguely at Ryan and Clyde. "Kate and Charlie were here," she said. "Gone down to Pedric." And almost at once she dropped into sleep again. The cast and bandage on her left arm looked heavy and uncomfortable. Her right arm lay across a red windbreaker, holding it possessively. Wilma stood beside her, holding the red jacket, too, keeping it firmly in place as the nurse reached to remove it, apparently not for the first time. At Wilma's angry glare, she paused and drew her hand back. Wilma's gray ponytail was awry; she looked as if she'd pulled on her jeans and navy sweatshirt while climbing straight out of bed. But she looked, even so, not a woman to defy, with that steady and uncompromising gaze. Wilma had intimidated her parolees for thirty years, until she'd retired from the federal court system. She didn't tolerate patronizing behavior from a person committed to easing the suffering of others, particularly of helpless patients.

"Lucinda wants the jacket near her," Wilma said. "She says it smells of pine trees, and of the hills of our village. What harm, if it comforts her?" Her stubborn grasp on the jacket, and Lucinda's own protective arm across it, even in sleep, didn't hide adequately the little mound beneath but, confronted by Wilma, and now with Clyde and Ryan's presence, the dark, sour woman seemed reluctant to push the matter. She smiled woodenly at the Damens, shook her head as if there were little she could do about unreasonable patients or visitors, and turned away leaving the jacket in place.

Moving to Lucinda's bed, Ryan reached beneath the jacket, speaking softly to Dulcie, smiling up at Wilma.

Wilma grinned back at her. "Lucinda thinks Kit's cuddled next to her. She's much more peaceful since Dulcie slipped into bed with her. If the nurses will just leave us alone."

"The best therapy," Clyde said, slinging his pack off,

resting it on the edge of the bed. "But there's no need for a stand-in now." And Kit peered out at them, her green eyes bright.

"Oh," Wilma said, reaching for her, pausing to glance out the door and then leaning to hug her. "Oh, you're all right, you're safe." She hugged Kit, squeezing almost too hard. "Pedric's been asking and asking for you, they've been so upset. That's made the doctor upset, he doesn't want Pedric stressed."

Ryan moved to the glass door and pulled it closed. She stood a moment looking out to the big, center island of counters and desks from which the nurses and doctors and orderlies could see into all the rooms. Only the canvas curtain offered privacy. When she closed that, too, leaving only a crack to look out, Kit slipped from the backpack, her dark coat stark against the white cover.

"Hurry," Ryan said, "she's coming back." Kit didn't crawl under with Dulcie, but returned to the depths of the canvas pack.

"Come on," Clyde said, slinging her over his shoulder. "We'll look in on Pedric. What time does the shift change, when does that nurse leave?"

"Twelve, I think," Wilma said, glancing at her watch. The clock above Lucinda's bed had almost reached eleven. Clyde and Ryan moved on out with their stowaway, leaving Lucinda sleeping happily with Dulcie as surrogate, and Wilma standing guard.

"How many cats," Clyde whispered, moving down past the nurses' station to the other side of the big, open square, "how many cats can you smuggle in, before you have Security in your face?"

"They let therapy dogs in," Ryan said softly. "If the cats wore those same little therapy coats, maybe . . ."

He gave her a lopsided grin. "Don't even think about it. This is dicey enough."

"What would they do if they caught us?"

He laughed. "What could they do? Two innocent little cats? At least we don't have to worry about Joe and Pan." They'd left the two tomcats in the king cab, both solemnly promising not to open the door, not to set foot outside, had left them pacing back and forth past Rock, who lay curled up asleep. Having completed his night's work, the silver Weimaraner didn't mean to be kept awake by a couple of edgy tomcats.

"I just hope those two are as good as their word," Clyde said.

"And how good is that?" she said nervously.

PEDRIC'S ROOM WAS brightly lit, the overhead fluorescents turned up high as if the softer lights of evening would too easily lull the patient to sleep when, with a concussion, he must be kept awake. Charlie and Kate sat crowded into folding chairs that they'd jammed between the wall and Pedric's bed. His head was wrapped in a thick white bandage. His thin, lined face was painted with black-and-blue marks down the right side and around his eye where Vic had hit him with the tire iron, bruises that made him look like a dignified clown halfway through applying his makeup. A young, redheaded nurse was fluffing his pillows, he was talking softly to her, the look on his face intense. Whatever he was saying made her uncomfortable. She turned away as Ryan and Clyde entered, bending to adjust the height of the bed. She glanced up embarrassedly at them and at Charlie and Kate, her face flushed, and silently fled the room. Behind her, Charlie and Kate exchanged a look of amusement.

"What?" Ryan said when she'd gone. "Pedric, what were you saying? You weren't coming on to her?" she said, laughing.

Pedric looked puzzled. "I was talking about the old country, the old myths, the old Celtic tales. I told her she looked like the princess from under the hill, but I guess she didn't understand. I guess I made her nervous." He looked vaguely up at them. "I guess if you're not into mythology, that might sound a bit strange?"

Charlie pushed back her red hair, where a loose strand had caught on her shoulder. "You got her attention, all right. Maybe nurses aren't into folklore. Maybe, when you work in a world of discipline and hard facts, slipping away into imaginary places can be unsettling." Though for Charlie that wasn't the case; she seemed, in her paintings and her imaginative writing, to live comfortably in both realms.

But Pedric's attention was on Clyde's backpack, which had begun to wriggle. When he saw Kit's bright eyes peering out through the mesh his face broke into a smile, he raised his arms to her as she struggled to get out to him. She was about to leap down beside him when another nurse, a blond, shapely woman, started across from the nursing station and Kit ducked down again. She was stone-still as the nurse entered. Her name tag said HALLIE EVERS. She opened the glass door wide, and opened the curtain.

"You can visit," she said, looking sternly at the four of them. "But not so many at once. One, maybe two if you're quiet. We don't want him excited, though we do need to keep him awake. We need to do that calmly, do you understand? Dr. Pindle will be in shortly. Are you all relatives of Mr. Greenlaw?"

"We're good friends," Clyde said. "The Greenlaws have no relatives. We came to do whatever we can for them."

She frowned. "He's been talking strangely, going on about some kind of fairy tale, about harpies and dragons as if they were real," she said doubtfully. "Maybe the concussion has stirred up some childhood fancy."

Kate hid a smile. Charlie frowned, looking down at her hands.

"That's not surprising," Ryan said, giving Nurse Evers her most beguiling smile. "Pedric's a folklorist, that's his profession. He *studies* the old, classical myths and folktales, he has an impressive collection of ancient literature, he tells wonderful stories. You should visit with him sometime, if you're interested in such things. But you're right," she said, her green eyes wide and innocent. "Four of us is too many, all at once." She turned to Pedric. "We'll take turns visiting, then, seeing that you don't sleep," she said gently.

Kate grinned at Charlie and rose, and the two of them left, highly amused by Nurse Evers.

"We'll be quieter," Ryan told the nurse. "How long must he be kept awake?" Still smiling, she stepped back, easing against Clyde.

"Until the doctor has done an evaluation," Nurse Evers said, "possibly longer, depending on what is found. Dr. Pindle will give you that information. Mr. Greenlaw's hurt his knee badly, as well. He seems to want to wait for treatment on that until he returns home to his own doctors. He's very vague, most likely due to the concussion. The doctor may want to talk with you about that." All this as if Pedric were not in the room with them or as if he didn't hear or understand her. "Vague, and then he'll start in again on those strange stories."

Clyde pretended to adjust his backpack, where Kit had begun to wriggle with impatience.

"He seems able to remember only fragments of the accident, but that's to be expected. He remembers more distant . . . things. I suppose," she said doubtfully, "if these stories are his profession, I expect he would remember those." She gave them a brighter smile as if to humor them, and she left abruptly, leaving the door and curtain wide open behind her. Returning to the nurses' station, she moved directly to a computer where she sat facing them, keeping them in view.

Ryan moved to the door, smiled across at Nurse Evers, then closed the door and drew the canvas curtain. She turned to the bed, where Clyde had lowered the backpack and opened it. Kit's black-and-brown ears emerged. As her little tilted nose pushed up over the edge of the pack, Pedric reached in to her, such joy in the older man's face that Ryan had to wipe her eyes and Clyde turned away embarrassed by his own emotion. Quickly Pedric lifted the sheet and Kit crept under, tucking down so close to him that when he'd covered her again, she was barely a lump in the thin white blanket.

"After the wreck," he whispered, "where did you go? Where were you when they found you?"

"Above the landslide," Kit said softly. "Rock and Joe and Pan found me and Ryan and Clyde right behind them and Ryan had her revolver, one shot at that coyote that was trying to *dig* me out of the rocks, and *that* mother died, serves him right, trying to eat a poor little cat, and those other two ran like hell and then Pan was there and, oh my . . ." She stopped talking, purring so loudly that anyone passing might have heard her. But then, suddenly yawning, she went quiet beneath the blanket, all worn out. Snuggling deeper against Pedric's side, she drifted off into a deep and healing sleep—while Pedric, longing for sleep, for a forbidden nap of his own, lay watching over her, as their friends stood guard.

15

IT WAS MIDNIGHT when Vic crawled into his sleeping bag on the floor of the stone shack, careful not to wake Birely and have him start whining again. The little turd was finally sleeping deeply, despite having to breathe through his open mouth. Even in the dim glow of the battery light, he was pale as milk. Vic had tried to get him to eat but he didn't want anything, just sucked at the water in the limp paper cup. He'd woken up once and talked for a while, his voice slurry, rambling on about his childhood again and his sister, Sammie, and how she came by all that money. Birely'd never say why the old man would send that kind of money to a young niece, send it clear up from Mexico, maybe didn't know why. They'd already found over a hundred thousand, and sure as hell Sammie'd had more down in the house. Weird, her growing old in that run-down place when she'd had enough to live high on the hog. Birely said she liked living the way she did. He said, look at Emmylou, her only friend, another recluse just like Sammie.

Strange, the change in Birely. He used to be a real wuss, a drifter, went right along with whatever anyone wanted him to do. But after Sammie'd given away what was his, now he was all anger, so mad at Sammie that he got moving, all right, looking for her hidden stash.

Birely never knew the old uncle, all he knew was what Sammie and maybe their folks told him. Old train robber did his share of prison time back then, Birely knew that much. Sammie was about nine when Lee Fontana made his big haul and lit out for Mexico, running from the feds, got out of the country shortly before Birely was born. Sammie called him the cowboy, Birely said. She claimed that sometimes she knew from her dreams what he was doing, knew what was happening to him even when he was halfway across the country. Well, you couldn't believe half what Birely told you. Birely said the old man's last robbery was big in the papers back then, and Vic could believe that, all right. Some kind of federal money, Birely didn't know exactly what. Said you'd get burned bad, back in them days, for a federal heist. Vic wondered if the feds kept records back that far. If, tucked away in some musty drawer of ancient files, some federal office had the serial numbers on those old bills.

But what the hell? Even if these cops here in Molena Point got their hands on the money, which wasn't likely, even if they figured out it was real old money, who would think to look back to the last century for some federal robbery? Who would even care?

Except, he thought, if that federal case was still open

and he did take Birely to some hospital and Birely started talking, who knew what the dummy would blurt out? Enough to make some nosy cop curious, start him rooting around into the past? Birely could talk on and on, and Vic didn't want to chance that—there were times when a man had no choice, when he did what was needed just to save his own neck.

THE DAMENS WEREN'T night people, Ryan and Clyde were early risers, they were often in bed by nine or ten, but somehow in the small hours of this long night they managed to stay awake and to keep Pedric awake, taking turns, one dozing, one asking Pedric for details about the wreck to keep him from drifting off.

Charlie had gotten two adjoining motel rooms nearby at Best Western, so they could all take turns sitting with Pedric; Ryan had stayed with him while Clyde left to take Rock and the two tomcats there, to feed them and get them settled in. Kibble and dog food for Rock, a nice spread of takeout for Joe Grey and Pan, of rare burgers and fried cod. He praised the three trackers lavishly again for their night's work before he left to join Ryan.

Rock, having bolted down his supper, was tucked up with Charlie on her bed. Joe sprawled across Wilma's empty pillow while she and Kate and Dulcie were still at the hospital; Pan didn't settle but paced restlessly, leaping onto the daybed that had been set up for Kate, aimlessly wandering the two rooms, missing Kit, wanting to be with her, still suffering the aftermath of his worry over her. *How strange is that?* he thought. Kit was his first true love, and he didn't quite know what to make of the condition, of the intensity and turmoil that had descended to change his carefree life. *Kit is all fluff and softness—over slashing claws,* he thought, smiling, *sharp teeth, and a will more stubborn even than my own.* She was brave as a cougar one moment, dreamy the next, always volatile, keeping him forever off balance. All he knew was that right now he missed her; he paced until he wore himself out, and then settled down next to Rock and Charlie and, like the softly snoring Weimaraner, Pan slept.

It was one a.m. The lights in most of the ER rooms had been dimmed, only Pedric's lights shone brightly behind the drawn curtain. Ryan had left the glass door cracked open, but the few nurses and attendants visible were busy at their desks, able to get computer records entered, now that most of the patients were sleeping. At this predawn hour a quiet lull held the ward, perhaps before the next sudden round of broken legs and stomach cramps that would have nurses hurrying again to minister to the wounded and accident-prone. Quietly, Clyde pushed in through the canvas curtain.

Pedric was sitting up in bed, in his skimpy hospital gown, a white cotton blanket around his shoulders, looking relaxed despite the fierce headache he said still plagued him. Beneath the blanket he held Kit safe, so happy to have her there. Ryan sat beside the bed, Clyde's backpack near, in case someone came to tend to Pedric; nurses were never shy about waking patients from sleep to administer pills, to poke and prod and straighten blankets.

"I can remember only fragments of this week," Pedric was saying worriedly, "a breakfast of Swiss pancakes, a cable car ride in the rain. Kit stretched out on Kate's windowsill," he said, smiling, "watching fog slip in beneath the Golden Gate. Whole mornings and evenings are blank.

"I remember Kate's stories more clearly, the granite sky, those cavernous sweeps of stone lit by the green glow of the subterranean daytime, a winged woman with a . . ." He went still then as the canvas curtain moved and was eased aside.

A doctor in a white coat stepped in. "Dr. James Pindle," he said, rigidly watching Pedric. He didn't offer to shake hands with him, or with Ryan or Clyde. He was a thin-boned man, narrow arms and shoulders, small hands. Milk-white skin against ink-black hair, eyes so black you couldn't see the pupils.

"I left orders for only one visitor at a time," he said accusingly. "I don't want him talking away like this, I don't want him stressed. Didn't the nurse *tell* you that?"

Ryan had risen, pretending to straighten Pedric's covers as Kit slid deeper down; too late now to slip into the backpack, and they were terrified Pindle would lower the rail to examine Pedric.

"At least you didn't let him fall asleep," Pindle said. "I hope he hasn't slept. The nurse must have told you that much, if you were allowed to stay in here with the curtain drawn. You *must* have been instructed what to watch for." He glanced out toward the nurses' station, where Nurse

Evers seemed totally preoccupied at her computer.

"You do understand," he said coldly, "that with a concussion he can't have drugs or painkillers or caffeine, and that he will try to escape the pain by retreating into sleep."

"We understand," Clyde said. "He hasn't slept. We've been very quiet, and he hasn't talked much."

"He just seems glad for the company," Ryan said. She didn't say which company had so pleased and calmed the patient. Pindle gave her a chill look and moved to the bed rail, forcing Ryan to step aside. He stood not inches from where Kit hid beneath the blanket, looking at Pedric. "One of you will have to leave. The patient is a bundle of nerves, surely you can see he's disturbed."

"Not at all," Pedric said, smiling easily at him, putting out his hand for a proper introduction. "In fact, I'm feeling better, the headache is less severe. I'd like something to eat, if there's anything available at this hour."

Pindle's face seemed frozen into scowl lines. "I'll tell the nurse. Maybe some crackers and applesauce." He looked at Clyde. "Is he still worrying about his *cat*?" he said with disgust. "This foolishness about a cat has him unduly upset. I can't have him worrying, certainly not over something so inconsequential. I'm moving him to the ICU in the morning, until he's stable. Blood sugar way too high, and that could mean any number of things. And the torn knee needs attending to. The hospitalist will be in shortly, he's the one who will admit him. I don't suppose either of you have a medical power of attorney?"

"We both do," Clyde said coolly. "As do Ms. Osborne, Wilma Getz, and Mrs. Harper. Ms. Osborne is down the hall with Pedric's wife. We are all listed on both of the

Greenlaws' health care directives. Mrs. Harper signed him in, so that should be on the chart."

"Then there should be no problem if further tests are warranted," Pindle said. "His wife will be kept in ER overnight. If nothing else shows up, she can go home. I'm on my way to look at her. We'll keep Mr. Greenlaw until the concussion has healed and the torn meniscus in his knee is repaired, though we may find that other procedures will be needed."

What other procedures, Ryan thought, here in a strange hospital? And who said Pedric and Lucinda weren't alert enough to do their own signing?

"Maybe Dr. Carroll can deal with him," he said without explanation, and without any comforting word to Pedric, he left the room, the canvas curtain swinging behind him. Ryan looked after him, rigid with anger, then hurried to catch up as he moved along the hall toward Lucinda's room.

"I'm not sure," she said, walking beside him, "that it's wise to separate Lucinda and Pedric, to send Lucinda home alone." She kept her voice loud enough to alert Kate and Wilma. One close call was enough, they didn't need this man finding Dulcie. Dr. Pindle didn't respond, he didn't speak or turn to look at her. He pushed past her, was just entering Lucinda's room when Ryan, glancing back, saw another doctor leave the room next to Pedric's, heading for Pedric's door.

Praying Kate and Wilma had heard her warning, she turned back again, to help Clyde get Kit out of there unseen, or try to get her out. But, stepping in behind the doctor, he didn't alarm her as Pindle had; his movements were easier and unthreatening as he turned to look at her.

He wore the requisite white coat with its little brass name tag, same dark slacks as Dr. Pindle, soft-soled black shoes. But this man looked relaxed, he had an easy walk, a big man, big hands, tousled red hair framing a face that looked sunny and thoughtful. As he approached Pedric's bed she saw Wilma hurry out of Lucinda's room carrying her heavy tote bag, the canvas bottom sagging. Had Pindle seen Dulcie and angrily sent them packing? Or had Wilma moved fast enough to clear the premises before they found themselves in a nasty tangle of red tape and security guards, mired in a diatribe that would leave both the cats and humans shaken, leave the two patients sicker than they'd been when they were admitted?

EVEN BEFORE RYAN left Pedric's room Kit was digging her claws into the mattress trying not to squirm, not to burst out hissing at that Dr. Pindle person. She felt trapped by his cold voice, trapped by the bed rails and the tightly tucked blanket that hid her, trapped even by the tubes and wires that confined Pedric, that seemed to confine them both. Hidden in the near dark against Pedric's warmth, she couldn't see out; she'd listened with growing anger to Dr. Pindle, had heard Ryan follow him out of the room, heard her voice moving away down the hall as if to warn Kate and Wilma, but still she felt he might appear again, and the man made her fur crawl. But then, crouched there listening, she sensed Pedric start to fall asleep. She felt

Clyde shake his arm, prodding him awake. "Talk to me, Pedric," Clyde urged.

Oh, don't talk about the Netherworld again, Kit thought, but already he was saying, "A world so green, like the green underworld of the old myths," and even as he rambled on again, to keep himself awake, she heard footsteps in the room next to them, a man's soft-soled step. "Green drifting out of the granite sky . . ." Pedric was saying, and she pawed at him to make him be still. She heard the next door slide open, the scuff of rubber-soled shoes approaching Pedric's door. She peered out searching for the backpack, but she couldn't see it. Yes, there, Clyde was holding it open. She tensed to slip out but she was too late. Another doctor had stepped in and with no time to hide she pushed closer to Pedric, her heart pounding.

He came to stand beside the metal rail. He would be looking down at Pedric, looking right at the covers where she hid. She tried not to move even a whisker, prayed not to sneeze or purr. Purrs weren't always controllable, sometimes they just slipped out.

He didn't smell like Dr. Pindle, he had a friendly scent, laced with a touch of spicy shaving lotion. His voice was easy, deep, and relaxed. "I was in the next room, Mr. Greenlaw. I'm Dr. Carroll. That was a fascinating tale you were spinning."

Kit swallowed. There was a long, awkward silence. She listened to Clyde and Ryan introduce themselves, standing near the foot of the bed. And Clyde launched into Ryan's explanation of Pedric's seemingly wild talk.

"Pedric's knowledge of Celtic folklore is remarkable," Clyde said, "he—"

Dr. Carroll stopped him. "Not necessary," he said. "I heard quite a lot, from next door." He smiled down at Pedric. "Dr. Pindle doesn't get it, does he?"

Pedric was silent, his body gone tense.

"The old tales are an interest of mine, too," Dr. Carroll said. "In my Scotch-Irish family, I grew up on the Celtic myths. Dr. Pindle seems concerned that you're delirious," he said, laughing. "I don't think that. Pindle has no feel for the ancient wonders. Maybe they frighten him."

There was another silence, Kit sensed the two men looking at each other. Dr. Carroll said, "Pindle seemed concerned that you are unduly distressed, Mr. Greenlaw. Over the loss of your cat? I understand she escaped from your car, after the wreck? I suppose he didn't understand why that would worry you. Has there been any word of her?"

Pedric's voice came stronger now. "She . . . she ran up the cliff, into the woods. But Ryan and Clyde found her, she's safe now, and that has eased my mind."

"I imagine it has," Dr. Carroll said, "and eased Mrs. Greenlaw, too." Kit felt him touch the blanket, and before she could slide away or think *what* to do he'd pulled the covers back. She stared up at him, stricken.

Dr. Carroll smiled. He looked straight down into her eyes, and it was a look she could never have feared. He reached to stroke her, his big hands gentle. His nails were very short, clean and neatly trimmed. His blue eyes were full of light, his red hair curly and wild, his freckles dark across his square cheeks. He spoke right to her. "The next time you hide," he told her, "you want to be sure you haven't left a tortoiseshell hair or two, on the white blanket."

Kit blinked, and then purred, but her poor heart was pounding so hard she knew he could feel it beneath his stroking hand.

He couldn't know that she understood him, but he spoke as if she did, he looked at her as if he knew what she was. He scratched her ears, then looked up at Pedric. "I'm glad she's safe, Mr. Greenlaw. I know you and your wife are relieved. Now that your little cat is here, I can already see the healing in your eyes, in your smile. This little lady," he said, "is the best medicine you could have. Don't be disturbed by people like Pindle. But," he said softly, "do keep her hidden."

He turned to look at Clyde. "Several of you came up from Molena Point to be with the Greenlaws?"

"Yes, my wife and three friends. Charlie Harper is the wife of our police chief."

"I know Max. We talked on the phone just a little while ago. You're not going back tonight?"

"Charlie got a couple of motel rooms, we plan to take turns sitting with Pedric, keeping him awake. If we're needed."

"It will be a big help. He mustn't sleep, yet." He gave Clyde a wink. "If you can keep their little cat close to them, maybe pass her back and forth, that will be good medicine for both patients.

"You've done well, so far, hiding her." He glanced up at the screen above Pedric's bed. "His vital signs are already stronger. Between the five of you," he said, "you should be able to keep the staff from discovering her."

"We're doing our best."

"Some of the nurses can get testy when a rule is broken." He scratched Kit's ears again, in just the way she liked. "If there's a problem, call my cell number. I'll be on duty all night, until six A.M." He jotted the number on two cards, handed one to Clyde, the other to Ryan. He winked at Kit, his blue eyes still laughing. He turned away, slipped out through the glass door, shut it, and pulled the curtain closed.

16

IT WAS MUCH earlier that night when Misto, wanting company, prowled the cool night looking for Joe and Dulcie or his son, Pan, to share the late and secret hours. Thinking that Pan might be visiting Tessa, he galloped away through paths of moonlight, through shadows as black as soot, trotted across rough oak branches above the narrow alleys, making for the crowded cottages that rose just above the village. Soon, from the roof of Tessa's small cottage, he looked down on the dark driveway where a reflection of light cut across from the kitchen window.

Backing down the pine tree by the front door and peering in, he watched Debbie at the kitchen table sorting piles of bright new sweaters and blouses and cutting the tags from them. He didn't scent Pan, and when he moved on to Tessa's window, there was no sign of him, no red tomcat. When he tried the screen, it was firmly shut and latched, and Tessa slept soundly. He wished she'd wake and talk to him.

He didn't hide from the child as Pan did, to keep Debbie from knowing he was about. But he didn't flaunt himself in front of the woman, either. Sometimes he'd come into the yard when Debbie wasn't watching Tessa, and the child would follow him, slipping away from her mother and sister up across the deserted streets into Emmylou's yard. If Debbie saw her, she'd drag her home again, she didn't want the child wandering off after "some stray cat. First that cat up in Oregon, that red-colored cat always hanging around. The fuss you made over it. And now this scrawny yellow one. What is it with cats, Tessa? Can't you play with one of your dolls and leave the dirty animals alone? I won't *have* it in the house, a dirty stray sneaking in and out carrying fleas and germs and dead mice."

But up at Emmylou's, the older woman was kind to Tessa, she liked the shy child, she talked to her just as she talked to Misto, never expecting an answer, just rambled on, and that put Tessa at ease. She would soon curl up on a chair or on the bed close to Misto, watching Emmylou and listening to her random comments and stories, and then she didn't look pale and pinched anymore. Now as he looked in at Tessa he heard Debbie's step, and saw the kitchen light go out. He dropped from the sill down into the bushes.

Heading away again, on up to Emmylou's house, he saw her windows were all dark, her lights already out, and he thought to curl up at the foot of her bed. It was lonely with his own family gone, even staying with the Damens sometimes it was lonely. Slipping in through the old, splintery cat door and through the dim house, he found Emmylou sound asleep. But before settling for a nap on her bed, he leaped to the dresser.

A finger of moonlight through the window reflected across the two pictures of Sammie. The little child. And the grown-up Sammie. Two photos taken sixty years apart, and that long-ago life nudged at him.

He thought about nine-year-old Sammie and how she had confided her fear of the man who followed her mother, and confided her dreams of her uncle Lee Fontana and his last big robbery, a lone bandit in the style of an earlier century making off with saddlebags full of stolen cash, never a hint of conscience or remorse, just a smug smile at the corner of his thin, leathery face. Was this, then, what these old musty bills were about, was this young Sammie's legacy from Lee Fontana that he'd sent her after he fled the country for Mexico? Misto's memory of that time was as fragmented as a shattered windowpane, only a few scattered moments coming clear, only a few snatches of that past life.

It was a noise outside from up the hill that drew him away, footsteps moving down the stone stairs from the little building above. Dropping to the floor and slipping outside again, he stood in the shadows of the porch, tail twitching, as the taller man eased down the stone steps carrying a bucket, a spade, and a heavy paper grocery bag. His jacket pockets bulged, too, and on the night breeze Misto caught the money scent. He watched him open the shed and disappear inside. The place was so small it was a wonder he'd gotten that long black car in there and been able to shut the door against its rear bumper. He came out again carrying only the spade and bucket. He knelt beside the stairs and began to dig, dumping crumbling dry earth into the bucket. There was a sense of hardness about him that Misto sometimes encountered in his travels, the cold brutality of some of the men around the coastal fishing docks that made him steer clear of them.

He expected the black car must be stolen, and he wondered what they'd done with their old truck. Maybe it had quit running and they'd traded it, in the way of thieves, for something far more grand. Easing down Emmylou's wooden steps and then up the hill for a closer look, he veered into deeper shadows as the man carried the full bucket inside and shut the shed door, shut it right in his face, never seeing him.

There was no way to see inside, no windows. The door itself, though ancient, was so tight a fit there wasn't a crack to peer through. The sounds from within were a dull clunking and gritty scraping, almost as if he were stirring the dirt in the bucket, and then a sliding, rubbing sound, then after a very long while there was another clunk and then silence. Waiting, he grew impatient, and at last he slipped on up the hill and up the stone stairs to the stone room to whatever he might see there.

The one window was crusted with grime, its screen fallen off, lying far away overgrown with weeds. The small pane of glass stood open to the autumn night, and he leaped up to the sill to look in. He could smell the stink of soured food in dirty cans, and of dirty clothes, could see a pile of clothes flung in one corner. The room smelled of the tall man, and of the smaller man and, sharply, the stink of sickness and blood.

Slipping in through the open window onto the short kitchen counter, he dropped as soundlessly as he could down to the grimy linoleum. The man lying in a sleeping bag didn't stir. He lay curled up like a hurt animal. This was Birely, the same man as in Sammie's grown-up photo of the two of them, still the same slanted forehead and fat cheeks as the tiny child he had known, same protruding lower lip caught in a permanent pout. His nose and face were a mess of blood and he was breathing through his mouth; he was doubled up in pain, he needed help, but apparently his tall friend didn't think so. He looked to Misto like he wasn't far from death. The old cat's instinct was to find a phone and paw in 911, to alert the medics. Leaping to the sill again, he was out the window racing down through the tangled yard to Emmylou's dark house, passing the shed where clicking sounds had begun again.

The phone was in the kitchen. He was through the cat door and up onto the counter. He could do it without ever waking Emmylou, he had only to whisper into the speaker, he thought nervously, hoping the call couldn't be traced, that the dispatcher wouldn't pick up Emmylou's number. Hoped Captain Harper and his detectives wouldn't start looking at innocent Emmylou Warren for the identity of the phantom snitch, for the source of so many informative phone calls over the years when, in truth, Emmylou hadn't a clue. The older woman had no notion about speaking cats or undercover cats who'd left their pawprints on so many village telephones.

But did Emmylou even have ID blocking? Not likely—why would she? This woman lived the simplest life, she didn't take a daily paper, didn't have a TV, didn't allow herself any amenities that he could see. Why would she pay for ID blocking? If her phone number *were* public knowledge, who did she have to fear? He had lifted a paw to the phone's speaker when Emmylou's bedroom light came on.

He heard her moving about and in another minute she came into the kitchen, in her robe and slippers. She glanced at him where he sat innocently beside the phone, and then moved silently out the back door. Stood on the porch looking up at the stone shed, listening to the faint scraping noises from within, then she moved silently down her steps, pulling her robe tighter against the chill. Moved up the hill in her slippers, the hem of her robe catching on weeds and on the overgrown bushes, stood to the side of the closed shed door, listening.

Two more taps, and then another long silence. When footsteps within approached the door, Emmylou ducked into the bushes, crouching comically, her tall form hunkered down among the tangled twigs, her long hair caught on the branches.

The door didn't open, the footsteps turned away again toward the back, and then again there was silence. So long a pause that Emmylou gave it up, just as Misto had done earlier. Rising, she looked up at the stone room above, stood listening, glanced back at the stone shed and then moved on up the hill as Misto had done, only pulling a small flashlight from her robe pocket and switching it on. The thin path of light picked out patches of wiry grass and the matted damp leaves trampled into a rough path. Twice she paused looking up at the house above her. The stone steps followed the ground only inches above it, and only near the top did she move from the yard up onto them, her damp slippers making no sound. On the little landing she switched the light off, and moved directly to the dirty window, again as Misto had done, and she peered in.

Even in the near dark she must have seen the figure doubled up on the floor, or maybe she heard Birely moan. She looked back down the long empty flight, making sure the man hadn't left the shed and was watching, then she shone her light in.

She stiffened when she saw Birely. Even with his bloodied nose, she had to know him from Sammie's pictures, and maybe she knew him, too, from when Sammie was alive? *"Birely?* Oh, my. What . . . ?" But even as she spoke, Misto saw the taller man slip out of the garage.

The doors had made no sound, only when he closed them was there the faintest scrape—but enough to startle Emmylou. As she turned, he saw her. He froze, then ducked into the bushes and was gone. Misto could hear him moving away, bumbling in the darkness crackling the branches, but then, as if gathering his wits, he moved on nearly silent as a cat.

Emmylou stood looking where he'd vanished, not where he was now. And then she ran, down the stairs and down the hill, up her own steps and into her cottage, and Misto heard the door lock behind her. Racing after her and in through the cat door, he watched her snatch up the phone and dial the three digits. He could hear the little canned voice at the other end, faint as a bee buzz, as the dispatcher questioned her.

When she'd hung up the phone, she fetched the crowbar, stood hefting it, looking out the kitchen window at the back porch. Misto rubbed against her ankles, wondering how Birely had been hurt so bad, wondering whether Birely would die, wondering why he still cared so much. Wondering why those lives, long past, had returned to haunt him so sharply, or why *he* had returned to this particular place and time. To play a part in Birely's sad life? Or, perhaps, so he could know the last, sad fate of his little Sammie?

17

HAVING LEFT PEDRIC'S room hidden in Clyde's backpack curled up atop his spare sweatshirt, Kit lay now beneath Lucinda's white covers pressed between the bars of the hospital bed and Lucinda's warm, familiar side. Her housemate seemed frail and vulnerable in her heavy bandages and cast, and wearing only the flimsy hospital gown. Whenever Lucinda slept, Kit drifted off, too. She woke when Lucinda stirred sleepily and stroked her back and head. Wilma sat close beside the bed in a folding metal chair, her brocade carryall hanging on a knob of the bed where Kit could slip easily down into it. Three times within the last hour, the nurse had come in. Each time, Wilma had risen to distract her, asking needless questions, going into useless detail about Lucinda's condition and care—maybe if she made a pest of herself the nurse would stay out of there for a while.

But nurses weren't easily distracted. This small, square

Latina woman had answered Wilma's questions briefly as she checked and replenished the IV bottle and went about tidying up, picking up discarded tissues and adhesive tape and paper wrappers from the metal table, and then bringing Lucinda a fresh pitcher of water. Clyde was down the hall with Pedric, but soon someone would come to relieve him and to pass Kit back to Pedric again—like a library book forever changing hands. The time, by the big round clock above Lucinda's bed, was three A.M. and despite Kit's satisfaction at being with Lucinda, the predawn hour made her incredibly lonely.

This was the cats' hour, the shank of the night, the time when, if she were at home, she would be bolting out her cat door and down her oak tree to hunt the hills with Pan. Or they'd be lounging in her tree house listening to little animal sounds bursting suddenly out in the silent dark. But tonight, here in this strange town and strange building, shut in this small unfamiliar room among unpleasant hospital smells, she felt edgy and dislocated.

She knew that Lucinda and Pedric, lying bound to their beds, felt much worse, helpless and so far from home, felt far more displaced than she.

There were no windows in the ER—when dawn did come Lucinda wouldn't be able to look out at the sky, at the first hint of sun as she so liked to do. She always rose from bed when the sky was barely light, would put on the coffee and then, with the house smelling deliciously of that dark brew, she would sit at the dining table sipping her first cup, looking out through the big corner windows enjoying the sunrise, watching its blush brighten and then slowly fade again and daylight spill golden onto their little corner of the world, onto the round and friendly hills and the intricate tangle of rooftops spread out all below her.

And Kit herself, if they were at home, as they should be, would soon return from hunting. Another two hours and she'd bolt into the house as dawn broke, Pedric and Lucinda up and showered and in the kitchen making breakfast. She'd sit on the windowsill cleaning up, washing off the blood of the hunt. She'd long for a nap but breakfast would win, the three of them would enjoy waffles and bacon and then head out for a walk up the hills or through the nearly deserted village streets looking in the shop windows.

Would they do that ever again? Would her housemates come home healthy and well, ready to enjoy their long, free rambles and simple adventures?

But she knew in her little cat bones that they would, just as she knew the dawn was on its way, just as any cat at this hour would wake and begin to prowl restlessly—knowing something good was coming. Soon her housemates would be home again, as eager and hardy as ever; stubbornly Kit clung to that thought with a keen and sharp-clawed resolve.

She could hear, up and down the ward, little clinking sounds as late-night medications were prepared or other mysterious routines attended to. The smells of alcohol and human bodily wastes were not Kit's favorite scents; she longed for the smell of new grass and its sweet, cool taste. Around her the ER, though still shrouded in the hush of night, was slowly beginning to stir, the steps of the nurses quickening as they attended to late-night medications.

Glass doors to several little rooms were slid open, curtains were drawn back. Whenever their night nurse left them alone, pulling the door closed as Wilma requested, the three of them talked in whispers. Lucinda sometimes slipped into sleep, but always when she woke she asked after Pedric.

"He's feeling better," Wilma told her, "the concussion's not a bad one. As soon as we get home, the knee will be repaired. Clyde's with him now, to keep him awake." And they talked again about that lost world where Kate had gone to learn about her forebears and had found only a dying civilization. All the anticipated magic was gone, only the cruelest creatures still blazing strong with their greedy hunger.

Wilma, like the Greenlaws, was comfortable with Kate's secrets. While Clyde, like Joe Grey, shied away from the tales. But, Kit wondered, what did Ryan think?

Ryan had cleaved easily enough to the knowledge that Joe Grey could talk, she hadn't been terribly shocked the first time the gray tomcat spoke to her—but still, Ryan had been raised in a hardheaded law enforcement family. Where were the limits of her sometimes willing imagination? What did she really think of a world teeming with remnants from the old Celtic tales that so embraced the cats' own history?

And what, Kit thought, *will Pan think, when he learns where Kate has been?*

She could imagine Pan's amber eyes blazing with a keen and hungry fascination, with a bold curiosity that would lead, *where*?

Kit herself had long ago come to terms with her own dreams of such exotic ventures, she had turned resolutely away from her own longing to descend down into the darkest pockets of the earth. When she was very young, when she first came to Molena Point, she had been drawn to Hellhag Cave that cleaved the hills south of the village, to its mystery, had sensed that dark fissure leading down and down, and down again deeper than any cat she knew had ever gone, she had longed to wander there, to discover whatever she might confront that would surprise and amaze her. Only fear—or a touch of good sense— had held her back. Then later she had been drawn to the cellars and caverns beneath the ruined Pamillon mansion that rose in the east hills above the village, intrigued by those dark clefts beneath the fallen buildings. But again she was afraid, she sensed evil there and a destruction she wouldn't dare to face.

But Pan was bolder. What would he do with Kate's secret? She thought Pan had never turned from danger. Her red tomcat had a hunger for adventure that had sent him traveling the coast of Oregon and half of California, one small cat alone never turning from a new and frightening adventure. *Oh,* she thought, *when he hears Kate's tale will he want to go there? Will he go away to follow the harpies and chimeras through that evil land, will he leave me for that adventure?*

Or would he want me to go with him down to that dying place that could destroy us both?

V<small>IC WATCHED</small> E<small>MMYLOU</small> hurry down the hill tripping on the hem of her robe, watched her double-time up her own steps and inside. She was going to call an ambulance or call the cops, the damned old busybody. He should have done Birely while he had the chance, and now it was too late. Unless he could stop her, push on in and grab the phone from her. Had she even locked the door? He'd started down, two steps at a time, but then he thought about the car.

He had to get the Lincoln out of there before the cops came swarming all over. Maybe he'd been foolish stashing the money there, but where else could he have hidden it? He thought about moving the money before the cops arrived because it was too late to move the car, but he didn't have time for that. He was reaching to open the shed when the whoop of the ambulance nearly deafened him, its flashing lights stabbing between the trees, a white medic's van pulling up into Emmylou's dirt driveway.

He eased back into the bushes as four medics in dark uniforms piled out and Emmylou came out her door onto the little porch and started down to them. He watched the shorter medic with the mustache follow her up the hill while the other three hauled out their trappings: stretcher, oxygen tank, black bags, and fancy stuff he couldn't name. Sure as hell, there'd be a patrol car right behind them. What he couldn't figure was, why would that old woman call the medics for a sick tramp? Why would she care?

And where would they take Birely? Some fancy emergency room? What if he started talking, if they gave him drugs for the pain and he got blabby, talking about the money, got some cop curious enough to start asking questions. Emmylou paused up on the stone porch while the medics hurried inside. That yellow cat had followed her winding around her ankles, damn thing gave him the shivers, he could see it there in the bushes, it kept looking at him, its yellow tail twitching in a way that made *him* twitch.

They took a long time in there. He grew cold in his light jacket. He crouched in the bushes hugging himself, antsy to get the car out. What had that old woman told the dispatcher? Had she said there'd been a break-in? Would she want them to search the whole damn property? Two medics came out of the stone house carrying Birely on a stretcher. Emmylou stood to the side, watching. Damned old do-gooder. A third medic, dark-skinned Latino, was asking her questions, writing down her answers on a clipboard. Vic watched her sign a paper when he passed the clipboard to her, and wondered what that was about.

She couldn't be making herself responsible for some tramp she didn't know, she couldn't be promising to pay his medical bill? Talk about a bleeding heart.

Or *did* she know Birely? Maybe Sammie'd had pictures, family pictures. Maybe this old woman recognized him and had got all sentimental over Sammie's little brother? Or maybe she knew Birely from when Sammie was alive? Birely had come here once in a while but Vic couldn't remember if he said he'd ever saw anyone but Sammie.

If this old woman had any sense, she'd let charity or

the government pick up the bill. The medics had to take Birely to the emergency room, it was the law, and the hospital had to treat him, the law said they couldn't refuse. So why *pay* for it? Hell of a waste of money. He watched the white van back around in the old woman's driveway and move on down the hill again, heading for some ER. Watched Emmylou head back down to her house, her bathrobe pulled tight around her. The black-and-white never had showed up. What had she told the dispatcher? Just that there was a man sick up there, and nothing about a break-in? Maybe said he was renting the place—all to protect Sammie's little brother? He waited a few minutes, was about to slip back down to the shed when she hurried out again, dressed in jeans and a sweatshirt, and got in her old Chevy. Hell, she was going to follow the van to the hospital. What a patsy. When she started the car it belched out a puff of dark exhaust. Yellow cat crouched on the porch watching her back out and head away following the medics, and Vic thought uneasily about Birely there in the hospital blabbing about the money.

He waited until the Chevy had disappeared, then headed for the shed, smiling. Maybe he could silence Birely right there in the ER, and wouldn't that be a laugh. Shut him up before he spouted off about the money and the fancy Lincoln they'd stolen or, worse, about some of Vic's own, earlier ventures. If Birely died in the ER before he started bragging about Vic's successful robberies, and maybe about that store clerk he hadn't meant to kill, if Birely died right there under the care of a doctor, how could he, Vic, be responsible?

18

HEADING FOR THE hospital following two blocks behind Emmylou, her old green Chevy nearly bumper to bumper with the ambulance, Vic spotted the turn-in to Emergency but went on by. He drove on half a mile farther, turning into a wooded neighborhood with big, expensive houses set back among the trees, their grounds softly lit by fancy lanterns but only a few windows showing lights, at this hour. Rolling his car window down, he heard no barking dog. There was no one on the street, no night joggers with their fancy, lighted shoes, no reflective gear of a cyclist who might prefer the empty streets of night, no late partiers headed home. Big houses, three- and four-car garages, but most of the driveways empty. He drove until he found a place with two cars parked in front, a Mercedes and a Jag, and a Toyota sitting on the street. Pulling over beside the Toyota and killing the engine, he got out, slipping a short, oversized Phillips screwdriver from his back pocket.

In less time than it would take the householder to hear some tiny sound and turn on the lights, he was driving away again with his new license plates on the seat beside him. He stopped ten blocks away and switched the plates on the Lincoln, smearing on a little of the Lincoln's damp mud to make them match the rest of the car. Then he headed back to the hospital, following the big red signs to the emergency entrance at the mouth of the underground parking garage, easing the muddy, dented Lincoln along the first level to the back row where cops coming into the ER might not notice it.

Parking, he hit the lock button on the pendant with the key and walked back to the emergency room's wide glass doors, thinking about somewhere secure where he could hide the Town Car later for a few hours, get it out of sight. He couldn't take it back to the stone shed; the minute the EMTs filed their report with the PD, the cops'd be all over the place, the stone shack and Emmylou's house, too. And, in the ER, they'd be all over Birely, wanting to know how he got hurt, asking who else was involved, asking him why he'd been staying in an empty house with only a sleeping bag and where was his friend that the other sleeping bag belonged to?

Approaching the glass doors of the emergency room, he saw an ambulance parked down at a garagelike bay, which stood open but was dark inside. He saw no activity there, no sign of any medics, no stretcher or gurney visible. He moved on up the few steps to the glass doors of the admittance room; they slid open automatically for him. He was hardly inside, moving on past the clerk at the desk hoping she wouldn't try to stop him, when he spotted Emmylou sitting in a small glass cubicle to his left. Her back was to him, facing a desk where a young man in a white shirt and V-necked sweater was filling out papers. Turning away, he moved into the general seating area, sitting as near to Emmylou as he could, hoping to hear what she was saying. She didn't know him, she'd never seen him that he knew of, but he picked up a magazine to hide his face. He couldn't hear much through the glass, and their voices broken by the conversation of passing orderlies and nurses going in and out, carrying clipboards, pushing wheelchair-bound patients on into the ER. He'd catch a few words and then the meaning would be interrupted. He was pretty sure Emmylou was passing herself off as Birely's sister, he heard her clearly when she said there were no other relatives. He waited until the clerk led Emmylou down a short hall to a set of heavy double doors and used his ID card to open them. Quickly Vic followed, slipping in behind them, moving on down the row of small glass rooms as if intent on his own business. Center of the big space was all open, with an island of counters and desks. The clerk at the nearest desk gave him a look. He nodded at her and moved on past. Maybe his stained chinos and worn-out windbreaker got her attention, and his mud-stained jogging shoes. If he had to make another trip here, he'd have to do something about clothes, find something to wear that didn't make him stand out. Several cubicles down, he turned back to see where the clerk had led Emmylou, and nearly ran into two employees, right behind him. They were both in blue scrubs, with ID badges pinned to the pockets. They stood blocking his way, their expressions bland but businesslike. The white-haired woman's badge said NELLIE MACKLE, RN. Short hair, thin, a small woman, maybe a hundred pounds, and no physical threat to him, but her dark eyes set him back, hard and challenging. "Are you looking for a patient?"

"My neighbor. My neighbor was brought in," he said. "At least I think they brought him here. Birely Miller? I heard he was hurt in a car accident, all the lights went on at the house and then I heard the ambulance and I thought . . . Well, he's kind of a loner, I wanted to know if he's all right, if there's anything I can do."

Nurse Mackle glanced back down the hall, where Emmylou stood in the doorway of one of the glass cubicles, number 12, then stepped behind a desk to a computer. She looked at the screen for a moment, returned to Vic, but said nothing. The man, whose hospital badge had no name, looked down at Vic from a healthy six foot four. Dark skin, dark brown eyes that looked soft and understanding, but with a gleam of challenge. Big hands loose at his sides, his fingers twitching just a little.

"Only family is allowed," Nurse Mackle said. "If you'll give us your name, we'll pass it on to his sister, she can let you know his condition."

Vic said his name was Allen James, that he lived four blocks down from Birely. He made up a phone number. She wrote down his information, nodded, and looked meaningfully toward the big double doors. Her dark friend's look, too, implied serious consequences if Vic didn't do as she suggested.

He left the two, feeling like a felon, turned away knowing their eyes followed him. He moved on behind another nurse who was headed for the big, closed doors just beside a unisex bathroom. Most California bathrooms were unisex like this one, the door marked with both his and hers symbols and, in this case, a picture indicating wheelchair access. When he glanced back, the two inquisitors had moved on away, but as he passed the last little room and was about to go on out through the big doors, voices made him turn back to a brightly lit cubicle.

Its glass doors and canvas curtain were open. The patient filled the whole bed, his broad shoulders crowded against the side bars, his feet pressed against the bottom rail. Beside the bed a small woman, round and wrinkle faced, fuzzy hair the color of old newspapers, stood talking with a dark-haired, white-coated doctor. "You might want to go on home, Mrs. Emory, and get some rest. In a little while I'll be moving Michael to ICU, I want to run some more tests, and watch him for a few days. That was a bad fall he took."

When he glanced up, Vic turned away, facing the door to the bathroom as if he were waiting his turn. "He can have one or two visitors at a time, Mrs. Emory, but they're not to stay long, you understand."

Vic turned his back to them, trying not to smile. With the patient's name, he had all he needed to get back into the ER without being interrogated. When the door to the bathroom opened and a woman stepped out, Vic stepped on in. He used the facilities, ignored the sign that said

WASH YOUR HANDS, and left. Keeping his back to Michael Emory's room, he pressed his hand to the mark on the wall as he'd seen the nurse do, watched the big double doors swing open. He moved quickly out through the waiting room to the dim parking garage; he still had things to do. He needed a change of clothes, and a haircut. Maybe a barbershop cut, not just him snipping around his ears with a pair of rusty scissors, making a mess. A haircut could go a long way toward keeping the cops off your back.

He'd gone through the packages in the Lincoln again, there was some expensive stuff there, all right. Maybe he could add a few things to it, unload the whole lot with that fence. Them bolts of heavy cloth for covering a chair or sofa, fancier, for sure, than the kind of upholstery goods they used in prison industries to cover the cheap office chairs they turned out. He'd found the old folks' two suitcases in the trunk under all the other packages, and had gone through them. Maybe he could sell the clothes, the woman's stuff had labels so well known even he recognized the value. But among the old man's stuff there was nothing for him to wear, even if it would fit. Two dress suits, white shirts and ties, the kind of clothes that would call attention to himself in just the opposite way from his own stained jeans and mended windbreaker.

Maybe when he returned to the hospital he could lift a pair of blue scrubs like everyone wore in there. He'd blend right in, except for the badge. Everyone he saw, nurses, orderlies, was wearing a badge. Did these people wear their scrubs to work, or put them on here? Maybe they got them from a supply closet, same as they'd get clean towels and sheets? And did they keep the closets locked?

He could think of a dozen ways to get tripped up, though, stealing hospital clothes. He kicked himself again for not snuffing Birely when they were alone and he'd had the chance. If he'd done him then, he'd be long gone by now, and wouldn't have all these details in his way.

But maybe Birely was so bad he wouldn't have to help him along, maybe before the night was over, the hand of fate would end the poor wimp's misery.

Heading upstairs to the main level, he glanced at his watch. Nearly four A.M. He found a phone, got the information he wanted. He was back down on the dim parking deck by four-thirty, easing the Lincoln out of the covered garage, turning down toward the freeway. Taking the on-ramp south, back toward the village, he wanted to get cleaned up, change his looks if he could, and get into some clothes that didn't make people stare at him.

He had the Lincoln's registration in his pocket giving the address, and now he had the phone number. One of the keys on the ring had to be the key to the Greenlaws' house, where the old man would have plenty of clothes. Let them two old folks give him a helping hand, it was their fault his truck was wrecked. If they'd been traveling at a decent speed he'd have been past the slide when the rocks fell, would have been well away from the damn delivery truck and would have never crashed into it.

Leaving the ER, he had wandered the main floor of the hospital until he found the courtesy phone on a little table in one of the seating areas. A nice amenity so patients' families like him, he thought smiling, could make local calls. Sitting down on the couch, he'd punched in 411, hoping Santa Cruz was in the same area code, because the phone sure as hell wouldn't reach long distance. Even these free spenders weren't going to let you call all over the country, at the expense of Peninsula Hospital.

But he'd lucked out, it was all the same code. He'd found the hospital pen he'd put in his pocket, jotted the names and numbers on a magazine, of the two Santa Cruz hospitals. He'd called Dominican first, asked for the room of Pedric Greenlaw, and he hit it right. The guy was there, secure in a hospital bed, maybe an hour away from Molena Point, and no way he'd be home tonight. He was advised that the patient was sleeping and that he should call back in the morning.

"And Lucinda Greenlaw?" he'd said, repeating her name from the car registration.

The operator would not disturb Mrs. Greenlaw, either, at this hour. "Try around eight in the morning, when the patients are awake," she'd said shortly.

Hanging up, he'd called local information again, for the Molena Point residence of Pedric Greenlaw. It was listed, all right—as if the Greenlaws had no idea someone would want their information for less than a friendly social call. When he was automatically connected, the phone rang twelve times before he hung up. He waited a few minutes and then called twice more, let each call ring a long time, but still there was no answer. Jingling the Greenlaws' keys, he'd headed back through the hospital and down the stairs, out through ER to the parking garage.

Before he pulled out, he'd gone through the glove compartment of the Lincoln again, found the local map stuffed in with a handful of Northern California maps, this one a colorful tourist edition meant for out-of-town visitors. He'd found the Greenlaws' street, and now he headed there, down the freeway and off into the hills above the village.

The neighborhood was wooded with scattered oaks, and dark as hell with no streetlights. He saw no light in any window. No house numbers in the village, either. But higher up on the hill there were numbers on the curbs, in reflective paint. Driving slowly, he found the Greenlaws' place and pulled up in front.

The drive and garden were lit by low lamps at ground level, real fancy. The driveway and walk were of stone, a huge oak tree overhanging the garage. He could see a tree house up among the branches, as if maybe these people had grandkids. He sat looking and listening. There was no sound, no lights, no window open with curtains blowing, all was dead still.

He looked for a button on the car's overhead that would open the garage door. How much noise would that make, to alert the neighbors? Some of them doors were as loud as a stump grinder. At last he decided to risk it. If there was no other car in there, that was one more good indication he was alone.

He finally found the button in the visor. The door slid up with hardly a sound. He smiled at the empty two-car space, pulled on in, and killed the engine. Hitting the button to slide the door closed behind him, he fished his flashlight from his pocket and stepped out of the Town Car.

He tried three keys before he had the inner door open. Shielding the flashlight, he moved in through a hall that opened to a laundry and bath, and then on into a big, raftered living room, high ceiling, windows all along two sides. The drapes were open and through the tall glass he could see the lights of the village down below, all pretty damn fancy. Garden lights at the back, too, a level lower, picking out a narrow deck that probably opened to a daylight basement. No light shone from that level out onto the deck or bushes, but in case anyone was sleeping down there, he took off his shoes. Still shielding the flashlight, he checked out the living room.

Big, flat-screen TV hidden in a cabinet, that should bring a nice sum but would be a bitch to haul around, there wasn't room in the Lincoln unless he dumped what he already had in there. CD and DVD players and music system were small enough to tuck in the car. Nothing else of much value in that room, a wall full of old, worn-looking books along the back, cracked leather bindings, nothing worth taking. In the dining room they'd cut a cat door in the window, at table height, he supposed for that cat they'd had with them. People were weird about their pets. There was a kind of study in one corner of the living room, desk and computer and more books, floor-to-ceiling books, all of them old. The money these people had, why didn't they buy some new ones, buy some of them fancy bestsellers with bright covers?

There was just the one bedroom, but it was nearly as big as the living room, with a bath and two closets, his and hers. In the old guy's closet he tried on several pairs of pants and sport coats, looking at himself in the full-length mirror. Everything fit pretty good. He settled on a tweed sport coat, tan chinos, and a brown cotton turtleneck, a pair of soft leather Rockports that were stretched enough to fit his larger feet.

In the bathroom he dared a light, closing the shutters first, pushing their louvers tight together. Rooting through the drawers, he abandoned the idea of a barber, he didn't want to wait until one opened, and he didn't want some guy to ID him later. Small town, cops poking around, in and out of places, asking questions. He found a pair of scissors and set about trimming off his long hair, and that took him a while. Felt strange as his hair dropped away, made him feel naked. Belatedly he spread out a towel to catch the mess, sweeping what had fallen onto it with his hand, trying not to leave evidence. When he'd done as good as he could, he found a razor and shaved the back of his neck, holding a hand mirror he'd found on the woman's side of the cabinets, twisting awkwardly to see.

He shaved off his short scraggly beard, which never would grow thick the way he wanted. He took a shower, using a big thick towel on the rack. He slapped on the old guy's aftershave, which had a lime smell. He found clean shorts and socks in a dresser drawer, and pulled on the brown turtleneck. Posing in the full-length mirror, he thought he looked pretty good. Except for his white, newly shaven cheeks and chin and the back of his neck. He rooted around among the woman's things, looking in the medicine cabinet and in drawers, but couldn't find any bottle of colored makeup to disguise the pale marks.

It took him a while, in the kitchen, working by flashlight, to figure out the fancy microwave. In the freezer he found a package of spaghetti, read the directions, opened it, and shoved it in. While he waited, he put his own clothes in the washer, threw his canvas jogging shoes in, too. While the washer rumbled away, and with the spaghetti smelling good, he opened a cold beer from the refrigerator door.

Retrieving his supper, he found a plate to put it on, and sat down at the table where he could look down at the village lights. He even found a paper napkin, tucked it in the high turtleneck to keep it clean. How would it be to live like this, in a fancy house? Well, hell, with the money he'd stashed in the Lincoln, and maybe twenty thousand more when he unloaded the car itself, he could live any way he wanted.

But not in a house like this. Not in a tame village like this where he'd be bored out of his mind. The kind of money he had now would put him in Vegas or some Caribbean island with plenty of action. Party all night, poker and roulette tables to help him double or triple what he had, and a choice of showgirls offering anything he could pay for.

Finished eating, he dumped his dish in the sink. He'd meant to make his way back to the hospital tonight, what was left of the night. Walk right on in, with his new, respectable look, take care of Birely and be done with it. But when he thought of going back there so soon, and maybe with those same goons on duty, he decided to hide the Lincoln first, maybe around Debbie Kraft's place, empty houses on the streets around her. He couldn't think of a better neighborhood. That woman contractor was around there some, but he could avoid her. Meantime, tonight, he wouldn't turn down a few hours' sleep, he thought, yawning.

Moving into the bedroom again, he undressed, folded his new clothes all neat on the upholstered bedroom chair, and climbed naked into the old folks' bed, sliding down under the thick quilt. Before he switched off the flash-light, its beam on the pillow picked out a couple of dark cat hairs. He flicked them off with disgust, turned the pillow over, got himself comfortable, and dropped into a deep, untroubled sleep.

19

Misto, having watched the four EMTs load Birely into the ambulance and head away for the hospital, sat now on Emmylou's porch, alone, pondering again Birely's presence there in the village, Birely whose grown-up photograph in Emmylou's house was neatly inscribed along the bottom with his name and Sammie's and the date the picture was taken, just a few years ago. Once when he'd hopped up on the dresser for yet another look, Emmylou had laughed at him. "You're an art critic now? I took that picture myself, with my old box camera, took it right out on the highway by the market where Sammie and I used to work. Took it one time Birely showed up, the way he did without ever letting her know, stopped off at the village from wherever he'd been wandering."

Misto had already died by the time Birely was born, the family already out in California, he was dead but he'd never left Sammie's side. Call him a ghost cat or whatever one liked, he'd stayed near her as they headed for the West Coast, stayed nearby through all that happened to her and to Lee Fontana, moving effortlessly in and out of their lives. Seeking to protect them, to face off whatever would harm the old man or the child. He'd been protective of Sammie's little brother, too, when Birely came along, and now in this different life he still felt protective of that little boy grown up and grown older. Birely was still irresponsible and maybe often useless in his ways but he was still Sammie's brother, lying alone in that cold stone house injured and hurting until Emmylou had discovered him and saw that he was cared for. When she'd left for the hospital behind the EMTs, Misto had paused at the edge of her yard, undecided whether to follow.

It was a long journey up to the hospital through tangled woods, down through a deep ravine, and across the busy freeway. Even if he could avoid the coyotes and occasional loose dogs, and dodge the fast cars, even if his aging bones didn't give out, it wasn't likely he could slip inside unseen through those bright halls, among so many people, and find Birely's room. Even if he got that far, how could he help Birely? He was only mortal, now. What could *he* do to help? He'd been more effective as a ghost without the limitations of a mortal body—and without the aches and pains. When he was spirit alone, he could appear suddenly wherever and whenever he chose, and more often than not he could subtly influence others with his whispers, just as he'd prodded tough old Lee Fontana.

He knew he'd had an effect on Lee's life, that he had hazed Lee away from some of the more shameful moves he'd considered. Even that last big robbery, when Lee held his forty-five to the head of the cowering postal clerk, Lee hadn't hurt the man. How much of that was due to Fontana's own sense of kindness, which he couldn't seem to escape, and how much to Misto's influence, would never be clear—though Lee's successful escape from the law was Lee's own sly plan. Misto couldn't take credit for that any more than he could be blamed for the darker presence that harassed Lee, and that Misto had sought to drive away.

But Misto's own ghostly power hadn't lasted long, and he found himself again among the living, encumbered again by a living cat's uncertain existence, by the forces of pain and of joy that the mortal world bestowed, and now by the pains and aches of old age descending on him once more; he didn't like that part of growing old.

Deciding against that perilous journey to the hospital, he left Emmylou's yard wanting companionship, wanting the other cats to talk with, Joe and Dulcie and his son, Pan. Scrambling up a pine to Emmylou's roof, he looked down upon the shabby neighborhood of small old cottages, to the village stretching out beyond, and to the vast expanse of lonely peaks and steep ridges that sheltered the coastal town. Tonight he had no heart for wandering, for roaming through the chill wind and the unforgiving dark, and he headed back to Joe Grey's house, to the most welcoming home he knew while his own two humans were absent. Maybe Joe was there now and would claw away his uncertain feelings, make him laugh again, and to hell with getting old.

Padding morosely over the roofs, the way seemed long tonight and the sea wind was unkind. He was deeply chilled by the time he reached Joe Grey's tower. Bellying in through one of the six windows, he found Joe's heap of cushions empty. Pushing on in through the cat door, leaving it flapping behind him, he crouched on the nearest rafter, looking over, down into the upstairs suite.

The big double bed had been slept in but was now empty, the covers thrown back in a heap. A fleece robe lay crumpled on the floor, a silk nightie flung over a chair. The doors to the walk-in closet stood open, a shirt dropped on the floor inside. Where had they gone, in such a hurry in the middle of the night? He looked down at Clyde's little office, his desk hidden by piles of papers, and through the open doors into Ryan's studio. The house smelled empty and sounded hollow, he had no sense of anyone there among the unseen rooms, not even Rock. The big silver dog, the minute he heard the cat door, would have been right there huffing at him, making a fuss. Rock was not in the house, the only living soul present was little Snowball, curled up on the love seat, so deeply asleep that even the flapping cat door hadn't woken her. The sleep of an aging cat, her sweet spirit floating deep, deep down among her hoard of dreams.

But what had gone down, here? Why had Ryan and Clyde risen in the middle of the night and left the house? Some emergency, someone hurt? Feeling a cold chill suddenly for his own humans, who would be traveling now on their way home, he dropped down from the rafter onto the desk, jolting his poor bones, and set about searching for a note or phone number jotted hastily, for some clue to where they had gone and, most important, for any hurried notation about John and Mary Firetti. Perhaps for some note from the veterinarian who was temporarily minding the practice and feeding John's feral band of shore cats.

He found nothing. Slipping down to the floor, he looked for some bit of paper that might have fallen. Again, nothing. He padded into Ryan's studio beneath its high rafters and tall, bare windows. Trotting beneath the big drawing board, circling the solid oak desk and blueprint cabinet, he looked out the west window, down at the drive where he had not thought to look before while he was still on the roof.

The king cab was gone, only Clyde's antique roadster was there, parked to one side and shrouded in its canvas cover. He circled the studio again, then prowled the bedroom, tracking Rock's scent back and forth as he'd followed close behind Ryan and Clyde from bed to bath to closet, back again to the stairs, and down. But then he thought, not only his own family was headed home. So were the Greenlaws and Kit. Could something have happened to them, on the road or before they left the city? He leaped onto the desk again, eyeing the answering machine.

He'd never used one of these. He nosed uncertainly at the flashing red light. Warily he punched the play button, hoping he wouldn't erase whatever was there.

Nothing happened. He punched again. There was a long, annoying buzz and the red light flashed and then died. The green light blinked twice and died, too. No lights now and only silence. He hissed at the uncooperative lump of plastic, hoped he hadn't erased anything, and turned away. His medieval life—what he remembered of it—might have been harsh, but one didn't have to deal with machines. And the machines of young Sammie's time had been simple ones, even cars had been slower and more predictable. Leaping from the desk to the file cabinet and across to the love seat, he climbed into Snowball's crumpled blanket close to her, and curled up. She woke only a little, looking at him vaguely. He spoke nonsense to her, as much to comfort himself as to comfort her. He washed her face and licked her ears, talking to her as Clyde and Ryan or Joe would do, telling her what a fine cat she was.

But soon she began to grow restless, to glance toward the stairs and toward the kitchen below. Leaping down, he led her down the stairs to her kibble bowl, which of course had been licked clean. He hopped from a chair to the counter, pawed open the cupboards until he found her box of kibble. With considerable maneuvering, and spilling quite a lot, he managed to tip the box on its side and send a cascade of little, aromatic pellets raining down over the side, some of it into the bowl. He sat atop the counter looking over, watching her gobble up the dry little morsels, watching her drink her fill at the water dish, her curved tongue carrying water into her pink mouth like a little spoon. She didn't offer to jump up on the counter, her arthritis was worse than his. Snowball's face was getting long, her belly dragging with age.

But she still handled the stairs all right, and when they headed back up, she settled into the exact same spot on her blanket again. When, purring, Misto stretched out near her, she looked at him expectantly. He looked back, puzzled—it was frustrating that his feline cousins couldn't talk to him, that, despite a vast repertoire of body language, they couldn't communicate their desires exactly, as a speaking cat could.

But he could see she wanted him to talk again, wanted to hear his voice. Snowball, too, was lonely, she wanted to hold on to the rambling cadences of a speaking voice. Clyde and Ryan often read to this little cat, the same way the Greenlaws read to Kit, or as Wilma Getz read to Dulcie, in bed at night. Just as Mary and John Firetti read to Misto himself, though John's reading too often involved veterinary journals that put him right to sleep. The difference was that the speaking cats understood all of the tale, while, for Snowball, the excitement and drama of the story lay in the tone of voice, in the emotion that one could impart.

Now, tonight, Snowball needed a story. To please her, and to distract himself from his own worries, too, he told her about his kittenhood in that long-ago Georgia time, about the steamy summers, playing in the grassy yard with small Sammie behind the white picket fence, playing with a little rubber ball she threw for him, or climbing together up the twisting oak tree that shaded the little front lawn. He left out the bad parts that happened later; and he left out the way he himself had died. He gave Snowball a happy tale, nothing angry in his voice to spoil her dreams, no dark shadow of Brad Falon stalking Sammie and her mother. Where was Sammie, now that she was gone from this world? Did humans, like cats, return to experience more than one life on this earth? Or did human spirits go on somewhere else altogether, wandering farther than Misto himself could ever imagine?

And what about a cat, once his nine lives were finished? Did he move on, too, as a human might? Did a cat at last rejoin his human companions? So many questions, and not even the wisest cat or human could know the true answer. All Misto knew was, there were more adventures to come than one could see from the confines of a single life. And that, from the other side, looking back, one saw many more patterns to the tangles of mortal life than were apparent while you were still there.

But, speaking his thoughts to Snowball and telling his tale, half his mind still worried uneasily at what had taken Clyde and Ryan out in the small hours. He didn't like the absence of the other cats, either, when usually one or another would come wandering in through Joe's tower, or he'd see someone silhouetted out on the rooftops, someone to race away with and laugh with. Thankful for Snowball's presence, he pushed closer still to the white cat and closed his eyes, and tried mightily to purr, to lull himself into a soothing sleep, too.

20

BIRELY LAY BENEATH the bright lights in the operating room, sedated but awake, his nose numbed by a local anesthetic as Dr. Susan Hunter leaned over him working swiftly, carefully rebuilding the shattered bone. With normal breathing impossible, with the breath sucked through his mouth too ragged and labored, she could not administer a general anesthetic. She was a thin woman, wiry and strong. Pale dishwater hair barely visible beneath her blue cap, long, thin hands, long fingers, a light, sure touch with the surgical instruments. Birely lay relaxed, deeply comforted by the welcome cessation of pain, his waking dreams happy ones; he was a little child again safe between his parents, not a grown man tramping some dusty road to nowhere, with no home to come to at the end of the day. No watchful traveling companions waiting to separate him from any small amount of cash he might have in his jeans, no overnights in a strange jail for some petty crime that, usually, his buddies had committed. His childhood memories were far different and more comforting—until the last memory grew frightening and he became restless, fidgeting on the table. .

Sammie had told him this story many times, it happened when she was just nine and Birely wasn't born yet. Her daddy was gone away in the Second World War, her mama working as a bookkeeper in their small Georgia town. The town had three gas stations, one of which their daddy would later buy, when he returned from the war. Sammie and her mother lived in a small rented house that would have been peaceful if not for an old schoolmate who, the minute her daddy was sent overseas, began to pester Becky, coming around the house uninvited wanting to spend time with her, a pushy man who frightened young Sammie with his cold eyes and slippery ways. Sammie had a cat then, a big yellow tom who liked the man no better. On the night Brad Falon came there drunk, knocking and then pounding, not beseeching anymore but demanding to be let in, it was the cat who at last drove him away.

When Falon pounded, Sammie's mother bolted the door and ran to the phone. Falon broke a window, reached in, and unlocked it. He swung through, grabbed the phone, and threw it against the wall. He threw Sammie hard against the table, shoved Becky to the floor, and knelt over her, hitting her and pulling up her skirt. As Becky yelled at Sammie to run, the big yellow cat exploded from the bedroom and landed on Brad Falon's face, raking and biting him. When Falon couldn't pull him off, he flicked open his pocketknife.

The cat fought him, dodging the knife. Becky grabbed up a shard of broken window glass and flew at Falon. He hit her, he had her down again, cutting her, but the cat was on him again. He leaped away when a neighbor man, hearing their screams, came running, a wiry young fellow. He saw the broken window and climbed through, but already Falon had fled, banging out through the front door. Their poor cat lay panting where Falon had hit him.

Now, on the operating table, Birely woke hearing Sammie weeping, the dream always ended this way, her weeping always woke him; but he knew the cat had survived, Sammie always ended the tale the same way. Groggy now and filled with the dream, he was jerking on the table. Dr. Hunter had drawn back. She waited, trying to calm him, until at last she could proceed.

After surgery, Birely was taken back to the ER for the rest of the night. The next morning he would be moved to ICU or to the observation ward. The ER doctor on the floor said that, with whatever emotional trauma he'd suffered there on the table, he could have no visitors. "Only his sister, and only if he calms down sufficiently." It was that order from the attending physician which, had it been strictly heeded, might have saved Birely's life.

VIC WOKE BEFORE dawn in a real bed, under smooth sheets and real blankets, and it took a moment to think where he was. Then, when he looked around at the big, fancy bedroom, he had to laugh. It was his room, now. Last night the bed had smelled of soap or maybe of that old woman's face powder. Now, did it smell of him? If those old people came home again to sleep in it, would they smell that he'd been there, and be frightened? He guessed that cat would smell him if they let it inside. Well, of course they let it in, they'd had it right there in the car with them. Good thing that cat couldn't testify how he'd roughed up those two, he didn't need no witnesses.

Climbing out of bed, he stood naked to the side of the open drape, looking out at the faint glow of predawn lights from the village. Watching the sky grow light in the east, he went over what he had to do before he made a last trip back to the ER, or to wherever they took Birely, if they meant to fix his smashed nose. He wondered again if Emmylou was paying for all that.

Maybe if he didn't go back too soon, they'd put Birely in a regular room where there'd be fewer nurses going in and out, and more visitors allowed. People wouldn't notice him so much; with his new "look," he'd blend right in, could take care of business without being bothered. Birely's final business. What more natural place to die than the hospital? You were there because something was wrong, people went to the hospital to die. He wondered how many folks had been done in there with help, and no one the wiser. How many cadavers did they haul out of there in a week, and no one suspicious that one or two hadn't died natural?

He went over, again, the way that paperback book had laid it all out, a book he'd picked up at the Goodwill when he was buying a pair of jeans, waiting for Birely to find a shirt he wanted. He'd got real interested in the story, had read that part four or five times, off and on, had carried the book in his pack for a long time. Well, it was sure as hell the foolproof way. How would you ever get caught? With a little adaptation, you could use it on a druggie, too. Just one more needle puncture. A little creativity, you could use it on just about anyone.

But in the book, this guy had died in a hospital exactly like he meant for Birely. All you needed was a 30cc or 50cc syringe, and he was sure he could pick that up around the nurses' station, there'd be syringes there somewhere, in a drawer or cupboard. If he couldn't find any, he could put on those rubber gloves he'd seen handy in the wall dispensers in the rooms, slip on gloves, dig a syringe out of the hazardous-waste bin right there in the room, too. Hospital was all organized for fast work, they made everything easy.

The way they did it in the book, you do the injection, the guy goes into some kind of fit or trauma, half a second later he's dead. Touchy part, you had to get out fast. Book said the minute the injected air hit the heart, the dials went crazy, alarms going off, the whole damn staff running in to save a life and you'd better be long gone.

Moving into the bathroom, he brushed his teeth with the old guy's toothbrush, and even took a shower. Felt strange to be so clean, didn't seem quite comfortable. First, before he went back to the ER and did Birely, he had to hide the Lincoln. Then he'd need wheels to get back to the hospital, Debbie's station wagon would do for that. How could she refuse, when he'd sold that stuff for her to the Frisco fence—that, plus what he had on her.

When he and Birely'd first moved in, up the hill, he'd seen her down there around her cottage, and then seen her twice in the village market, light-fingered and quick. He'd drawn back into the shadows, to make certain, knowing he'd find the information useful, one way or another.

Two days later, he saw her come out of a village dress shop pushing one of them fancy baby carriages. She didn't have no baby that he'd ever seen, just the two girls. She came out of the store with the sun hood pulled over, the "baby" all covered up with a blanket, and the older girl walking beside her.

After that, a couple times he'd watched her return home, haul the carriage out of the station wagon all folded up, no sign of a baby, but she always carried four or five bulging shopping bags inside. For a few days he'd followed her, too, walked into town when she left. It wasn't far, and it was never hard to find that old brown Suzuki station wagon, the village was so small. She liked to park beside the library where there was more shade than on the street. She often had the twelve-year-old with her, but never the smaller girl. He'd see Debbie take off with both girls in the morning, come back without them as if she'd dropped them at school, but in the afternoons, she'd have only the older one in the car again. Or maybe the little one was in the back where he couldn't see her. The older kid, Vinnie, she was a smart-ass, but when she shopped with her mother she was quick, fingers nearly as slick as a professional.

He'd gotten acquainted with Debbie, walking down there of an early evening as her kids ate supper, walked the roundabout way, coming up from below. When he'd let her know he knew what she was up to, that had scared her. She'd denied it until he told her exactly what he had seen. The woman was feisty but she was easy enough to intimidate. He got her to show him what she had, and some of the stuff was high-end, from the Neiman Marcus and Lord & Taylor stores in the village plaza, and that had surprised him. Molena Point might be small, but there was money here, and Debbie had gone right for it.

Once he'd complimented her on her skill, she came around real nice, got real friendly. He noticed that, heading out for those high-end stores, she dressed real slick, tried to look like she belonged in there. She said she was selling what she lifted through a consignment shop up in San Jose, the guy was a second-rate fence, using the shop as a front. Said she'd drive up there once a month. She'd told him what they paid, and after a couple conversations, they'd struck a deal. He said he knew a fence in the city— well, he knew *of* him. Said he could get way better prices, that he'd sell what she stole, keep his share, and still make more for her than she was getting. He wasn't sure why she trusted him. Or why he bothered. Except she was a looker, and she had a snotty little way that he liked. Who knew, maybe something more would come of that.

Out the bedroom windows, the sky was growing lighter. He dressed in his new clothes, folded up the old ones, clean now from the washer. Carrying those, moving into the living room, he looked down from the front window to make sure the street was clear, then moved on through the laundry into the garage. Locked the door behind him, and slipped into the Lincoln. He'd thought to eat something, there in the house, but he wanted to move on out of the neighborhood before people came out to walk their dogs, take kids to school or go to work. Starting the engine, he hit the button to open the big door, checked the street for cars as he backed out, closed it again fast. On the street he saw only the same three cars that had been parked there the night before, their windows fogged over. Moving on away, down the hill, he studied the houses as he passed. No one out in any of the yards, no kids, no one on their porch or looking out a window, that he could see. He had a good feeling about the day ahead. By tonight he'd be miles away from the coast headed inland and north with the Lincoln and the money, and he wouldn't have to worry about Birely anymore. By tonight, Birely would be history.

IT WAS THE next morning that Pedric was transferred down the coast from Dominican Hospital in Santa Cruz to Molena Point's Community Hospital. Joe peered through the mesh in Ryan's backpack as she walked along beside Pedric's gurney, approaching the ambulance. Wilma stood with Clyde, Dulcie looking up over the edge of her carryall. Clyde's backpack bulged with Pan and Kit crowded in there—a four-cat entourage to accompany Pedric's careful transport home.

But in Clyde's pack beside Pan, Kit couldn't be still. Fidgeting and staring out, her gaze followed Pedric worriedly as he disappeared into the ambulance. "He's so hurt. All that talk about MRIs and arteriograms, whatever they are, and about maybe a tumor and more blood work to do and—"

"Those are just tests," the red tom said, his tail twitching irritably. Did she have to fuss so, in the confined space? "Only tests," he said, "precautions. They don't necessarily mean anything."

"But Dr. Carroll said Pedric's blood sugar's high, and he's having trouble with his eyesight, and—"

"He said there could be any number of causes. It doesn't *mean* anything, Kit. He just wants to be sure. Will you settle down?"

"He said there might be something going on in Pedric's *brain*," she said, her voice quavering. "He talked about a *brain scan. That* means something, *I heard* him say they'd look for a tumor, maybe a pituitary tumor, whatever *that* is, and an abnormality in an artery, and—"

Pan hissed at her impatiently. "Those things can be fixed. Would you rather they *didn't* look, and missed something important and Pedric got worse?"

"I'd rather he wasn't hurt at all and we hadn't been in that wreck and that *scum* hadn't hit him in the head and we were all home right now, all safe at home and they had never been hurt," she said, shivering.

Pan fixed her with a hard gaze. "You can't help Pedric by crying, and you can't help Lucinda if you're all weepy." Reaching out a paw, he tucked it around her paw, and licked her ear. "They're lucky to have you, and they're lucky to have good doctors. Now can't you settle down?"

Kit settled, glancing sideways at him, and together they peered out through the mesh, watching the ambulance pull out of the parking area, to the street. They watched a nurse wheel Lucinda out from the ER in a wheelchair and help her into Kate's rental car, which was the newest and most comfortable of their three vehicles. When Lucinda was settled inside and the nurse had gone, Clyde leaned in and Kit and Pan slipped out of his backpack onto Lucinda's lap. Lucinda was a bit groggy from the pain medication; she smiled sleepily at the two cats. Kit licked her hand, which tasted of disinfectants. Through their open car door, they watched Charlie settle Wilma into her Blazer, setting the carryall by Wilma's feet, watched Dulcie emerge and climb up into her housemate's lap. The rented Lexus and the Blazer pulled out, with the Damens' red king cab behind them, Joe Grey and Rock peering out the side window, the little parade moving through the quiet morning, heading home.

21

The click, as Clyde unlocked the Greenlaws' front door, echoed hollowly in the deserted house. Outside in the drive, Kate's rented Lexus stood next to the Damens' red king cab. Charlie had gone on to the hospital, to offer moral support as Pedric was admitted. She would swing by Wilma's first, drop Wilma and Dulcie at home where the two meant to tuck up for a mid-morning nap; their all-night vigil in the motel, broken by only a few hours of sleep, had left both woman and cat yawning, and a bit fuzzy in their thoughts.

Clyde and Lucinda moved on inside, Lucinda leaning on his arm, still groggy and unsteady from the pain medication. The room was chill and smelled musty even after only a week's absence. Ryan and Kate followed them in, but tortoiseshell Kit hung back, looking off where Joe and Pan had raced away. The moment the two vehicles came to rest in the drive, Pan had taken off for the rooftops, his amber eyes flashing with anger. Joe Grey had followed him, perplexed, uncertain how to think about Kit and Pan's sudden conflict.

In the car, driving down, Pan had been fascinated by Kate's tales of the Netherworld, but Kit had soon gone sullen and cross. She'd always been drawn to the thought of mystical lands that might link to their own history, but this morning suddenly, faced with Pan's enthusiasm, she hadn't wanted to hear about Kate's journey.

Now, she watched the two toms race away, and then quietly she entered the house. There she paused, shivering at its neglected feel. The kind of gloom that makes folks hurry to flip on the lights in the middle of the day and open the windows, as Ryan was now doing, to let in the fresh ocean breeze. But Kit, entering, sensed more than abandonment. Nervously she scented out and backed away, curling her lip at the smell.

She watched Clyde settle Lucinda in her chair before the hearth and then turn to lay a fire, arranging logs from the stack in the wood box, and striking the gas starter. She could hear Ryan in the kitchen filling the coffee maker, and taking a lemon cake from the freezer, as Lucinda had asked her to do. Kate settled in Pedric's chair, near Lucinda, looking questioningly at Kit when she didn't leap up into Lucinda's lap.

With the smell of that man in the house, Kit turned away to prowl the empty rooms—hopefully empty. *He used Lucinda's keys to let himself in*, she thought. *If he's still here, he's cornered, and he's even more dangerous.* Giving Clyde a look, she moved off toward the bedroom. Watching her, Clyde picked a short length of firewood from the stack behind Lucinda's chair, and followed. Kate looked after them, frowning, then rose to tuck a lap robe around Lucinda.

"Kit's just in a mood," Lucinda said. "All this stress. She'll be all right, in a while."

"That was my fault," Kate said, "that argument in the car, my fault for telling Pan about the dark world. His interest didn't sit well with Kit."

"They'll have to work it out," Lucinda said sadly. "They were so happy. But it wasn't your fault at all, Pan had to hear the story sometime. How could he not, when Joe and Dulcie both know about your journey."

The drive down from Santa Cruz had started out pleasantly, the morning bright and cool, the sea on their right a deep blue beneath stacks of high, blowing clouds. Pan had curled up on the seat between Kate and Lucinda, while Kit snuggled in her housemate's lap, her tortoise-shell coat dark against Lucinda's white bandages. But then as Kate spun her tale, Pan sat up straight, listening eagerly, and soon he was asking excited questions, his tail twitching—and soon Kit grew restless watching him, her ears back and her own tail lashing hard when Pan talked about going down himself, about going there with her. Kit had once dreamed of that land, but not the way it was now, she didn't want to go there now. What was Pan thinking? Kate had had a reason to go, searching out her mother and father's own history, but Pan had no such excuse.

It was in San Francisco that Lucinda had asked Kate, "Your journey down into that world? It was your father's old journals that led you there?"

Kate nodded. "Yes, the diary he left me. And the jewelry I found there and brought back, it's so like the pieces he left me. The same ancient Celtic jewelry style that has haunted me. And so many pieces with cats worked into the design."

"I remember you sold a few pieces, those without cats."

"Those lovely pieces stashed away for nearly half a century, in the back of a walk-in safe."

It was the grandson of the attorney who gave Kate the first pieces of jewelry, who had journeyed with her down through the caverns. He had found her again, up in Seattle, got her address from the San Francisco designer firm she'd worked for. He meant to retire, to leave the firm, and he had the trip all planned. He'd wanted her to go because of what her parents had done in trying to save that land. "He wanted to know if I'd like to join him."

"You said yes, just like that," Lucinda said.

"Oh, I did some research on him, as much background check as I could, by myself. I didn't want to involve anyone else. From what I found—mostly what I didn't find—from the holes in his own family background that were so similar to mine, I decided to trust him."

She moved into the right lane; they were making good time. The sea wind had turned warm now, as the sun rose higher. "I knew it was risky, but I was burning to see where my mother was raised." She had described for Pan the vast caves of the Netherworld, the rich veins of gold reaching down miles below California's own depleted gold fields. And then, in the car, when she talked about the shape-shifting beasts and the winged lamia, Pan's paws kneaded with excitement—and Kit's claws kneaded with unease, and as they'd passed Seaside, just north of Molena Point, the two cats had begun to argue.

Pan wanted to descend down into those dark tunnels despite the dangers, and he expected that Kit would go with him. Kit said that if *he* went, that would be the last adventure he'd live to see, and Pan didn't see why she was suddenly so timid. Her hissing refusal sent them into a snarling argument, the matter ending when Kit leaped into the backseat, curled up in a dark little ball with her back to them all. In the front seat, Pan had crouched forlornly between Kate and Lucinda looking helplessly from one to the other, not knowing what to do, not wanting Kit's violent anger, but unwilling to give in to her.

The minute they pulled into the Greenlaws' drive, and Kate parked and opened her door, Pan leaped out and took off across the yard, vanishing among the neighboring oak trees. Kit dropped to the drive and headed for the house, looking at no one, her ears flat to her head, her eyes blazing, her fluffy tail lashing with rage. Glancing back once, she saw Joe jump out of the Damen truck and follow Pan and she hissed at him, too. Joe didn't know what had happened but he was with Pan all the same, as if he were certain that it was her fault.

Now as Kit explored the house, Kate looked after her, dismayed. "I thought Kit loved my stories. It wasn't until this morning that I saw the truth."

She hurt for Kit, and for Pan; she had no idea how this clash of feline stubbornness would resolve itself.

They could hear Clyde in the bedroom opening the closets and cupboards. They watched Kit return, her nose to the carpet, moving on through to the kitchen.

"What?" Lucinda said. "What is it?"

Kate shivered, listening to Clyde's movements as he

investigated the house. Someone had been in there but was gone now, she'd heard Clyde open every closet, every door. Their assailant had Lucinda's car and house keys; and Lucinda's muzzy, sedated condition had left her without her usual sharp perception.

Kit, returning from the kitchen, looked up at Lucinda, lifting a paw. "The man who hurt you and Pedric, he made himself at home. He ate, he messed up the kitchen, he rummaged through your closet. He slept in your bed," she said, hissing indignantly.

Ryan appeared from the kitchen, wiping her hands on a dishtowel. "There's a dirty plate in the sink, an empty container from frozen spaghetti, a crushed beer can."

Clyde came out of the bedroom. "He took a shower, left wet towels on the floor. Hair all over the floor, long hair, and more wrapped in a towel. As if he's cut off a pigtail. Left a hell of a mess."

Lucinda rose, and they followed Clyde back to the bedroom. She looked with disgust at the mussed bed, which she had made carefully before they'd left for San Francisco. She inspected the dresser drawers, and then the closet. "Pedric's tweed sport coat's gone," she said. "He didn't take that to the city. His tan slacks, too, with the stain on one cuff."

"And the dark brown Rockports," Kit said, "that he wears to walk the hills." She looked up at Clyde, her ears flicking uncertainly. "If he wanted clothes, the suitcases were right there in the Lincoln. Did he have to come in here, invade our house, mess it up, and leave his smell everywhere? What a pig."

"What else has he done?" Lucinda said. "What else has

he taken?" She moved back to the dresser, began opening drawers to examine them more carefully, lifting layers of sweaters, socks and underwear, leaning awkwardly with the weight of the cast.

Kate opened the carved pine armoire, but the big, flat TV and the DVD player were in place, the rows of CDs lined up on the shelves beside them. Ryan, stepping out to the living room, opened that armoire but returned shaking her head. "TV, music system, looks like it's all there."

"He means to come back," Lucinda said.

Ryan put her arm around Lucinda. "I'll call the locksmith again, get him on out here pronto." But Kit looked worriedly at Lucinda. Even if the locks were changed, Lucinda and Kate would be alone tonight.

With only me to guard them, she thought with dismay. Despite the angry, predatory twitch of her claws, despite knowing she'd do her best to protect her humans, she was no hundred-pound police dog. *Even with new locks*, she thought, *he can break in easily enough.* Now, since the accident, her housemate seemed so frail, hindered by the cast and the pain, her senses dulled by the drugs that were meant to ease her pain.

Ever since she first met Lucinda and Pedric, up on the grassy slopes of Hellhag Hill when she was a very young cat, she had looked on them as invincible. She'd never before known a human in her short, wild life. She'd had no idea they could be like these two, so wise; two humans who understood her, who saw at once her true nature as a speaking cat, and delighted in their discovery. That first day as she spied on Lucinda and Pedric while they enjoyed their picnic, as she listened to Pedric recite the same ancient Celtic tales that she herself loved, Kit had felt as one with them. It hadn't taken long for them to coax her out with gentle questions and with smoked salmon, and that was the beginning of their friendship. Despite Kit's wild and independent life roaming the hills alone, she soon went home with them. She had never left again, they were her family, two strong humans she could trust with any problem, any secret, could trust with her very life, the two humans who would be there for her forever, wise and indestructible. But now suddenly she might have to protect Lucinda, or try to. Now suddenly Kit had a hard glimpse into human mortality, and she didn't like it much.

She listened to Ryan calling the locksmith back, watched her hang up the phone, looking at Lucinda. "He'll be here within the hour. I'll call the department, they can photograph, and run prints."

"Do we have to?" Lucinda said. "There's nothing else missing, a jacket, a pair of pants, and a pair of shoes. Clothes that Pedric *could* have packed and forgotten though I know he didn't, clothes he might have left in the city. The TVs and computer are still in place."

"It's vandalism," Ryan said. "Whatever they find, including prints, might help as evidence later, if . . . when they recover the Lincoln."

"Call them," Lucinda said at last, resigned. She didn't want to be disturbed, she only wanted her house to herself again, cleaned of every trace of the man, wanted to wipe away every invading trace of him with scrub rags and disinfectant.

As Ryan made the call, Kit watched Clyde pack a

duffel bag to take to Pedric's hospital room. She showed him where Pedric kept his robes and pajamas, his shaving things. She watched Kate put fresh sheets on the bed, throwing the used ones and the bed pad in the washer, with Clorox that made the whole house smell. Ryan brought Lucinda a bed tray with coffee and some lemon cake, helped her change into a nightie and tuck up under the covers. It had been a long morning, Lucinda was yawning and already half asleep; everything was hard for her, with the use of only one arm. When she was settled in bed with the tray and her snack, Kit lay down close beside her, daintily accepting small bites of icing; and only now did Kit let herself think about Pan again, let the whole sorry episode fill her heart.

She told herself that maybe Pan never thought about danger. Maybe, traveling all over Oregon and down the California coast, cadging rides with strangers, maybe he'd just done what he wanted, fought when he needed to, and then gone happily on his way again undeterred by worries. So now, he expected her to do the same, to follow him on what he said would be the greatest adventure of a cat's life. She tried to think about it from his viewpoint, but lying close and safe beside Lucinda, Kit's anger burned anew when she thought about the fiery pit that Kate had approached, the flaming mouth of hell itself, and about the beasts that had crawled out of it to attack anything mortal. She loved Pan, but she was sickened that he blithely expected her to go there, into that dark and deathly realm.

How is it that when I was younger I would have leaped at such a journey, would have longed to go there—how close I was to venturing down into Hellhag Cave and, later, down alone among the dark Pamillon caverns—how is it that now I'm so afraid?

She told herself she was grown up now, that she wasn't so foolhardy anymore, but all she really knew was that Pan wouldn't give in, and she wouldn't give in, and his short-sighted stubbornness hurt her clear down to her very cat soul, to her frightened and uncertain soul.

22

 **IT TOOK VIC** a while to hide the Lincoln. On leaving the Greenlaw house he had detoured past the village market, parked on a side street, and walked back. Bought a jar of peanut butter, a box of crackers, and a cup of machine coffee that tasted like boiled sawdust. The market wasn't two blocks from the PD, and that gave him a thrill of fear. But who was going to recognize him, all shaven and cleaned up? The cops had never even seen him, all they knew was what that old couple told them: two men, shaggy hair, old wrinkled clothes, and him with a ponytail. No one was going to look at him twice now, dressed all proper like some village shopkeeper on his way to open up the store.

He'd eaten in the car parked under some low-hanging eucalyptus trees, then headed for Debbie's place. Passing Emmylou's, he'd checked for her green Chevy. Just as he'd hoped, it was still gone as if she hadn't returned from the hospital, had stayed there all night worrying about that little wimp, about her friend's baby brother.

Easing on by, he turned down onto the cracked streets of the neighborhood below among the small, ragged cottages, expecting the streets to be empty as they usually were. Not so. Here came a fat woman walking a skinny old dog and, overtaking them, a pair of joggers dressed in tight black spandex like earthbound skin divers, and from the other direction a young boy in a blue jacket cruising on a bike, the whole damn neighborhood suddenly crowded with people. He circled through, parked on a side street. Waited until the streets were empty again, then headed back to Debbie Kraft's place. Her station wagon was gone, and that annoyed him.

Passing on by, he turned into the drive of the place he'd spotted earlier, house and narrow garage sat way at the back, all secluded back there, bushes rangy and tall; the dirt-crusted Lincoln looked almost at home there. He pulled clear on back to the garage. Cracked gray paint, heavy wooden garage door hinged at the side. Getting out, he tried to open it but it was securely locked. He moved around to the side. That door was locked, too, but this was one of them old-fashioned skeleton-key jobs, older than dirt. Fishing out his pocketknife, it didn't take him long, he had it open. The power to the place was shut off, and with no windows it was dark as hell in there. Moving to the big door, he turned the knob for the lock and pushed it open, lifting where the door wanted to sag and scrape on the cracked cement drive. Jury-rigged kind of arrangement, only one door and not two, even if this was just a one-car garage. Good thing he hadn't heisted a *stretch* limo to hide here, he'd be flat out of luck.

By the time he'd finessed the Lincoln inside and had the door closed again, he was sweating like a pig. Shutting the big door, leaving the place looking as deserted as he'd found it, he'd walked on over toward Debbie's place hoping she'd got home, meaning to give her the money and talk her out of her car. But when he came in sight of the house, the drive was still empty. Walking on up her drive like he belonged there, he looked in the garage window.

Garage was empty except for some boxes of junk, kids' broken toys, some dried-up paint cans. If she was out "shopping," light-fingered and involved, she might be gone for hours. Turning away, he headed on up the hill, past Emmylou's. Her car was still gone. He moved on up the stairs of the stone house thinking to pick up the sleeping bags, stash them somewhere up the hill in the bushes, clear the place out before them cops showed up. Maybe even wipe the place down of fingerprints, he thought, amused. Like some big-time criminal. When all he ever did this time was borrow a car and lift some money that was *already* stolen, for Christ's sake.

PAN AND JOE, having raced away from Lucinda's house as their human friends moved on inside, were wandering the rooftops above the center of the village, Pan still grousing about Kit's stubborn nature, when they saw Debbie Kraft walking down Ocean Avenue wheeling her empty baby stroller. The interior, as usual, was swaddled with a concealing pink blanket. They watched her approach the drugstore and wheel her "baby" inside; they had watched this routine before, they knew too well what she was up to. Joe, pausing on a shingled peak, his paws in the damp gutter, looking down at Debbie, wanted badly to nail her. This was the first time in his life he had turned his back on a thief, the first time he hadn't called the department the minute he saw a crime coming down. Shoplifting might seem like a minor offense, but even in their small village hundreds of thousands of dollars of merchandise vanished every year. The local shopkeepers were having a hard enough time, with the sharp failure of the economy. They didn't need any light-fingered visitors trashing their livelihood; he itched to snatch her up like a struggling mouse, and turn her over to the law. He didn't like Debbie anyway. He had bristled at her nervy attitude when she'd moved in with Ryan and Clyde uninvited and had disliked her even before she first arrived in the village just from her pushy letter. It would be a real treat to see her cooling her heels in Max Harper's jail—but if he turned her in, what would happen to Tessa? To both her little girls?

Beside him, Pan had already tuned Debbie out; all his anger, for the moment, was still directed at Kit, at her puzzling disdain for adventure. "Even my pa never explored such a land. If Misto ever once set paw there, he'd be bragging about it, rambling on so you'd never shut him up."

Joe said nothing. The Netherworld made him nervous, he knew exactly how Kit felt. What was so inviting about a dark world that had decayed and fallen to ruin? No way *he'd* venture down there into those crumbling caverns. Maybe their heritage did have its roots among the ancient Celts, and maybe some strain of those races *were* down there beneath their own coast, emigrants from an ancient time, but so what? That didn't mean he had to launch himself into some nightmare encounter with a world that should be left to complete its own destruction. The very thought made his paws sweat.

They watched Debbie emerge from the drugstore, tenderly arranging the pink blanket over her baby, taking care that the little tyke was warmly covered. She smiled sweetly at two uniformed officers coming out of the coffee shop, heading for their black-and-white. The younger officer smiled back at her, but Officer Brennan was busy brushing crumbs from the ample front of his uniform.

"She's going to get caught," Pan said softly, finally paying attention. "Caught without any help from us. Are those guys taking a second look at that stroller? Did you see Brennan glance back? Maybe," the red tom said, smiling, "Debbie's little operation is going to hit the fan. But then," he said, dropping his ears, "where does that leave Tessa? If Debbie's arrested and goes to jail and has to do prison time, what will happen to Tessa?" He didn't mention Vinnie, he didn't give a mouse's ear what happened to that little torturer. Too many times up in Oregon Vinnie had poked and teased him, tormented him until he raced out of the house, often into the snow and rain, and it would be a long time before he came creeping back—only to be with Tessa, with his own small human.

"The girls have one aunt," Joe said. "Debbie's older sister. I guess by law they'd go to her, if she'd even take them. That would be a pity for Tessa. Sour woman, no use for kids." They watched Debbie move on up the street leaning over the stroller, whispering tenderly to her baby. "Tessa has a half brother," Joe said, "but Billy's only twelve. He'd take her if he was older, just like he adopts stray cats and cares for them."

Billy Young had lived with Charlie and Max since his grandmother died, an arrangement they'd made when his father went to prison for the murder of Billy's mother and, later, of Sammie Miller. Billy was a caring boy and dependable. Ever since his mother died when he was eight, he'd worked on the neighboring ranches, he was trusted with their horses, and proud to help in his own support, as boys did in past generations, taking pride in doing a man's work. Then when Billy's grandma died shortly after Christmas, and neither Debbie nor her sister wanted him—not that Billy wanted to live with either of them—he had moved up to the Harper place. Had gone where he was wanted, had taken over the Harpers' stable work before and after school in exchange for his room and board and "a little to put aside in the bank," Max had told him. But now, for the Harpers to take in two little girls as well, both with emotional problems, would be, in Joe's view, an exercise in calamity.

The two officers still sat in their black-and-white, Brennan in the right seat filling out paperwork, the rookie in the driver's seat talking on the radio, both men watching the street only casually, barely glancing at Debbie as she passed. Whether Brennan's instinct alerted him was hard to say, neither Debbie's amateur ruse nor her body language seemed to touch the older man. The cats, trotting away over the roofs, followed Debbie's progress on the sidewalk below, watched her looking covetously into the shop windows. Over the cool rooftops, they moved through shafts of sun and through pools of shade, beneath twisted oak limbs and splayed pine branches that overhung the shops. When Debbie turned into the little village market they eased down a bougainvillea vine, deftly avoiding its thorns, dropped to the sidewalk and followed her. They had, looking back, seen the black-and-white move away from them, heading toward the shore.

The village grocery kept two cats of their own, assigned to rodent control. The customers were used to seeing them wander among the shelves, so why would they be surprised at a visitor or two? Slipping along through the aisles, and through the shadows at the base of the produce bins, they found Debbie in the canned goods, dropping one can of soup or beans in the little basket she'd picked up, and easing two more in under the pink blanket. By the time she headed for the checkout, the padded vehicle was so full she had a hard time pushing it along between the narrow aisles.

Easing into the shortest of the three checkout lines, she arranged the purchases from her basket on the moving belt and then set the basket on the floor beneath. Pushing the stroller along ahead of her, she paid for her groceries and moved quickly on out, looking smug with the success of her morning's venture, both in resaleable merchandise and in food for her little family. Carefully arranging the three grocery bags down onto the lower shelf of the stroller, she headed around to the small parking lot at the side of the store. The cats saw, only then, that she'd left her station wagon at the back beneath a row of low-growing pepper trees that sheltered the adjoining building. Vanishing in among these, they climbed a few feet until they were hidden beneath its foliage.

Debbie set the grocery bags on the ground by the tailgate and then opened the side door. Leaning in, she retrieved some additional paper bags from under a tangle of toys. Opening them, and rolling the stroller close, she began to unload her take from beneath the pink blanket. When the bags were full she put a few groceries, a loaf of bread and packages of chips, in on top to hide the telltale new clothes and handbags. As she opened the tailgate and folded up the stroller the cats peered in at the tangle of toys, small sweaters, and empty drink cans. Lifting the stroller in, she laid it on top, squashing a cloth bunny and a sandal caught in the folds of a plaid blanket. Even as the cats watched, the blanket moved, a thin little arm flopped out, and Tessa turned over, a hank of pale hair straggling across the plaid cover, her dark lashes shadowing her soft cheeks. Waked by the intrusion of the stroller, she looked up at her mother, groggy and flushed. Her nose was running. Debbie fished into her own pocket for a tissue, reached in as if to blow the child's nose, but Tessa turned away, turned over again, sniffed loudly, pulled the blanket higher around her, and closed her eyes. Had Debbie left her alone in the car all the time she was shoplifting? At least the vehicle was in the shade, and she'd left the windows down a few inches, apparently unconcerned that anyone would want to bother the child.

Had she kept Tessa out of nursery school because of a cold but, because she was sick, didn't want to leave her home alone as she so often did? That was more motherly concern, Joe thought, than Debbie would normally exhibit. When she turned away from the open tailgate the two cats dropped down onto it and slipped inside, fast and silent. Pan hid at once among the rubble, concealing himself from both Tessa and her mother. They wanted to see where Debbie was headed and, of even more interest, to see if Brennan's patrol car might show up again, if the two officers were, indeed, watching her.

AT THE GETZ house, as Wilma slept away her midmorning nap, Dulcie sat alone on the desk in the soft glow of the computer, her restless mind too busy to let her sleep. Last night as the cats and humans crowded into the two motel rooms, the human contingent taking turns napping and one then another returning to the hospital to keep Pedric awake, Kate's tales had filled Dulcie with such wonder that the pictures and words just crowded in. The grimness of that world had turned her incredibly sad; the pictures that filled her head grew dark, and this poem, now, was not like her usual ones, not sly and humorous verses that would make Joe laugh. She didn't know what her tomcat would think of this effort but she didn't care, she needed to get the words out, to make sense of what she felt for that lost land. Just as Joe was driven to slaughter the wharf rat, and catch the thief, her words must be brought to life. Needs were needs, and a sensible cat attended to those urges.

Down and down on silent paws
Deep into the earth I go
Down and down through caverns black
Stones hang like spears above me

Green light glows from granite sky
Harpies fly above me
Castles fall around me
Farms lie dead around me

Herd beasts dead around me
Bones all white around me
What was grand is lost
Twisted into ruin
Magic shattered now
Used too long for evil
What was loved is lost

Gone, that earthen magic
Gone, those magic people
Used too hard for evil
Used by greed and power
By the cold hard lust of evil

She didn't know if it was a good poem or without value. She didn't care, she needed to write it. She wrote quickly, changed a few words, and then sat reading the lines back to herself, her small cat being filled with sadness for that land where, now, neither she nor Kit would ever want to venture.

23

I RAN OVER TO look at the leaky plumbing," Ryan said, pulling into Debbie's weedy driveway beside the station wagon. The dark-haired young woman was unloading her grocery bags, and at Ryan's voice she turned, startled, a secretive look crossing her face, replaced at once by a too bright smile. Ryan smiled back, and killed the engine. She had, for the last few minutes, been sitting up the street in her truck beneath some overhanging juniper branches, watching Debbie haul a baby stroller out of the back, open it up and pile grocery bags into it. She had also seen, the instant Debbie opened the back of the wagon and turned away, a flash of red and of gray leap out, the two tomcats streak across the drive behind the woman and disappear up the pine tree near the front door. What was that about? Now the cats crouched on Debbie's roof, peering over; Ryan didn't dare look up at them, she kept her eyes on Debbie.

"You came to fix the leak now?"

"I came to look at it," Ryan said. "To see what's needed."

"Go on in, then. It's the kitchen sink," Debbie said, turning away, busying herself with the stroller.

Ryan went in, watching through the kitchen window, pretending to be occupied with the faucet as Debbie wheeled the stroller up to the little porch. Hauling it backward up the three steps with its heavy load of groceries, she passed on by the kitchen and parked it in the bedroom. She returned with three bags of groceries, leaving the rest in the stroller. Outside the window, the two tomcats seemed just as interested as Ryan was. She watched them scramble down the pine again, to pause among the lowest branches, intently looking in. Ryan, herself, had no chance to look at the remaining bags, under Debbie's gaze.

Returning to the truck, she let Rock out, snapped on his long line so he could roam the yard, and tied that to the pine tree. He didn't like being tethered; but she didn't like his propensity to take off suddenly on some track he considered too urgent to ignore. Already he was sniffing over some scent, his ears and tail up. Maybe a deer that had been in the yard, or a raccoon. Whatever had crossed the dry grass, Rock had that look in his eyes that told her she'd better keep him under control. The Weimaraner's long generations of breeding for a powerful and single-minded hunter and tracker had produced a strong-willed individual. This, plus his lack of any early training, had produced a dog eager to outstubborn human orders in deference to his lust for the hunt.

Rock was eighteen months old when he and Ryan

had found each other; he'd been roaming stray in a wild stretch of country north of Molena Point. Unclaimed and untrained, his habits already indelibly formed, he came to her defiant and headstrong, with a burning power to do as he pleased. She had worked hard to redirect his talents, sometimes with the help of the gray tomcat. It was Joe Grey who had taught Rock to track on command, to heed to his handler and stay irrevocably on the scent when seeking a felon or a lost child. Joe's method of tracking with nose to the scent himself as he gave his commands, could not have been accomplished by any human trainer. Now when the gray tomcat spoke, the big dog paid attention; though still, Ryan's own commands were not always heeded.

As she moved on inside again, Debbie was just coming out of the bedroom. Saying nothing, Ryan stepped past her into the little room crowded with its twin beds. The loaded stroller stood against the far wall, five grocery bags lined up on the floor beside it, a loaf of bread sticking out, and boxes of crackers. Behind her, Debbie had returned nervously to the kitchen as if hoping she would follow. Ryan gave the bags a cursory look and followed her back into the kitchen where she turned her attention to the sink. She knew what was in the bags, but right now she was too tired to play games; it had been a long day, after a sleepless night.

She and Clyde, after leaving Lucinda's house, had dropped Pedric's duffel off at the hospital. Charlie was still there, waiting with Pedric for the ICU doctor, and she seemed to have everything in hand. Pedric was in better spirits, now that he was back in the village, and soon Ryan and Clyde had gone on, stopping for a bite of lunch in the hospital café before heading home, sitting at a small table beside the café's big reflecting pond. They'd left Rock in the truck, snoring away in the backseat. The shallow water and plashing fountain shone brightly where the sun struck down through a great, domed skylight. Waiting for their order, they'd watched the red and black koi fish, as strikingly patterned as Japanese kites, dashing mindlessly through the water from one onlooker to the next, hoping for a handout. After lunch she'd dropped Clyde at the shop and headed on for Debbie's, having promised to look not only at the faucet but at an electrical plug that had stopped working.

She had never been fond of Debbie, she hadn't seen her since their art school years in San Francisco, then suddenly Debbie had gotten in touch. She wrote that she was moving down from Eugene, was divorced and claimed to be destitute, and was needing a place to stay. Joe Grey said, "Demanding a place to stay," and that was closer to the truth. It was Joe who discovered Debbie wasn't broke at all but had a nice wad of cash tucked away in her suitcase. Between Debbie's patronizing ways, and Vinnie's rudeness and loud tantrums, her sojourn in the Damens' guest room had lasted one night. Neither Ryan, Clyde, nor Joe himself wanted her there. Rock, who liked most children, kept his distance from Vinnie, his lip curling in warning, though he let Tessa climb all over him.

Unwilling to put Debbie out on the street, in desperation they had offered her the empty cottage which, later in the year, they intended to remodel. She was to clean up the cottage and the yard, and do as many repairs as she was capable of, under Ryan's direction. So far, she had pulled a few weeds, which she'd left lying in a limp pile in the driveway, and had made a poor stab at painting the one bedroom, abandoning half-used paint cans in the garage with their lids off, leaving the unused paint to grow dry and rubbery. As for any temporary plumbing repairs, the woman was sullen and evasive. "A busy mother," she told Ryan, "with two children to support and care for shouldn't have to be doing a man's work." Ryan wasn't sure what a man's work consisted of, but Debbie seemed to know, and the prospect of pliers and wrenches didn't appeal.

She glanced in again at the loaded grocery bags. If they had held only groceries, one would have to wonder where Debbie had gotten the money for such a large purchase. Debbie'd said she was looking for work, and sometimes Ryan did see her go out dressed as if for an interview. But so far no job had materialized, not even the most menial employment—though Debbie didn't think much of cleaning houses or bagging groceries, those pursuits didn't fit her idea of a suitable lifestyle.

It was Joe Grey who had first told her about the shoplifting. "How long," he'd said, "before someone peeks under that pink blanket, baby-talking, and finds themselves prattling on to a pile of soup cans and designer jeans?" But neither Ryan nor Joe wanted to blow the whistle on Debbie. There seemed no way to nail her and yet leave Tessa unscathed. Examining the faucet, she saw it would be better to replace it. The thing was shot, several parts loose, its joints rusting beneath the chrome. Knowing how particular her men were, she thought maybe she'd do this job herself, just a temporary fix. She and Clyde had bought the house to remodel, they expected to replace the ancient plumbing at some point.

The building was old but solid, its frame was good and the ceilings were nice and high. It was hard to lose money on a spec house in Molena Point, particularly in a hillside location with a view down over the village—hard to lose, she thought, once the economy turned around. She hoped that *would* happen soon. Stepping outside, she fetched her tool belt from the backseat of the truck. Moving into the garage, to the junction box, she turned off the master breaker so she could look at the malfunctioning wiring. As she stepped out again, Debbie came down the steps headed for her car. Leaning in over the open tailgate, she dragged a rumpled blanket heavily toward her. Ryan saw Tessa stir within, knuckling at her eyes as if she'd been asleep, heard her grumble as Debbie lifted the child out.

"She was in the car all the time you . . . shopped?" Ryan asked.

"I parked in the shade, she slept the whole time," Debbie said innocently.

"How long?"

"How long, what?"

"How long was she in the car? She looks flushed."

"She has a little cold," Debbie said. Saying no more, she headed for the house carrying the child, the blanket dragging behind her along the drive. Ryan followed her into the bedroom, watched her tuck Tessa under the covers, and then move to the kitchen where she poured canned orange juice into a glass. Moving to the bed, Ryan put a hand on the child's forehead. She was warm from the car but didn't seem fevered. Behind her, Debbie had set the juice on the dresser and was rooting in the closet. Turning, she threw a blanket over the stroller as if that were a handy place to put it down, letting it trail across the grocery bags.

"Shall I give her the juice?" Ryan asked.

"I'll do it." Debbie grabbed the glass, pulled Tessa up, propped her against the pillow. The child drank sulkily, but she drank it all. Looking past her mother, up at Ryan, her resignation was far beyond her years. When Debbie spoke to her she didn't respond. When Debbie turned away, Ryan smoothed the child's pale, damp hair. Tessa gave her the tiniest smile and reached to touch her hand.

But then she turned over again and burrowed down beneath the cotton spread. As Ryan stood watching her, Pan appeared at the window, looking in and glancing warily toward the kitchen where Debbie had disappeared. Deciding the coast was clear, he remained there watching the sleeping child, disappearing only when Debbie's footsteps approached again, vibrating on the hard linoleum. Standing by the dirty window Ryan could see him below her on the brown lawn, but instead of racing away he stood frozen, looking up along the side yard to the street in front, his ears twitching uneasily.

When she looked along the side of the house, all she could see was a slice of empty street and part of a ragged cottage on the other side, crowded by overgrown cypress trees. Below her Pan turned and looked up into her eyes with a smug little cat smile, and when she looked at the street again, the nose of a squad car was slipping into view, the black-and-white moving slowly along, the young officer at the wheel scanning the driveways and cottages. Beside him she could see Officer Brennan's heavy profile.

When she turned, Debbie stood behind her, occupying herself with the child. "It's just a cold," Debbie said, "she'll be better tomorrow." She leaned to straighten Tessa's covers, and when Ryan looked back out the window, Pan had gone and the squad car had moved on, she could see it moving away up the hill toward Emmylou's. She spotted Pan and Joe two roofs over, keeping pace with it as it cruised slowly along.

Turning to Debbie, she said, "I guess nursery school doesn't want Tessa there, with a cold."

Debbie nodded. "So much sickness."

"She'll be going back, when she's well?"

Debbie looked up at her, her expression flat. "The nursery school's too expensive, I took her out. Why doesn't the village have a free preschool? Not everyone can afford . . ."

"So, you take her with you when you . . . shop," Ryan said, "and leave her in the car?" Moving toward the stroller, she lifted the loaf of white bread and a box of Sugar Pops from the nearest grocery bag. Beneath, neatly folded, lay an assortment of cashmere sweaters, cherry red, turquoise, lime green, all still bearing their sales tags.

"Why would you buy so many sweaters, when you don't have a job, Debbie? When you can't pay for nursery school, or pay rent?"

"They were on sale, they were really a great bargain."

"Debbie, you have a choice here. Do you think that squad car was cruising this street by accident?"

Debbie just looked at her.

"You can clean up your act, take these things back to the store, and stop any further stealing. Or you can move out, find somewhere else to live. We can't let you stay here," she said, trying to be gentle, "when we know you're shoplifting, when Clyde and I are connected to MPPD. Our friendship with Chief Harper and Charlie, and the fact that my uncle Dallas is one of Harper's detectives, doesn't leave any choice. You will quit stealing and return every item you stole to the store it came from. You can beg them not to report you, not to press charges. If you don't do that—and I'll know whether you did—you will be out of here by the end of three days.

"If you do neither, I'll report you. You'll be arrested and most likely held, unless you can make bail. Your two girls will be taken to Children's Services." It broke Ryan's heart to say that, to think of the children being taken away. She didn't tell Debbie she meant to talk with the store owners. She knew several of them and was hoping, if Debbie followed through, they wouldn't press charges. Turning back to the grocery bags, she went through them all, writing down in the back of her purse calendar every stolen item, its brand, and the name of the store as it was printed on the price tag. Maybe those two officers already had that information, maybe they had already made Debbie when they'd followed her, or maybe not. Maybe they were just cruising, keeping an eye on this problem neighborhood with its empty cottages and foreclosures.

She said nothing more to Debbie. She left the house disturbed equally by Debbie's thieving and by her neglect of Tessa—and with no idea at all how to resolve Tessa's plight, how to prevent Debbie's foolishness from coming down hard on the forlorn little girl.

24

FROM HIGH ABOVE the stone cottage among the cypress trees Vic watched that woman contractor, that Ryan Flannery, back her red pickup out of Debbie's drive and take off. He'd stashed the sleeping bags deep in the bushes, their dirty clothes rolled up inside, had pushed the bundle under the tangled branches of a deadfall. Now, the minute the pickup left, he moved on down through the woods, watching for that cop car that had pulled by Debbie's place, half expecting it to come back.

But maybe they weren't looking for him, were just cruising the area, a mindless routine while they sucked down their doughnuts and coffee. They hadn't stopped at Emmylou's, and hadn't looked up toward the stone house—but after Emmylou called that ambulance, you could bet your bippy MPPD would show up sooner or later, nosing around.

Moving on down onto the empty streets of the small neighborhood, he turned up Debbie's driveway, pausing beside her station wagon to look it over. Old Suzuki was ready to fall apart. He looked in to see if she'd left the keys but she hadn't. The car was a mess inside, even to him, and he wasn't real picky how he kept a car. He was wondering if the old heap would hold together for the few hours he needed it when movement above on the garage roof startled him and he swung around to look.

Couple of cats up there pawing at something in the metal gutter, maybe a dead bird. Nasty beasts. Turning away toward the front door, the only door, he saw a light on in the kitchen but, approaching the window, he couldn't see Debbie inside. He didn't knock or call out, he moved on up the three steps, tried the knob, found the door unlocked, and pushed on through.

JOE AND PAN watched the man enter. On the little fitful breeze they couldn't catch his scent, but they looked at each other, puzzled. He was familiar, but different. He was well dressed and his clothes were familiar, too. Even from the roof they could hear the scuff of his loafers across the linoleum of the cottage. They heard him pause at the kitchen and then head for the bedroom, his rubber soles grating across something gritty. Quickly they scrambled down the pine tree to the ground, and only then did they find his scent. "The guy from the stone shack," Joe said, "the one with all the hair." And, as they sniffed around the door, a mix of familiar smells hit them that made their fur stand up: the ripe male smell from the stone house overlaid, now, with the smell of lime shaving lotion and, making them hiss in consternation, the personal scent of Pedric Greenlaw, distinctive and familiar. From within, they heard Debbie yip, the beginning of a startled scream.

The man's voice was low and flat. "It's just me."

Debbie's voice was cranky. "You could have knocked," she snapped. "What do you want? You scared me half to death."

The cats, pushing the door in, slipped on inside, past the kitchen and into the shadows outside the bedroom door. The two stood in the middle of the bedroom, the man's back to them. Debbie had turned from Tessa's bed, scowling up at him. She didn't seem frightened, just annoyed. "You have my money?"

"I got it."

Joe studied the guy. He was wearing Pedric's tan slacks with the spot on one cuff, Pedric's tweed sport coat. The guy's brown hair was newly trimmed, the skin at the back of his neck as white as a baby's bottom. His cheeks and chin were pale, too, and he'd used too much of Pedric's Royall Lyme shaving lotion.

"You got yourself cleaned up fancy," she said. "What's the occasion?"

"You like it?" he said, leaning close to her.

Debbie laughed, a squeaky little giggle. "I hope you didn't spend my money on that fancy sport coat!"

"No way, baby. The money's all here." He sat down on the edge of the bed, crowding the sleeping child as if she were only another pillow. The cats, crouched beside the door, watched him remove a wad of greenbacks from his jacket pocket. Using the bed as a table, he began to count out hundred-dollar bills, fanning the stack like a deck of cards and then dealing them out across the covers. Debbie moved closer, watching greedily. Behind them, the cats slipped through the room into the shadows of the baby stroller, beside the five grocery bags—a swift flash of gray and red, their paws silent on the grainy floor. Behind the cats, the closet door stood just ajar. With a silent paw Pan eased it open, preparing for escape, watching Vic warily.

Dealing out the bills, Vic said, "Like to borrow your car."

"Why would you need my car? Where's your truck?"

"Just for a little while, an hour or so. Had some trouble with the truck."

"Where is it? What kind of trouble? You wreck it?"

"It's in the shop."

"So why do you need my car?"

Laying down the last hundred-dollar bill and smoothing it out, he drew her close to the bed and put his arm around her. "Just for an hour or two, baby. Some errands I need to run." He picked up the stack of bills, tapped it against his palm to align the edges, and handed it to her. "Twenty-four hundred bucks. I did pretty good. Agreed?"

"I'd hoped to get more than this," Debbie said crossly. "Those Gucci bags . . ."

"Those Gucci bags were last year's models. I did a hell of a lot better than you'd have done, trying to peddle that lot to someone here in the village or trying to sell it through some consignment shop. Or on eBay. That'd bring the cops down on you."

Behind the stroller, Joe and Pan smiled at each other. The actual sale of the stolen luxury items put a nice footnote to Debbie's thieving ways.

But what the cats didn't understand was the connection. How did Vic and Debbie know each other? He and his friend couldn't have moved here to the village just to act as her go-between, where was the profit in that?

Had they just happened on her, down in this adjoining neighborhood, and got acquainted? Maybe Vic liked her looks, started coming on to her. One thing led to another, and first thing you know, he's easing in on her profits. They listened to Debbie argue about the amount of money he'd offered, but then rudely she snatched it up, pulled up her sweater, and stuffed it in her bra.

"What about the car?" he said. "Just for a little while, baby."

"I don't think so, I need it for the children, I need to pick Vinnie up at school."

"School's four blocks away. Vinnie can walk." Vic hugged her close, his voice teasing. "Come on, baby. You got to have more stuff for the fence by now, with your clever ways. What's in them grocery bags over there, under the bread and cookies? You want me to handle that lot? I will if you loan me the car."

He argued and wheedled until at last she gave in. "On one condition," she said, and now there was a smile in her voice. She turned, indicating the bulging grocery bags. "Load those in the back under the blankets, get them out of here until that contractor's done nosing around."

"And them cops," he said. "You wouldn't want them

cops to see all this, the ones that were cruising up here."

Debbie shrugged. As if she wasn't worried about cops.

"Will you be going back up to the city again, when you get your truck?"

"Might."

"When will that be?"

"Two, three days for the truck to be ready."

"Take that lot with you, sell it for me like you said, and you can borrow the car for two hours. No more."

In the bed, the cover stirred and Tessa peered sleepily out, watching Vic and her mother. The little girl, Joe thought, observed more than people imagined. Vic said, "When I get the truck, what if I head for the city with your stuff but don't come back this way for a while?"

"Send me a money order," Debbie said smartly.

"You trust me with the money, baby?"

"You brought me this much," she said softly, picking up her car keys, looking toward the stroller.

Panicked, the cats slid into the closet. From among the tangle of shoes and dropped clothes, they watched Debbie hand Vic the bags, loading four into his arms, piling the last atop the others in the stroller, watched her wheel the stroller out, escorting him to her car.

Slipping out of the closet, Joe Grey followed. But Pan leaped up onto the bed beside Tessa, worrying over the child, sniffing at her to determine just how sick she was.

Outside, skinning up into the branches of the pine, Joe watched Vic load up the grocery bags and cover them as Debbie had instructed, watched him back the station wagon out, turning downhill in a direction that would put him on Highway One, and watched Debbie turn back to the house with a smug and self-satisfied smile. No stolen goods on the premises now, no evidence to any crime.

Was this the last of her shoplifting, had she paid attention to what Ryan had told her? Or was she thinking Ryan would get busy with other matters and forget her threat? Was it possible that Debbie, now that she'd been caught red-handed, *would* stop stealing and look for a job?

Not likely, Joe thought. *Not bloody likely.* Clawing farther up the pine tree to the roof, he watched Debbie head for the garage with the empty stroller. Maybe she meant to fold it up and stick it in the corner behind her trash and boxes, get it out of the way, too. Behind her, Pan slipped out the door and scrambled to the roof beside him.

"Why does he need her car?" the red tom said. "Has he already sold the Lincoln? Sold it with Kate's treasure inside, with millions of dollars hidden in there just inches from his greedy fingers and he doesn't have a clue, no idea he's dumped a fortune for a few hundred bucks, to some scuzzy dealer?"

"You find that amusing? You think that's funny, if he let Kate's hoard get away where no one will ever find it, where not even the law might get a line on it?"

"I didn't mean it that way," Pan said contritely. "MPPD will find it. If he *has* sold it, it'll just take them longer."

"Or maybe," Joe said, "maybe he found the jewels before he sold it, took the door panels off himself to hide his stolen money, and found everything. Maybe right now he has Kate's treasure stashed somewhere else. Or," he said, "is the Lincoln still here somewhere with Kate's treasure still in it?" He looked up the hill to the woods, where the narrow dirt drive led down to the stone shack. "*Could* he have gotten the Town Car down through the trees? *Would* it have fit in that narrow shed?"

"Like a rat stuck in a jam jar," Pan said. "None of us were here to see him hide it, we were all up at the wreck. Except my dad," he said. "Except Misto."

"Vic's hardly had time to sell a car," Joe said. "Maybe everything *is* in the shed, and he's afraid to drive the Lincoln, afraid Harper's men will spot it, maybe that's why he wants Debbie's car. Let's have a look before he and his pal take off for good."

"Maybe the other guy's too hurt to travel. Kit said the man in the wrecked truck never stopped moaning, as if he were injured real bad."

Approaching the shed, looking up at its solid door, Joe leaped up at the padlock, striking and pawing at it. The big lock swung heavily but was closed tight. Pan tried, but with no better luck. Together they clawed at the door itself, trying to pull it away enough to see under or see through a crack at the side, but the heavy construction of bolted planks wouldn't budge. But then when they sniffed along the molding they caught Vic's fresh scent, and when they pressed their noses to the thinnest crack between door and molding they could smell a faint breath from within that made them smile: a distinct new-car smell, the smell of fine leather seats, the same comforting aroma as when they'd ridden in there with Kit, the smell of the Greenlaws' Town Car.

And when they examined the dirt apron of the drive itself, the faintest tire tracks led up to the shed door, the sharp tread of new tires just visible on the hard earth. Another set led away again to vanish where the narrow drive was covered with rotted leaves, where only vague indentations compressed the damp mulch. And only now, sniffing along the ground, did they catch Misto's scent where the old yellow cat had indeed padded along following the track of the Lincoln.

"Did they bring the Lincoln directly here from the wreck?" Pan said. "While we were headed up the mountain with the Damens, did my pa see those two men hide it in here?" He lifted his nose from the old cat's scent. "While you and Dulcie and I, and Rock and the Damens, were setting off to find Kit, did Misto know all along where those two men had holed up? He couldn't know who they were or what they'd done, and he couldn't know the Lincoln was stolen, but he knew where it *was*," he said, smiling.

"He knew they'd put a car in there," Joe said. "But would he recognize the Greenlaws' nice Town Car if it has heavy damage, dents and crumpled fenders, dirt and gravel from the landslide? And now," he said, "is it still parked in there behind those plank doors, or is only the smell there, and the Town Car gone again?"

"Secrets within secrets," Pan said as they moved away, wondering where else to look for the stolen vehicle. "This old place reeks of secrets. Only a few months ago, you and Dulcie find Sammie's body buried right down there under her own house. Then Emmylou inherits the house and starts finding money hidden in the walls. Those two tramps come here looking for it, too. And then those same two men wreck the Greenlaws' car or are involved in the wreck, one of them attacks Pedric and Lucinda and could as well have killed them both."

"And," Joe said thoughtfully, "even Sammie's death itself might be tied in. It was her money."

"Tied in how?

"The department's file on Sammie says she was killed because she saw Debbie's husband, Erik Kraft, kill Debbie's younger sister after he got her pregnant. Killed his own wife's little sister. But did Erik kill Sammie because of the money, too? Could he have known Sammie had hidden money? If he found out somehow, could he have tried to find it himself, tried to force her to tell him where it was? When she wouldn't, he killed her?"

"Maybe," Pan said thoughtfully. "I guess we'll never know. Whatever happened, Erik Kraft is scum, I always hated him. With a father like that and a mother like Debbie, it's no wonder Tessa has problems. Do you think," he said, "Vic hid the Lincoln nearby, where he can get at it in a hurry?"

Both cats glanced down the hill where the little cottages stood crowded close together beneath their overgrown cypress trees. "Come on," Joe said, "it's worth a look, half those places are empty." And off they went, past Debbie's house, down among the FOR RENT signs and the neglected foreclosures, to peer into garage windows and under doors, searching for a car worth maybe twenty thousand but loaded with treasure worth many times more.

25

RYAN DROVE HOME from Debbie's feeling dead for sleep and out of sorts, wishing Debbie Kraft had never returned to the village, and cursing her stupidity that she'd allowed Debbie to entrench herself rent-free in the little spec cottage. She had no idea whether her ultimatum to Debbie would have any effect on the woman. If it didn't she'd give the department a heads-up—if they weren't already watching Debbie. She hated that this would jeopardize Tessa. Even rude little Vinnie didn't deserve to be swept into the maw of Children's Services. Looking at her watch, she saw it was only mid-afternoon, just after two, but she'd love to crawl under a quilt for a few hours. Last night's desperate phone call from Kit seemed like weeks ago, a whole lifetime seemed to have passed since Kit's lonely cry for help.

Racing up to Santa Cruz, searching the dark cliffs and then that business with the coyote, their relief at finding

Kit unhurt and then hurrying to the hospital and their long vigil there, had left her limp with fatigue. Their trek home this morning behind the ambulance, getting Lucinda settled, and finding that lowlife had been in there pawing through their personal things, stealing Pedric's clothes, that was enough without Debbie's sour defiance to top off the long and exhausting drama. Was she getting old? she thought crossly. But no long day on the job, no amount of hard physical work on a construction project, exhausted her as these stressful hours had done. Now, pulling into her own drive and killing the engine, she glanced in her side mirror to see Clyde turning in behind her, in one of the shop's loaner cars.

He had put in less than an hour, since she'd dropped him at work to clear up some irksome detail about Jaguar parts lost in shipping. She watched him step out of the silver Mercedes, yawning. Despite his aggravation at a delay in the repair schedule and, consequently, an annoyed client, it was nice to own your own business, to feel comfortable taking some time off when you needed to. The minute she opened the truck door, Rock bolted out and straight for the house, nearly upsetting Clyde as he unlocked the front door. When he pushed it open, swinging it wide, Rock bolted through heading for the kitchen.

Grinning, Clyde put his arm around her and they followed Rock in, found the big silver dog checking the kitchen floor for stray food. They stood watching him lick Snowball's empty bowl clean then sniff along the countertop—whatever enticing trail he found led him out of the kitchen again and up the stairs to the master suite. They moved up behind him, Clyde carrying their duffel and backpacks, to find Rock had followed the scent of the old yellow cat.

On the love seat in Clyde's study, Misto and Snowball woke only a little, curled together sleepily. On the desk the message light was flashing, but neither Ryan nor Clyde wanted to listen to messages. They watched Rock nose at the two cats, licking them all over. The little white cat was used to the big dog's attention, his wet caresses made her smile. Misto batted at Rock with velvet paws, hissing halfheartedly—but then the yellow tom caught a whiff of the backpacks where Clyde had set them on the floor. He rose to investigate. He smelled the canvas with a puzzled look, then looked up at Ryan, questioning. He sniffed the ocean smells the canvas had collected, the scent of fresh pine needles, the scents of Kit and Joe Grey and Pan. He dropped his ears and backed away.

"Coyote," he said, scowling up at them. "And blood," he added, drawing his lips back at the metallic scent.

"The Greenlaws had a wreck," Ryan said. "They're in the hospital. Kit ran off and was lost and called us, and we went after her. We found her, she's fine, but . . ."

Behind her, Clyde had flicked the replay on the answering machine; she paused until it had played its messages. The first two were about problems with the house she was just finishing, but nothing serious. The third call was from Dr. John Firetti; his recorded voice brought Misto to full attention. Leaping onto the desk, he nosed at the machine.

"*We're home!*" Firetti said.

"*We're home,*" Mary chimed in, "shall we come get Misto? We so missed him, could we—"

But Misto was already on his way, leaping up to the rafters like a young cat and through Joe's cat door, his yellow tail vanishing as he bolted out through Joe's tower. They heard him thudding across the roof at a dead run, his gallop soon fading and then gone; they imagined him flying across the peaks above Ocean, making for the veterinary clinic and the cottage that stood beside it, making for home.

He'd left the Damens' without knowing much at all about the wreck or about Kit's fearful adventure, and with no idea the Greenlaws' car had been stolen, that the black car he'd seen pulling into the stone shed did, indeed, belong to Lucinda and Pedric. He left Ryan and Clyde equally ignorant, as well, of where the Town Car might now be hidden.

D EBBIE'S CLUTTERED AND smelly station wagon was a big change for Vic, from driving the pristine new Lincoln. He'd quickly grown used to the heavier, smoother ride, and even with the Town Car's dents and coat of mud its interior had been better suited to his new, cleaned-up persona. Though in truth the Suzuki, stinking and littered, was more what he was used to, more like the comfortable old truck with trash on the floor, discarded socks, the smell of accumulated dust, stale crackers, and empty drink cans.

Heading for the hospital, he meant to use patient Michael Emory's name to enter the ER through the locked doors, to be admitted without a hassle. He planned to head for Emory's cubicle as if to visit, but then move right on by to Birely's room. It wouldn't take a minute to do Birely, inject the air the way the book said, bending the IV tube to keep air from going up into the bottle—just stick the syringe in below the bend, and push the air in. As simple as that, the air goes down through the IV, through the vein and up into Birely's heart. Half a second and he's dead, his life snuffed like a match in a blast of wind.

Vic knew he'd have to move fast, get out in that split second before the alarms went off and the place exploded into action, nurses and doctors running in with their expertise and their machines to bring Birely back to life; that part worried him, hoping he could escape before anyone saw him or realized he'd been in Birely's room at all.

And who knew how long it would take before he could even be alone with Birely without them nurses going in and out? The hour he'd spent in there before dawn, when he'd followed Birely's ambulance and pushed on in, the place had been pretty quiet. But now later in the day he imagined it might be real busy, people in scrubs hurrying every which way, phones ringing, maybe gurneys pushing by him coming or going from X-ray, white-coated doctors moving with deliberation from one cubicle to the next. If it was like that, he'd be lucky to get half a minute alone. He could hardly hang out there for hours waiting for the right moment without someone asking questions.

Pulling into the underground, he found a parking slot near the glass doors into the ER. He figured no one would take a second look at the old Suzuki, would think, just one more patient with no money and no insurance, go-

ing into the ER with the flu or a backache, going for help
where the doctors wouldn't refuse to treat you even if you
couldn't pay. The wide glass doors opened automatically.
At the admitting desk, he gave his name as James Emory,
told the nurse he'd come to see his cousin Michael.

"Mr. Emory has two visitors, that's all we allow at one
time. If you'll have a seat here in the waiting room, we'll
call you when you can go in."

"No problem," Vic said. "You got a Coke machine
handy?"

"There's nothing on this floor. You can go up to the
cafeteria, they have Cokes, coffee, and sandwiches." She
pointed down the short hall, where he could see the lower
steps of a stairway leading up. "That's the shortest way. At
the top just keep going to the big central atrium."

He didn't know what an atrium was but he guessed
he'd know when he saw it. He went up the steps into a
wide, bright corridor, glass walls on his left looking out to
manicured trees and gardens. Passing well-dressed people
who looked like they belonged there, he felt out of place
until he remembered he looked just like them now, no
more shabby clothes, he was so cleaned up it took him
a minute to recognize his own reflection in the tall windows. Hell, he looked pretty damn good, for a hobo.

The atrium was high ceilinged, with a towering round
skylight at the top, and a big indoor fishpond with a small
tree growing in the middle. He bought a Coke in the cafeteria, sat down at a table beside the pond. All kinds of
space led away into bright halls and more open spaces, and
he could see two more sets of stairs leading down. All so
damn clean it made him uncomfortable. What kind of

money did it take to build a fancy place like this? Molena Point was even richer than he'd thought.

He drank his Coke watching some kind of large, brightly colored fish swim back and forth, then got himself a sticky cinnamon bun and a cup of coffee. How long would it take for those people down in the ER, visiting Michael Emory, to get tired and leave? He felt edgy to get back down there and get this over with, and nervous, too, not wanting to go back. What time did the nurses change shift? Maybe better to wait until then, when they were hurrying to go home, others hurrying in to work, looking at records, playing catch-up to which patients had checked in or checked out or died—best to get down there when they were all distracted, do the deed, slip out to the parking garage again and vanish.

He got more coffee and settled back, watching the circling fish, checking his watch every little while. Just before four, several young women dressed in scrubs hurried out, and several others double-timed in from another parking lot that lay beyond the gardens. Young women walking fast, all businesslike, they knew where they were going and were in a hurry to be on time. Rising, he left his trash on the table.

He was headed for the stairs when he saw that woman contractor come in through the glass front doors, and he stepped back, frowning. No mistaking her, same jeans and red sweatshirt she'd had on at Debbie's, only now she was wearing one of those backpack purses, an expensive leather model. Looked like, the way she held her head, she was talking to the damn purse, but then he saw she was talking on her cell phone. He turned away and sat down at the table again. Did she recognize him from around Emmylou's place?

As far as he knew she'd probably never noticed him there—yet when he glanced around again, she was looking straight at him. She saw him looking, said something into the phone, and went on past the pond toward a set of stairs that descended on the far side. Well, he'd seen *her* for sure, around Debbie's and up at Emmylou's, too, helping out with the old woman's carpentering. Were these women all friends? He didn't rise until she had disappeared, moving on down the steps, making him wonder where she was headed, what was down there in that direction. He waited a while and then descended the other way, to the ER, trying to calm his jumpy nerves.

R YAN HAD AWAKENED in late afternoon to the ringing of the phone. Clyde, sprawled beside her on the king-sized bed, hadn't stirred. An afternoon nap was a rare occurrence in their lives, she didn't like being woken up. Grabbing the ringing instrument, she'd eased out from under the coverlet that she'd tossed over them.

"It's Kate. I hope I didn't wake you."

"Only a little."

Kate laughed. "I'm sorry. Pedric called, he's feeling better, he asked if I could bring Kit over, he misses her, he wants to know if I can smuggle her in. I don't want to leave Lucinda alone yet when she's on the pain meds, but he sounded so forlorn. I think Kit's ordeal up on the cliffs has left him more upset than she was, he wants her close to him, he asked if Lucinda could spare her for a while. Could you . . . ?"

"Of course I'll come, I'll take her over there to him." Beside her, Clyde turned over, mumbling but hardly waking; Clyde had sat up the longest last night with Pedric, he deserved to be sleepy.

"I'm just running Kit up to the hospital," she said, "Pedric's asking for her."

"Take the Mercedes," he said, waking fuzzily. "Keys are on my desk. I'll drop the truck off at the shop before the mechanics go home, I don't like the way it's running."

She thought it was running fine, he was so picky about their cars. She grinned at him, nodded, pulled on her boots, and found her purse. She dropped her keys on the desk, took the Mercedes keys, and told Rock to stay home. The Weimaraner, having hauled himself from sleep and surged off the love seat, was more than ready to go with her. She told him, "No," and hugged him, but he looked after her ruefully. She moved on down the stairs and out, slipped into the silver Mercedes, and headed for Lucinda's house.

When she pulled up into the Greenlaws' drive, tortoiseshell Kit was waiting on the steps shifting from paw to paw, lashing her fluffy tail with impatience. Ryan set the emergency brake and then opened the driver's door. Kit leaped up into her lap, her expression a strange mix of eagerness and sadness.

"What? What's wrong? Lucinda's all right?"

"Fine," Kit said, snuggling down close to her, pushing her head into Ryan's ribs.

Ryan rubbed Kit's warm little ears, but she didn't start

the car. "Tell me." She sat frowning down at Kit. "Is it Pan? Is it because you argued?"

"Because . . ." Kit pawed at a tear seeping into the dark fur of her cheek. "Because the most important things to Pan are so different from how I see things. I didn't know that about him. We can never . . ."

Ryan took Kit in her arms. "You're not opposite at all. You're perfect for each other. You're male and female, that's all. That's what makes the world work. Females go more for security, they'll fight tooth and claw to protect their home and kittens but tomcats' hearts are strung for adventure. They go searching for challenge, that's the way *they* protect their brood. That's the way you're made, you and Pan."

Kit looked up at her and her pink tongue came out, licking at another tear.

Ryan looked down into Kit's wide yellow eyes. She didn't know what else to say, she didn't know how to resolve this. Their story was as old as the very concept of male and female. "Maybe," she said, "if you could talk without hissing and spitting at him . . ."

"Pan does all the hissing," Kit said untruthfully. Ryan gave her a sideways glance, settled Kit in the seat again, put the car in gear, and headed for the freeway.

"Maybe I hissed a little," Kit said, "but he was so—"

"If Pedric sees you all teary, you'll make him feel worse than he does now."

"I know," Kit said contritely. She crept up into Ryan's lap again, curled up in a tight little ball, shivering. She was being so dramatic Ryan wanted to scold her, but this was the way Kit reacted, the little tortoiseshell was a born drama queen. This was the way she was made, her wild little spirit knew no compromise, her wild heart blazed with the passion of an unruly youngster, and Ryan knew she would never change. Taking the off-ramp for the hospital, she headed up the hill, made a right, and a left into underground parking. Cruising the first level for a space, she passed Debbie's old station wagon pulled in beside a pillar. What was she doing here? Had one of the children been hurt? Or maybe Debbie had brought Tessa to emergency for some free cold medicine, that would be her style. But then when she did find a parking place, she was two cars down from an old green Chevy that was a ringer for Emmylou's car, so much like it that, telling Kit to wait in the car, she walked back and looked in.

She could see Emmylou's ragged tan sweater on the front seat, no mistaking the tear in the sleeve. The presence of the two familiar cars there at the hospital unsettled her. Uneasily she returned to the car, where Kit was standing on the dashboard, peering out. "Debbie's car, and Emmylou's?" Kit said. "What's that about?" And neither of them could answer.

Opening her small leather backpack, Ryan watched Kit climb in and curl up at the bottom. Kit didn't like this pack because she couldn't see out, like the big canvas one with the net insets, but to Ryan the oversized purse seemed less obvious. She buckled the flap loosely enough so Kit could crawl out if she had to, she would never confine any of the cats beyond escape. "Smile for Pedric," she said, "he needs you now, even more than Pan does." She slung the pack over her shoulder. "Who knows," she said, "maybe Pan will get some sense and change his macho mind, maybe he'll look at your side of the argument."

Kit didn't answer.

"Maybe," Ryan said, locking the Mercedes, "if Kate describes her journey in more detail, if she tells him more graphically exactly why she will never, ever return to the Netherworld, maybe he'll listen. Maybe," she said, "he'll think a little more about the dangers to his beautiful lady." Heading for the elevators, stepping in and pushing the button for the main level, she took her phone from her pocket so she could talk with Kit in public looking perfectly natural. Stepping out of the elevator onto the open terrace, she crossed to the glass doors, moved inside into the vast, airy court with its sun dome and pond, its information desk and cafeteria, its light-filled corridors leading away to the various hospital wings. The hospital walls were made of white concrete in a bas-relief pattern that made her think of Aztec monuments, the occasional paintings hanging against them offering rich islands of color, oils and watercolors by well-known local artists, dating back into the last century. The smell of coffee and of onion soup rose sharply from the cafeteria kitchen. A man stood beside the pond half turned away seeming to watch the red, black, and white fish swimming aimlessly, but in fact he was watching her, a furtive sideways glance. Did she know him? The back of his neck was so white he must have only recently decided to change his hairstyle. Pale cheeks and chin, too, when he turned.

But he was no one she knew, and she headed past the fishpond, for the far stairs that descended to the ICU, hoping she *could* slip Kit into Pedric's room without getting caught. The nurses in the ICU stuck pretty close to their patients. They'd pushed their luck enough, up in Santa Cruz. Their own Peninsula Hospital, being larger, seemed somehow more intimidating. Who knew what contempt a furry feline visitor, discovered in the ICU against all bureaucratic regulations, would stir among the medical staff—what lack of sympathy that would generate for a needful patient?

26

Ryan descended the stairs, not talking to her hidden passenger even with the ruse of her cell phone. The scrutiny of that man by the pond had made her edgy. Light from the main pavilion shone from behind her down the wide stairs; she imagined Kit peering out beneath the leather flap at the sunny vistas and at the paintings spaced along the walls, oils and watercolors, many of the bright California coast. At the bottom of the stairs she followed the signs through a long waiting room; three women sat at a little round table at the far end, all talking at once. Passing them, she moved on down the hall to the ICU. As she entered, no one paid any attention to her, the nurses were all busy with patients or at the computers. When she found Pedric's glass cubicle, the clear doors and the canvas curtain were wide open. His hospital bed was empty, the white covers neatly turned back. When she turned, a slim, dark-haired nurse stood behind her, green scrubs, gold earrings, hair sleeked into a bun at the back.

"Where's Pedric? Mr. Greenlaw? I thought he was in room 7."

"You are . . ."

"Ryan Flannery," she said. "I'm a friend, I'm on his health care directive." Did they keep *lists* of those permitted in the ICU? The nurse moved to a desk within the open nurses' station, peered into a lighted screen and pushed a few keys, then glanced up at Ryan. "Mr. Greenlaw is having an MRI. Later today, sometime after he returns, he'll be moved over to the west wing, into a room there."

"Why is that? He's not worse?"

"Oh, no, his own doctor wants a few more tests, that's all. And he wants the surgeon to go ahead with the arthroscopy on his knee, for the torn meniscus. That's usually an outpatient procedure, but with the other complications, Dr. Bailey wants it done while he's here, wants him to stay for at least a day or two."

"Can you tell me where the new room will be? What number?"

"We don't have a number yet, they're still cleaning the rooms. If you want to come back in, say, an hour, we should know."

Ryan nodded, and left the ICU, glancing in at the rows of bedridden patients, each tethered to their iron bed like a prisoner, she thought dourly. Heading for the waiting room, she thought that Pedric must not have known he would be having another scan and then would be moved, or he wouldn't have called the house asking for Kit.

In the lounge she chose a love seat as far from the three noisy women as she could. The room was furnished with dark rattan chairs, small rattan tables, and three leather love seats. Potted schefflera plants the size of small trees cast the room in gentle shadows. The place smelled of coffee, from an urn sitting on a console against the longer wall. Paper cups, a basket full of artificial creamer and fake sweetener, all the accompaniments a health-conscious hospital would want to furnish. Setting the backpack down beside her on the cushion of the love seat, she fished out her cell phone. The pack shifted only slightly as Kit peered out the top, scowling at the boisterous women, at their frantic exchange as each tried to get in one more word. "Why do women go on like that," Kit whispered, "tearing their husbands apart? *You* don't do that, none of *my* human friends do that."

Ryan shrugged, holding her cell phone to her ear. "*You* said a few things about Pan," she pointed out.

Kit said nothing. Inside the pack, she curled up again, closed her eyes, and tucked her nose under her paw. Maybe, Ryan thought, after her long and arduous night she would sleep now, would drift off into happier dreams and would wake less angry. Ryan closed her own eyes, but the women's too-loud voices racketed into her thoughts as sharp as hail on a metal roof; when she did doze off, her dreams were filled with fog and craggy cliffs, with the gleam of a coyote's eyes and the sharp smell of gunpowder, with regret at the kill but with deep satisfaction that Kit was safe.

WHEN VIC CAME down from the cafeteria into the ER, the nurses were too busy to pay attention to him. He moved on past the nurses' station glancing into each glass cubicle trying to look like he knew where he was going. He walked the entire square, all four sides, but Birely was not in any of the rooms. At last, revving up his nerve, he asked a nurse.

"I'm his neighbor, I stopped in to see how he's doing."

The little blonde was young, her hair tumbled up atop her head like a bird's nest and secured with a strip of white bandage. "Mr. Miller just returned from surgery, he's over in the ICU. They repaired his nose. It'll be some time, after that heals and his breathing's steadier, that he'll be ready for surgery to remove the spleen."

This had to be more than the nurses were supposed to tell a stranger, and Vic smiled at her in a friendly way. "Sounds like he's getting good care. I'll stop over there a little later, then, when he's feeling stronger."

Leaving the ER, he had a time finding his way to the ICU. The halls led every which way, and many of the heavy double doors were locked. By the time he found Birely his hands were sweating with nerves. The layout was pretty much the same as the ER, big room maybe fifty feet square, nurses' station in the middle fenced off by open counters with their ever-present computers.

Big chrome machine on the counter near him with spigots for hot and cold water, another machine for brewed coffee, regular and decaffeinated, just like a fancy café. Again he circled the nurses' station but when at last he found Birely there was too much traffic around him, nurses moving in and out of the other rooms. Be-

neath the white blanket, Birely looked small and weak.
He had a white bandage across his nose, a tube sticking
out of each nostril so he could breathe, and the usual
IV tube attached at his wrist, held in place by heavy
tape. His eyes were closed, as if he slept. Even as Vic
watched, a nurse moved past him and inside followed by
a white-coated doctor. Vic glanced at them casually and
stepped on along as if heading for a room around the
corner. Damn place was crawling with doctors and several of them glanced at him, looking him over as if he
had no business there. He moved along paying no attention to them, as businesslike as he could manage, until
an older nurse stopped him, an overweight redhead in
blue scrubs, braces on her teeth, asked what patient he
was looking for. He gave her Michael Emory's name. She
carried a trench coat over her arm, and a brown leather
purse as if she were headed home. Stepping to a computer, she said Michael Emory was over in the ER, and
she told him how to get there. She was pretty nice, she
didn't treat him like scum. It had paid to get cleaned up
and wear expensive clothes. It was nearly five, and he was
sure the shift had already changed. Eight to four, four to
twelve, midnight to eight, that was the way most places
broke up their time. He waited until he saw the redhead
leave, hurrying down the hall carrying her trench coat
and jingling her car keys. When he was sure no one was
looking, he slipped into an empty room where he could
see they hadn't cleaned up yet, bedsheets wadded in a
heap in the middle of the mattress, trash can overflowing
with blue plastic pads of some kind and lengths of used
tubing. Metal table cluttered with pieces of bloody gauze

and used tape, and two used syringes with no needles in them.

He found the rubber-glove dispenser on the wall beside the door, pulled a pair from the section marked LARGE, worked one onto his right hand, and dug into the trash. When he couldn't find a syringe he turned to the hazardous-waste bin, which was also attached to the wall.

The first three syringes were useless, just the blunt plastic end. Digging deeper, he found one that someone hadn't broken off the needle. Retrieving it, he hoped to hell he wouldn't pick up some kind of lethal disease that'd put *him* in the ER or leave him sick and helpless.

Well, hell, if he didn't pull this off he'd be looking at worse than a hospital bed, looking at a lumpy metal cot behind steel bars. If the cops went nosing around Emmylou's after she'd called the ambulance, if she told them she'd had a break-in and they were camping up there, and the cops came up here to the hospital asking Birely questions, and the dumb little twerp started talking about the money, that would put him on the hot seat. Cops picked up even one fingerprint in that stone shack, ran it through the system, they'd have his whole damn record.

Dropping the syringe in his pocket, he left the ICU still trying to look casual. Made his way out to the stairs, thinking to wait a while until maybe there was less action in there and until people forgot they'd seen him looking in the rooms. He was passing the waiting room to the ICU when he saw her again, that dark-haired woman contractor sitting right there only a few feet from him, and he stepped back out of sight.

She sat in there drinking a cup of coffee and talking on her cell phone. Sounded like she was talking to a carpenter, going on about door sizes and the delivery of some kind of flooring. She sat turned away from him, and silently he slipped on by. What was she doing here?

Well, hell, people got sick. Birely didn't have a corner on the market. He moved on down a long hall to another part of the hospital thinking to wait a while until people forgot about him, then go back and take care of Birely. He knew he was putting it off, he told himself he was being cautious, that he wasn't scared. He wandered the halls until he'd got himself thoroughly lost again and began to feel shaky.

Finally, passing a big, glassed-off garden right in the center of the building, he saw the cafeteria ahead, and knew where he was. He stopped off there, had himself another cup of coffee to steady his nerves, and another one of them cinnamon rolls. Jangled nerves always made him hungry. That garden he'd passed, big as a city lot, hospital rooms and glassed hallways facing it on all four sides, garden had a big rock formation with a waterfall, three stories of rooms looking out on it. Pretty damn fancy, he wished he had half the money it'd taken to build this place. What couldn't he do with that kind of cash?

Finishing his coffee and sticky roll, he headed back to the ICU. Moved on in past the nurses' station and across to Birely's room. He was about to step inside when he saw a nurse in there and another doctor. He moved on by, glancing around, and into the room next door. The patient was sleeping, snoring softly. Slipping past him to the connecting wall, he stood listening.

The doctor's voice was deep, it reached him easily, he must be standing right there on the other side. The glimpse Vic had had of him, he was a big man, his shoulders rolled forward as if maybe he had a weak back. He was talking about the IV, giving the nurse instructions. "Keep him on fourteen milligrams of Demerol every three to four hours, until his nose is less painful. I want him to lighten up a little now, not so deep under. I want only nurses in here, no trainees, I want him handled with care. I don't want any pressure on the abdomen. None. Do you understand?"

Vic couldn't make out what the nurse said, her voice was too soft. He was so intent, listening, he almost missed seeing Emmylou pass by, he barely glimpsed her through the crack between the curtain and the wall as she turned into Birely's room.

Had she seen him out there, coming into the ICU? But hell, *she* didn't know him, either. He was too edgy. Just because he recognized someone didn't mean they knew him. If Emmylou'd ever seen them and knew they were living up there, she'd have called the cops long ago. And with his change in looks, his long hair gone, why would she recognize him now? The doctor was telling her that when Birely's nose had healed some, he'd go back into surgery and they'd take out his spleen, same as that nurse had said.

"If the spleen doesn't rupture," Emmylou said, "before you get him back into surgery?"

"We're taking the best care we can," the doctor said coldly. "You have no idea what happened to this man?"

"None," she said. "I found him hurt like that, lying in a sleeping bag half-conscious and moaning."

"Found him where?"

"In an old vacant house at the back of my property, no one was supposed to be in there."

"You reported it to the police?"

"I called the ambulance. I don't plan to file a complaint, so why call them?"

There was a long silence. The doctor said no more. Emmylou said, "I'll come back in a while, see if he's awake. He . . . I'd like a word with him, when he wakes."

Vic watched through the crack as she left. Soon the doctor left, and then the nurse. He watched the nurses' station as personnel moved back and forth, going about their business, all so damned organized. The ward grew quieter, some of the nurses disappeared into patients' rooms, the pace seemed to slow. Vic moved out of the room past the sleeping patient, his rubber-gloved hand in his coat pocket, caressing the syringe. He was about to slip into Birely's room when two nurses came around the corner wheeling a gurney, came straight toward him. He stepped away, looking with curiosity at the patient, his head all wrapped in white like a turban, his face white as death itself. They turned into a room two doors down, both nurses looking up at him. He smiled at them and nodded, annoyed that they looked right at him, that they could identify him in a damn minute entering Birely's room. Angrily he moved on out of the ward, down the hall and out of sight. He'd wait a while and go back. Or come back tonight after another change of shift, when maybe the ward would be quieter?

Right, and when every visitor would stand out all the more. Best to walk the halls a while and then go back again, get it over with, this time, before he lost his nerve altogether. Strolling the hall pretending to look at the pictures on the walls, he stopped at a picture of boats in a stormy harbor, the water wild with whitecaps that made him cold just looking at them. He walked on, feeling shaky, and at last headed back to the ICU. Passing the waiting room, he saw that carpenter woman was still in there, and Emmylou had joined her, she sat right there beside her, talking earnestly. Moving on beyond the open door past the big leafy plant beside it, he paused in the shadows to listen.

27

KIT WAS SO warm inside the backpack she couldn't help but squirm, she had to poke her nose out for one breath of cool air. She ducked back when Emmylou appeared in the doorway. What was she doing here? "Come sit," Ryan said, moving Kit's leather pack off the love seat, setting it on the floor. "Have you come to see Pedric?"

Emmylou crossed the room with a soft scuffing sound, and sat down. "Pedric Greenlaw's here? Oh, my. What happened? What's wrong?"

By the time Ryan had explained about the wreck, Kit had crawled halfway out of the backpack again, listening. Ryan explained how Kit had run off from the wrecked Lincoln, which was the natural thing for a frightened cat to do, and how they had gone to search for her.

"Poor little thing," Emmylou said. "How lucky that

you found her, up in those dark woods. She must have been terrified."

I was terrified. And ready to bloody those damned coyotes.

"She came to us," Ryan said. "She had the good sense to do that."

Well, of course I did.

"And you spent the rest of the night at the hospital up there? You must be dead for sleep. And they're here, now, in the hospital? Pedric and Lucinda?"

"Pedric is," Ryan said. "They brought him down in an ambulance. They'll be moving him over to the other wing for a few days, but Lucinda's at home. Our friend from San Francisco is staying with her. Lucinda's happy to *be* home, and so is their little cat."

"I'm sure of that," Emmylou said. "Cats don't take well to that kind of stress. But now they're both safe in their own place, and that will help to heal them." Emmylou had a special fondness for the concept of *home*, for a safe haven of one's own, having recently lived homeless in her old car, and before that in a wind-riddled, one-room shack from which she had been evicted. Her work on her snug house, as she remodeled, was thoughtful and loving. Was, in its own way, deeply restorative to the lone woman, a home at last that no one could take from her.

But, Kit thought, *we're not all home, Pedric's not home yet. And I feel like I've spent half my life in hospitals hiding under the covers having to be quiet and still and my very fur smells of hospital. Pedric has to feel just as trapped, all the bandages, the needles stuck in his arm, the nurses doing things to him he'd rather do for himself. We're not all home yet, we're not all three of us back together yet.* The brush of a footstep in the hall, the silence as it paused startled her. She rose up out of the leather pack, to look.

Beyond the open door a shadow shifted where someone stood listening, his shadow half hidden by the big floppy leaves of the schefflera plant that hid, as well, most of the hallway. Emmylou was saying, ". . . squatters. Two sleeping bags, empty cans of beans, beer cans, trash. They left a mess. Well, this man that I've come to visit, he was in there in his sleeping bag on the floor, and he was hurt real bad. I don't know what happened but he was all alone, moaning and bleeding, the minute I saw him I hurried down to my place and called the ambulance."

Listening to Emmylou, trying to make sense of what she was saying, Kit watched the shadow shift again, and when she breathed deeply she picked up the sweet smell of sugar and cinnamon, and then . . . What? What was that she smelled?

Pedric? The faintest scent of Pedric? But then even stronger, over Pedric's scent and the smell of sugary cinnamon, came a familiar odor that made her swallow back a growl. It was all she could do not to bolt out of the bag and leap at him, slash him as she had up on the mountain when he'd hurt Lucinda. Why was that man here at the hospital? The same hospital where Pedric was. What did he want, what did he mean to do?

"Well, to make a long story short," Emmylou was saying, "the hurt man is Sammie's little brother, Birely. Can you believe it? Her homeless brother who came around once or twice a year. Birely who never admitted to being among the homeless, who called himself a hobo. Whenever he showed up, she'd take him a sandwich or a hot supper from the deli. Sometimes I went with her, we'd sit under the Valley Road bridge, the three of us like homeless folks, having our picnic."

"Was Birely here for her funeral? I don't . . ."

"No," Emmylou said. "He probably didn't know she'd died, until now. Came back all these months later, after Sammie was buried, came up to the property but didn't tell me he was here. Broke into that stone shack with one of his cronies. How long have they been there, and I didn't have a clue? Not until I heard some noises up there last night, and went up to see and there was Birely, lying there only half alive."

The shadow had moved closer, pressing against the door, Kit could see the flap of his jacket now, through the crack between the wall and the open door. His smell came stronger again, hiding Pedric's scent. Emmylou said, "Days earlier, I *had* wondered, when Misto started watching the place, sitting in the yard, looking up there. And then when I saw your Joe Grey and little tabby Dulcie up there, saw them come down off the windowsill as if they'd been inside. I thought, then, there were rats up there, there are wood rats all over these hills. I decided they were hunting in there, and I thought no more about it."

In the shadow of the love seat, when Ryan turned away, Kit slipped on out of the backpack, to the floor. Ryan said, "When he learned Sammie had died, why didn't he come to you? Was he too shy, did he move in there out of loneliness but was too shy to let you know he was there? But then," she said, "what happened? How did he get hurt?" Behind her Kit fled belly down across the dark tile floor and into the shadows of the potted schefflera tree. "Last night," Ryan said, "when you called the ambulance, why didn't you ask for the police, too?"

"Those two hadn't *hurt* anything," Emmylou said. "They were trespassing, but nothing more. My concern was all for Birely."

"Emmylou, you don't know anything about the other man, or, in fact, about Birely . . ."

"Oh, Birely isn't mean, just irresponsible. Maybe a little dim. Sammie always tried to take care of him. She was nine when Birely was born. She said he was always shy and rather slow, that the other kids teased and harried him. Their parents did their best to see he wasn't bullied and to teach him to fend for himself, but then their father was killed. Birely was seven, Sammie sixteen. After that, I guess they all had a hard time.

"When Sammie died she left me everything she had, the house and the money. She asked me to take care of him if I could, so of course I feel responsible for him, I couldn't betray Sammie, I have to help Birely."

"She left you money? I hope enough to pay the taxes and insurance."

Emmylou smiled. "Oh, my, yes. She . . ." She glanced down the room at the three women, but they were still talking all at once, as frantically energized as sparrows on a pile of bread crumbs. "She left money hidden in the house," Emmylou said softly. "Quite a lot of money."

"I'm glad of that," Ryan said. "That helps with the re-furbishing, too. I hope you have it safe in the bank, now. But, Emmylou, if Birely's friend knew he was hurt, why didn't *he* get Birely to the ER? He just went off and left him? Doesn't that tell you something?"

Kit, hidden among the leaves of the schefflera, wasn't six inches from the man who'd hurt Pedric and Lucinda, who'd gone into their empty house and trashed it. He looked different now, smooth shaven, with short, neater hair—having left his pigtail scattered across their bathroom floor, she thought, twitching a whisker. He was wearing Pedric's sport coat, the missing tweed sport coat, and Pedric's missing Rockports that, when she sniffed them through the crack, still smelled of the Molena Point hills, of bruised grass and damp leaves. He had used Lucinda and Pedric's house key to steal Pedric's clothes, and now he was here at the hospital. Come to visit his hurt partner? Or to nose around Pedric's room? For what reason?

Emmylou said, "Maybe Birely's partner didn't have any money to take him to the hospital, maybe he left Birely to go for medicine, to help him the only way he could, maybe—"

"You know better than that, Emmylou. Medicine, for a smashed nose? Everyone knows you can check yourself into the ER with no money, that, by law, they can't refuse to treat you. Where *is* this friend, who couldn't bother to bring Birely here?"

The man beyond the door had turned away, moved silently, heading down the hall toward the ICU. Silently Kit followed him. Bellying out from under the schefflera and out the door, she hoped no doctor or nurse came along the hall and made a fuss, called security to chase that cat out of the hospital. Behind her the voices faded as Kit streaked across an intersecting hallway close behind the man's heels. The floors were no longer dark so he blended in; the linoleum was white now, against her black-and-brown coat as she followed him into the big, open expanse of the Intensive Care Unit.

IN THE WAITING room, Ryan knew she should be returning to the ICU, to see if Pedric was back in his bed. She imagined Kit sound asleep in her backpack, worn out from last night's excitement. Emmylou was saying, "I read Sammie's letter over and over. I kept it for only a few days and then I burned it. I was afraid someone might find it, and find the money. Sammie had invested some of it, and she did all right, enough to live on, and to work only when she wanted to. She kept most of the original money at home, she said her uncle'd taught her never to trust banks.

"After he left the states, Sammie thought he was afraid to write or call, afraid that might put the Mexican Guardia on his trail, afraid of being extradited back to the U.S. He must have been a tough old guy; he was one of the last legendary train robbers, a man right out of the Old West, and he was a real hero to Sammie. She prayed he'd come back, but he didn't, not until she was nearly thirty. Came back to California to die.

"She was living up in the Salinas Valley then, working as a bookkeeper, when the uncle showed up again. He was real sick, lung disease. He was bone thin and weak, and could hardly breathe, she was surprised he had made it up from Mexico, came by train all the way. She got him into the hospital," Emmylou said, "but he only lasted a week, lying there white and helpless, she said, and then he was gone. Dead from emphysema and pneumonia.

"Her letter was with her will. I was surprised she had a lawyer, she lived such a simple life, was so reclusive." Emmylou laughed. "Like me, I guess. Well, the lawyer gave me the sealed letter, and the newly recorded deed in my name, a check for what little she had in the bank, and the letter he'd sent her with the money some years before he died."

"That's why you were tearing into the walls," Ryan said, "that's why you're remodeling, looking for the money. Oh, my God, Emmylou. What if there'd been a fire?"

"It was wrapped in sheets of asbestos," Emmylou said, "some kind of insulation, maybe what they used to use in houses before the laws got so strict."

Ryan closed her eyes, imagining packets of old, frail treasury bills, wrapped in asbestos that probably wouldn't help much if those ancient, dry studs went up in a hungry blaze. She wondered if, in those simpler days when every crime was more newsworthy, that robbery had been in the California papers. She wondered if the case was still open, perhaps, was still on the books after all these many years—and if the feds would still like to get their hands on those old bills? It was only after Emmylou had left, and Ryan reached down to pick up her backpack and head for the ICU, only when she felt the pack swing up too light, light and empty, that she panicked.

28

MAKING SURE HE had the rubber glove, Vic patted the syringe, safe in his pocket. At the door to the ICU he tried to look casual, walked on in past the chrome coffee machine, scanning the glass-fronted cubicles. His plan was to use patient Michael Emory as his cover, pretend to be visiting him. The nurse had said he was being moved over there from the ER. With luck he'd be there already and maybe asleep, sick people slept a lot. If the wife wasn't in there he could sit in there himself, like a visitor, could watch Birely's room from there until the coast was clear. It would take only a second to do Birely, bend the tube, inject the air, and get the hell out—and talk about luck! There she *was*, that Mrs. Emory, coming out of number 15, the same small dumpy woman with the round, wrinkled face and yellowed fuzzy hair. Congratulating himself on his perfect timing, he watched her leave Emory's room pulling the canvas curtain halfway across as if maybe Emory *was* sleeping. As she passed the nurses' station and moved on out the double doors he stepped over to the coffee urn, filled a white foam cup with coffee, added sugar and cream. Carrying this, he headed on around the nurses' station to the other side. If anyone questioned him, he was here to visit with Michael Emory. He smiled and nodded when one or another of the nurses glanced up at him. They were all busy, no one paid much attention to him, busy doing their routine chores of one kind or another, oblivious to Vic's purpose there.

STALKING THE MAN was an exercise in fast judgment and heart-thumping panic. Kit made it down the hall and around the corner into the ICU having to dodge only twice into open doorways, where she barely missed being seen. Slipping behind his heels into the ICU, she was engulfed by the smell of alcohol, adhesive tape, disinfectants, and human urine. The ward was brightly lighted, and on the white linoleum she stood out like a raven on a white bedsheet. There was not one dim recess near her in which to hide, to camouflage her dark coat, not one shadow except, yards away, where the occasional cart or wheeled cupboard was parked against the open nurses' counter. Twice she dodged behind rolling electrical equipment that looked like it could shock her straight into cat heaven.

If this man was visiting his wounded friend, wasn't it a little late? Why would he care about Birely after leaving him to suffer and maybe die all alone? Her sense of Birely, after listening to Emmylou, had softened, had left her feeling only sorry for Sammie's pitiful brother. It wasn't Birely who had hurt Pedric and Lucinda and stolen their car, it was Birely's visitor.

The soft pad of a nurse's approaching footsteps sent her behind a stainless steel machine with a cord hanging down like a noose. Next to it against the counter stood three rolling storage cabinets, polished steel carts with doors and drawers, with who knew what inside them? Towels and warm blankets? Or lethal and radiating medications that could sear a cat's very liver at this close range? The carts stood on casters, four inches off the floor, leaving narrow, bone-bruising spaces beneath. Flattening herself, she crept under.

Squeezed against the cool linoleum floor, concealed within the cupboard's shadow, she peered out at the man in Pedric's sport coat. He stood with his back to her looking in through a partially open glass door, the canvas curtain drawn halfway across. She watched him move on in, to disappear inside. Whatever he was up to, his body language and his nervous smell made the fur along her back stand stiff.

But this wasn't Pedric's room, his was around the corner near the double doors, she'd seen it earlier from Ryan's backpack. Relieved but curious, she looked both ways as if crossing a busy street, and slipped behind him across the wide walkway to the open glass door. She crouched there frantic to hide herself before a nurse spotted her, but she was afraid to push inside where *he'd* see her.

The canvas curtain didn't reach the floor; whoever had designed the flimsy barrier hadn't envisioned anyone interested enough to peer underneath from a four-inch vantage. When she looked under, his back was to her. She crawled under and crouched against the glass beneath the curtain's edge.

The patient was either asleep or unconscious. He lay unmoving, his eyes closed, his nose covered with a thick white bandage. A thin plastic tube snaked out of each nostril, she could hear him breathing through them. The man she'd followed stood over him. She had to force her tail to be still, not switch with anger. He stood looking down at the tube that ran from a vein in Birely's wrist up to the hanging jar that was the IV dispenser. He reached to examine the tube and then looked up at the screen, watching its moving graph and changing numbers. When he fished a syringe from his pocket, she shivered at the long needle.

He took the IV hose in his other hand and bent it double, stopping the flow of liquid. She watched him lay the needle along the tube as if preparing to stick it in—for what purpose? All Emmylou's sympathy for Birely hit her, and all her own hatred of the man who had hurt her humans. She leaped screaming at him, landed on his shoulder clawing hard.

He hit and grabbed at her trying to pull her off, then swung around as if to run. She clawed down the side of his face, down his neck. When he raised the needle to jab her she dropped off and dove under the bed, up onto its heavy metal stand. He leaned over, looking. He kicked at her, swearing. Even as she dodged away, she saw him drop the needle, straighten up, and draw back his fist over the patient.

His fist struck straight down with all his weight, into Birely's stomach. Birely screamed a gurgling cry and then was still. Bells went off on the monitor, the graph of Birely's heartbeat went flat, the gauges blinking in distress. An alarm shrieked from the nurses' station. Birely's attacker was gone, racing away, dodging nurses who came running. He shouldered through them shouting, "Help, someone help . . . Get a doctor, call the doctor." Pointing and shouting, he fled through the open double doors and vanished. Kit flew through behind him, flicking her tail away as they swung closed.

Racing past the surprised clerk at the admittance desk, she could see him out beyond the glass doors running through the dim parking garage, nearly trampling three children coming in with their heavily pregnant mother. His running feet echoed on the concrete, heading for an old brown station wagon. Debbie's car? Puzzled, she raced for it. The instant he jerked the door open she streaked behind him into the back, into the dark tangle of Coke cans, mashed food, and little stray shoes. As he started the car, grinding the engine, she barely heard, behind them, a little child's voice, "A cat, Mama . . . a cat chasing . . ." He took off with a squeal of rubber, the concrete roof passing over them, but at the entrance he slowed, easing sedately out of the covered parking into daylight.

Turning left on the tree-lined highway, she knew he was headed toward the freeway. She braced into the right turn, up onto the south on-ramp as if heading back toward the village. She heard no siren behind them, and there'd been no one in the parking lot to note his frantic flight, no one she'd seen except the woman and three children. She couldn't believe he'd escaped past the running nurses without alarming any of them. Couldn't they see what he'd done? Crouched behind him among the litter of toys, she scared herself thinking she could have been crushed in the slamming ICU door and then in the slamming car door. She scared herself even worse, knowing she was alone with this man whom she'd twice attacked and bloodied, who might do any terrible thing to her if he got his hands on her.

29

EMMYLOU HAD HEADED back to the ICU when Ryan reached down to her backpack, found it empty, and panicked. She stared around the lounge, rose to look behind the two chairs in the corner, behind the other three love seats, all unoccupied, behind the green scheffleras that spread out as lush as small trees. She studied the three loud women down at the end, scanned the shadows around their feet, but there was no darker shape, and why would Kit be there? She looked out to the hall, and with an uneasy feeling she headed for the ICU. She was halfway up the hall when she heard women shouting ahead, heard some kind of alarm go off. She ran, saw someone roll a machine across the ICU to a cubicle on the far side where nurses were crowding in. "He's flat-lined . . ." Two white-coated doctors pushed inside, shouldering Emmylou away where she was stretching up trying to see over the crowding nurses.

"Birely," she was crying, "let me in, let me by." Ryan saw a running man disappear out through the open double doors and—her stomach sank—a dark cat chasing him, leaping through the closing doors behind him. She ran. They disappeared in the direction of the admittance desk, the closing doors clicked together in her face even as she fought to open them. Had they locked down automatically, like prison doors? She remembered a nurse touching the wall earlier, just there where that little black hand was painted. Maybe an electric eye? She hit the wall.

Slowly the doors swung out again, so slowly. She threw her weight against them, squeezed through, raced across the reception room startling a red-coated volunteer pushing an empty wheelchair. Dodging him, she was out through the wide glass doors into the dim underground parking garage, nearly falling over a woman and three children. They stood staring after him, the taller girl pointing and shouting, "A cat! Look, Mama, a cat chasing that man." Tires squealed, she saw Debbie's station wagon pull out fast and then slow as it moved up the ramp, as if the driver didn't want to attract attention. Dodging past the children, racing for the Mercedes, Ryan barely glimpsed the man driving. Whatever he'd done back there had enraged Kit. She had no notion what happened or why he had Debbie's car, only that something violent had occurred and Kit didn't mean to let him get away. Had she leaped inside his car? Yes, a pair of pointed ears were visible for an instant, then gone again. Starting the Mercedes, she followed, glad she didn't have her truck. A red pickup with a ladder on top wasn't so good as a tail. The Suzuki turned onto the freeway. She entered the heavy traffic two cars behind, sliding into a narrow slot. Whatever emergency had brought the nurses running, the patient in trouble had to be Birely Miller, the way Emmylou was yelling.

Was this man Birely's traveling partner? What had he done to Birely? Had he stolen Debbie's car? She tried not to think about Kit in there with him, she could picture her hiding in the back among the children's castoffs, and she was sick with fear for her. She was angry as hell, too. After they'd searched for her half the night up among the cliffs thinking she was dead, why did the crazy little cat have to launch into another crisis? Moving in and out of traffic, changing lanes while following the Suzuki, she was needled by too many questions. Had Kit gone back to the ICU looking for Pedric, seen the commotion, was startled by the cries of distress, saw the man running headlong and guilty, and had impetuously given chase?

Ryan played back Emmylou's talk about Birely that had made her feel sorry for him and would have made Kit pity him, too. Or did Kit already know the man, and maybe know Birely? Was this the man who had broken into Lucinda's house? Kit would know him by smell, if nothing more. She thought about Birely camping in the stone house. Was this his partner? Were they, and the men at the wreck on the cliffs, the same? Was this the man who had hurt Pedric and Lucinda, and who now had apparently hurt Birely? No wonder Kit was angry. Up ahead a car pulled out of her lane moving to the left, and she was right behind the Suzuki. She looked for a lane to dodge into, but already he was watching her, studying her in his rearview mirror, glancing ahead and then back at her. She was still trying to cut into another lane, away from him, when a siren whooped behind her.

She tried to nose over into the right lane to let it pass but horns honked and no one would let her in. Easing precariously near the car on her right, she barely let the emergency van squeeze past, giving her an angry blast of siren. Ahead, the Suzuki managed to swerve across, nearly hitting a blue convertible; tires squealed and a horn blasted as the station wagon spun off onto Carpenter Street. The traffic surged on, bearing her with it, she couldn't get over to turn and follow. By the time she managed to change lanes she was at Ocean. She swung off there, knowing she'd lost him. Nothing ahead of her now but a green panel truck. Taking a chance, she made a right onto a small, wooded street, heading for a tangle of narrow, twisting lanes where it might be easy for the driver of the battered old station wagon to get lost among a maze of similar cars tucked into every narrow drive and wooded crevice. Moving as fast as she dared on the little residential streets, she scanned every side street, every hidden drive, praying for Kit and shaky with fear for her.

ROCKING ALONG IN the back of the station wagon, crouched in between a dozen loaded grocery bags, Kit peered out between them watching the driver. Earlier, coming down the freeway, she'd watched him look repeatedly in the rearview mirror at the cars behind him as if he were being followed. She could only hope he was, and hope it was a cop. She couldn't creep up again to look, he'd be sure to see her—but when he'd swung fast off the freeway almost getting them creamed, she'd glimpsed a silver Mercedes and the driver was a dead ringer for Ryan. But then, screeching off the freeway onto Carpenter, he must have lost her.

Still, though, he checked behind him as he negotiated the narrow and twisting residential lanes, and at last he pulled over onto the shoulder beneath a clump of eucalyptus trees, the car hidden by the overhanging branches of the dense trees in front of the small, crowding cottages.

He must have taken a cell phone from his pocket, must have punched 911, she listened to him describe a silver Mercedes four-door, "Moving south on the freeway," he said, "headed for Ocean or maybe on beyond. A woman driving. Dark, short hair, red sweatshirt. I saw her pick up a man running out of the hospital, looked like he was being chased. I thought . . . Looked like there'd been trouble in there, that maybe he'd robbed someone. He jumped in the backseat of the Mercedes, ducked down so you couldn't see him. The way he acted, I thought maybe you'd be looking for him . . ." He paused, listening.

"A sport coat, I think. Maybe brown, sort of rough . . . like tweed . . ." He listened again, but then abruptly he hung up. Maybe the dispatcher had asked for his name, maybe asked him to stay on the line. He sat looking around him into the wooded neighborhood as if planning what to do next. She wondered if he'd borrowed the car from Debbie, or stolen it? Swiped it before she had a chance to unload her groceries, Kit thought, amused. But when she nosed at the paper bags, she realized they didn't smell like groceries, no scent of cereal boxes or fresh fruit.

Maybe everything was canned, that would be Debbie's style. Feed the kids on cans of soup and beans. She tried not to think about being trapped in there with him, tried not to scare herself. Trapped until he opened the door, or until she opened it herself behind him, fought the handle down, leaped out and ran like hell.

But she wasn't ready to do that, she wasn't finished with him yet, she wanted to know where he was headed. If he'd killed Birely she meant to see him pay one way or another. Maybe he'd hole up somewhere for a while. Then, when he thought he was safe, she could slip out, find a phone, and call the department. She just hoped he didn't take off for good, putting long fast miles between him and the cops—and between her and home.

She wasn't sure why she cared so much that he'd hurt Birely. Except she'd felt bad when they'd found poor Sammie's body, and now it didn't seem fair Sammie's little brother would be murdered, too. Not fair the killer would get away with it, just as Sammie's killer had almost gone free. She didn't like when human criminals didn't pay, she wanted to see them face their accusers and squirm, wanted to see them suffer due consequence. *That's the way the world's supposed to work, that's the right balance*, she thought angrily. *If you have to live among the dregs and put up with their evil ways, then you should see some retribution.*

30

HAVING LOST BIRELY'S attacker, Ryan still didn't call the department. She wanted Kit out of there first, and safe, before the cops descended on him; they wouldn't be polite in taking down a killer, if in fact Birely was dead. They'd run his attacker off the road if they needed to, fire at him, do whatever necessary to take him into custody, and Kit would be right in the middle.

She could keep on cruising the village backstreets looking for the Suzuki among the winding, wooded residential lanes, which would, she thought, be an exercise in futility. Or she could go back to Debbie's, park the Mercedes out of sight, and watch. See if he showed up there—perhaps to return the car, if he hadn't stolen it. If Debbie had let him use it, then did Debbie have a role in this, whatever it was? Was she into more than shoplifting? Ryan thought angrily. Moving on through the village and up the hill, she parked two blocks above Emmylou's on a narrow backstreet roofed over with its giant cypress trees, their lower branches reaching out across the street half covering the Mercedes. Getting out and locking the car, she walked on down to Emmylou's.

The Chevy was still gone, Emmylou would still be at the hospital. Maybe she was being questioned by the police, or maybe she was asking questions of her own. Was she mourning poor Birely now? Ryan wondered. Moving up the back steps, she tried the door but found it locked. She sat down on the top step, in the shadows where she could see down across the street into Debbie's scraggly yard. Into *her* scraggly yard, that Debbie had never bothered to clean up. She could see the full expanse of Debbie's empty drive but no sign of Debbie, no light on in the kitchen. Was Tessa still in there alone, tucked up in bed?

Watching the shadowed bedroom, she began to make out a silhouette, a small figure looking out. As if Tessa were kneeling up on the bed, looking out watchfully at the neighborhood, much as she herself was doing.

She was scanning the empty streets, the empty yards, when Debbie's station wagon came into view slipping slowly along a side street. The driver didn't turn onto Debbie's street, he paused at the corner and then turned, circling back, moving down along a stand of pines. She watched him turn into a narrow, overgrown property two blocks to the south. He pulled down the long, weedy drive to the back, where a one-car garage stood beside the forlorn gray house. Parking at one side of the drive, two wheels on the yellowed grass, he nosed the Suzuki into a pile of scrap lumber, gray with age. The minute he opened the driver's door a dark streak exploded out behind him, fled across the lumber pile and up into a pine tree. Ryan eased back with a sigh of relief. Among the dark foliage, she could barely see Kit slip out onto a branch, to peer down.

Stepping out of the station wagon, the man moved to the old-fashioned garage door and stood fiddling with the lock. She could imagine the hinges rusted, the cracked driveway beneath stained with scrape marks where the old door swung out. With his attention diverted, Ryan moved on down the stairs, had started down the hill, heading in his direction, when she heard the ratcheting squeal of wood on concrete as he eased the door open. Within, beyond the open door, something dark loomed. The hood of a dark car, its lines sleek but its narrow chrome and its headlights dulled as if with dirt; they were the smooth lines of the Lincoln. Snatching her phone from her pocket, she punched in 911.

She ended the call just as fast, clicking off.

She didn't want the law there, taking over the stolen car, declaring it out of bounds to everyone but the department, impounding it for evidence. Not with what was there—what she hoped was still hidden there behind the door panels. Instead, she hit Clyde's number.

When she got no answer she left a message, irritated, and clicked off. Turning away among Emmylou's trees, she headed back to the Mercedes, through the overgrown yards. Slipping in behind the wheel, she hoped he wouldn't hear the engine start, or would think it was just some neighbor pulling out. Easing down the street and onto his street, she couldn't see the garage now, it was on the other side of the forlorn gray cottage; not until she was level with the house did it come into view again.

As she turned into the drive, the dropping sun was in her eyes, it was hard to see inside past the Lincoln. She could sense him watching her, as if maybe he stood deeper in, where the shadows were dense. Letting the engine idle, she hit Clyde's number again.

Still no answer. She eased on down the drive toward the garage, glancing up toward the pine tree where Kit crouched among the thin branches. *Stay put, Kit, just stay where you are.* He came out of the garage fast, heading for her car as if he meant to jerk the door open. She didn't kill the engine, she let it idle. As she hit the master lock she dropped the phone, felt frantically along the seat for it. When she looked again he had moved to the edge of the drive. She watched him grab up a short length of two-by-four, and turn. He came at her fast, swinging at the window, his pale eyes flat and mean. She ducked, fishing under the seat for some weapon, maybe a wrench left by one of the mechanics. She found nothing, but then scrabbling deeper she found the phone. He swung his makeshift club, and she covered her face. The window shattered, crazing into a pattern like snowflakes. She gunned the engine, put it in gear, gave it the gas again as if to back away from him up the drive.

Instead she sent the Mercedes leaping forward, braking only as her front bumper rammed the back of the Town Car, solidly blocking it. He came at her again, striking at the broken window, glass flew around her in a cascade of particles. He hit it again and reached through, grappling for the lock. She snatched up the phone, brought the end of it down hard on his wrist. He yelped and drew back and then lunged at the door. He had reached in, grabbing for her, when darkness exploded from above him from the roof—and the world was filled with cats, a tangle of clawing, screaming cats.

EARLIER IN THE day, having searched the neighborhood for the Lincoln, Joe and Pan had given up at last and headed away into the village. Their fur smelled of juniper bushes, every garage they'd investigated stunk with overgrown foliage crowding its old walls. Where they'd been able to find a thin crack beneath a tight-fitting door, they'd detected only the smells of empty oil cans, caked dirt, and mice. When they'd leaped up at dirty garage windows they'd seen nothing within but a broken chair, old cardboard boxes filled with who knew what refuse, and a rat-eaten couch, the cotton stuffing leaking out across the concrete. They'd searched for the Lincoln until both were cranky and hissing at each other, then they hit the rooftops hoping to see the Town Car parked on some farther-off, out-of-the-way lane. But soon, growing discouraged even with that futile effort, they simply ran, working off their accumulated frustration. In the center of the village they raced up the stairs of the courthouse clock tower, to the parapet high above.

Leaping to the rail, they had prowled along it looking down at the rooftops and crowded streets, focusing on each long black car they spotted, but knowing that this, too, was an exercise in futility. They were circling the rail yet again when Dulcie came racing up the stairs, looking up at them. She paused on the little tile balcony.

"There's been a murder," she said, "at the hospital. Those men staying up behind Emmylou's, looks like one killed the other. Killed him right there in the ICU. Emmylou'd found the one man hurt, lying in that stone house behind her place, she called the ambulance and . . ."

The two toms dropped down to the tiles beside her, giving her their full attention.

"Pedric heard it all from Emmylou when they took him back to the ICU before they moved him to his new room. He got a glimpse of the man from his gurney, he was just being tucked up in bed again when the whole place exploded in an uproar and Pedric saw him running out. Pedric swore the guy was wearing his sport coat, the tweed one. He and Emmylou called Lucinda, she called and told Wilma, and I came to find you. Emmylou said Ryan ran out chasing the guy, that a nurse just coming back from her break saw them, she knew Ryan, she said the man took off in a battered brown station wagon. Debbie's car? The nurse said Ryan chased him in a silver Mercedes, I don't know where she got that car but the nurse swore it was Ryan. If he has Debbie's car and goes back there, and Ryan follows him there, if that's where he was headed, and Ryan's all alone . . ."

"Come on," Joe said. He leaped down the stairs hitting every fourth step, but halfway down the last flight, before he hit the street, he sailed onto the adjoining roof. The three cats, racing away over the peaks, their heads filled with questions, made straight across the village and up the hill toward Debbie's hoping he *was* going there, where they could help Ryan if she needed help, and where they could summon the law. They were a block from Debbie's cottage when they saw, between the pines, Kit crouched on the edge of a roof looking over, precarious and intent.

Leaping the chasms between cottages, they gained the roof beside her, to the accompaniment of breaking glass below as the man in the tweed coat swung his crude club, then yelped and drew back, then lunged at the door, reaching in grabbing for Ryan. The cats sprang, exploding down on him in a whirlwind of teeth and claws.

He twisted, shouting and flailing, and dropped the two-by-four. Fighting them off, reaching down for it, he lost his balance. Ryan was out of the car, pounding at him. He went down under her blows. She snatched the two-by-four away, and kicked him in the groin. He curled into a ball, whimpering. She yelled at the cats to back off, but Kit kept at him, raking and biting, she stopped only when Ryan pulled her away, forcing her clinging claws out of his arm.

Kneeling, Ryan held the end of the two-by-four hard against his throat as she frisked him. He looked at the four cats crowding over him growling, their teeth bared, and he lay still. She had pulled two packets of hundred-dollar bills from his pockets, stuffing them into the front of her zipped jacket, when he struck out again, hit Ryan in the face, and struggled to his feet. He ran—but not to the Lincoln, it was useless to him, blocked by Ryan's car. He headed for the station wagon, jerked the door open, Ryan could see the keys dangling in the ignition. She grabbed

Kit away as he swung in. Clutching Kit, she moved away fast as he gunned the engine, dodging the car as it shot backward burning rubber, careened the length of the drive, racing backward into the street, and took off.

Ryan held Kit tight against her, both of them shaking with rage. He was gone, but the Lincoln was safe. Her heart pounding, Ryan flipped open her phone.

This time, Clyde answered. "Sorry," he said, "I was talking to the supplier, he thought he had the part, but he doesn't."

"You're at the shop?"

"Just leaving."

"I'm a couple of blocks south of the cottage, down from Debbie's. Old gray house with the garage way at the back? Can you bring me those two tools your body guys use, to take the panels off a car door?"

"You found the Lincoln."

"We did."

"You okay?"

"Fine," she said.

"You call the department?"

"Not until you bring the tools."

"On my way."

"Pick up some gloves," she said.

He laughed, and hung up. It wasn't twenty minutes until he pulled into the drive in her king cab. The cats, crowding into the dim garage behind them, peered up into the Lincoln as Clyde, putting on a pair of cotton gloves to prevent leaving fingerprints, removed the door panels. Lifting them off one at a time and reaching in, he began to remove the small white boxes, and he lifted out the little plastic containers of coins, too, all tightly sealed. Ryan placed each item carefully in a stained paint bucket that she'd taken from the back of her truck.

But it was Joe and Pan together who, leaping up into the backseat of the Lincoln, rooting among the tightly packed bundles, found the scent of the old musty bills. Sniffing at bolts of fabric, at boxes and bags scented of far places, the two tomcats rooted down under the Greenlaws' diverse and expensive purchases, and came up grinning.

"Try here," Joe told Clyde.

Pulling packages away until he was able to examine the center console beneath, Clyde pulled down the armrest, revealing the small black tray with its cell phone connections.

"There," Joe said, sniffing at the small square hole in the front. "Musty. The money's there. Take the screws out." Already Ryan was headed for the truck. She returned with a Phillips screwdriver, which she handed to Clyde. He unscrewed the tray and lifted it out.

There it was, the rest of the money, thick packets of hundreds stuffed tightly into the small space. He handed them out to Ryan, she packed them in the stained bucket atop the little boxes, filling it to the dented edge. Turning away to the king cab, she locked the bucket in one of the metal tool compartments along the side, arranging heavy coils of electric drop cords in front. Only then, locking the compartment, did she call the dispatcher.

She told Mabel they'd found the Greenlaws' stolen Lincoln, and gave her the location. But as they talked, she watched Kit and Pan, up on the roof again sitting near but not looking at each other, both staring away into space—

looking as if they *wanted* to make up, but both still too stubborn. She could see only a touch of Kit's superior "I'm right, you're wrong" expression. Pan, though he glanced sideways at Kit, sat tall and macho, still with a "I'm not changing my mind" look in his amber eyes. Both cats so hardheaded, Kit refusing to understand Pan's hunger for new adventure, Pan just as obstinate, wanting Kit to thrill to *his* view of the world. Neither cat, even after their bold and concerted attack on the thief, willing to understand the other. And Ryan could only watch, disappointed with them both.

31

KIT LAY SPRAWLED on the dining table among the last pieces of jewelry that Kate and Lucinda had not tucked away in one bank or another, the gold and sapphires and emeralds reflecting bright shafts of light where the setting sun slanted in through the oak trees. With a soft paw she patted at the brooches and pendants, feeling like a queen counting her wealth, though it wasn't hers at all. Lucinda was in the bedroom napping, Kate in the kitchen making a light supper, filling the house with the scent of grilled cheese on rye and herb tea.

It had taken Ryan and Clyde only a few minutes, yesterday, to strip the jewelry and money out of the Lincoln before they called the department, before the police were all over the car, lifting fingerprints, taking blood samples, and impounding the vehicle itself for closer inspection. But it had taken the two women all this morning and most of the afternoon to rent seven safe deposit boxes, each requiring them to open an accompanying bank account, to take the necessary cards and papers up to Pedric at the hospital to sign, and then return them to the banks. And then at last to retrieve the treasure from the Greenlaws' padlocked freezer and tuck it securely away where, they hoped, the banks would keep the gold and jewels safe.

It was last evening after the police arrived to meet Ryan and Clyde at the small garage and go over the Lincoln, that Kit had trotted home shaky from their attack on Vic, and had made a follow-up call to the department. Talking to Max Harper himself, she had laid out in every smallest detail Vic's murder of Birely Miller there in the hospital. She had hung up abruptly, of course, when Max asked for her name, as he always asked. Both knew he didn't expect an answer to that question. Secrets upon secrets, she thought, pawing at the mysterious jewelry, and smiling.

Kate and Lucinda, after finishing with the banks, had kept back just this handful of antique pieces that lay scattered around her, now, each one featuring a cat or some mythical creature in its design. Patting at those Netherworld images, Kit thought about Pan's hunger for that world, and she wondered if he would go there without her. But, then she wondered, would his attachment to Tessa keep the tomcat from leaving, after all?

That very morning when Ryan returned to Debbie's, to put in the faucet herself, Tessa had whispered to her all about the man with the black car. It was the morning after the cats' attack on Vic, and Tessa had told Ryan all about that, too, she had seen it all from the window above her bed. She had, much earlier in the day, seen him hide the Lincoln, too. The child had seen more than anyone guessed. "I didn't tell Mama," she whispered.

"Why didn't you?" Ryan had asked her.

"She'd say I was lying. I'm not, that's what I saw, that's what happened. My Pan and those other three cats attacked that man to save you. My Pan is back," she had said, smiling. "But, where is he now? When will he come to live with me again, to be my cat again?"

To that, Ryan had no answer.

No one owns a cat, and yet Kit knew that Pan, in his secret spirit, was indeed Tessa's cat, just as Tessa was his person. *Maybe*, she thought, *maybe Pan will stay here for Tessa, if he won't stay for me.*

But how will I feel about that? she thought, and she wasn't sure.

She lay watching as Kate set the table around her, arranging the jewelry in a wicker basket that she put on the buffet. Kit watched her bring in the teapot and cups, watched her go to call Lucinda and help her get up; Lucinda's cast was heavy and cumbersome, and was tiring to haul around. Walking out with Lucinda, Kate seated her in her own chair and brought in the sandwiches, steaming hot and oozing pale cheese with slices of salami peeking out.

Kate cut Kit's sandwich in small bites and set the plate on Kit's own place mat. Over supper they talked about Pedric's knee surgery, a noninvasive laser technique that was scheduled for early the next morning; they discussed Birely Miller's simple burial, which would also take place in the morning. Not until after supper did Kate read to them from her mother's diary, from the later pages that she had found hidden among the moldering Netherworld volumes in the library of a fallen palace, the long passage disconnected from whatever the previous pages had told, from whatever had gone before or after those faded lines.

> . . . *all along. We have done our best to battle the royal families that would bring this world down. Inconceivable that the very rulers who benefit most from the labor of the peasants are now destroying their only source of food and goods, of the labor to produce what they need. Hatred, not logic, drives them. Hatred and greed. An evil drives them that comes straight from the hell pit and, in the end, will drag them down into the pit themselves. Soon we must get the baby out of here, must make the journey up into the surface world and find a home for Kate. I pray our one friend there, with Netherworld connections, can watch over her until she's grown. Will there be any Netherworld left, when Kate is grown? I cannot bear to leave her, but we must return here and rejoin the battle, we must keep fighting.*

There Melissa's journal pages ended, the last page torn at the bottom as if whatever came after had been ripped away. "Maybe buried somewhere among the rubble of the palace," Kate said, "buried in a world where no one reads books anymore or hardly knows what they're for.

"Do you remember, Kit, the year I was given that other jewelry, by the old lawyer, the pieces he'd held so long for me in his office safe? That big old walk-in safe, the box hidden way at the back containing my mother's journal, too? Do you remember how excited you were when you first learned of another world, how you had dreamed of such a place?"

"I remember," Kit said quietly. "But that world was bright and happy, not crumbled and cold, it was not a dead world, then."

Kate said, "You remember, Lucinda."

Lucinda said, "Most of the earlier entries in your mother's journals were bright. There was destruction even then, failure of the magic, but the world still held much of wonder. That was only the beginning, the failure of that magic that your parents tried so hard to prevent."

Supper ended in sadness, which none of them had intended. Kate rinsed the dishes, and they sat for a long while in the living room before the fire, Kit curled in Lucinda's lap. She looked up often at Kate, still caught and grieving in the remains of that sad world where her parents had died.

BIRELY MILLER'S FUNERAL, early the next morning, was indeed simple, only a few words spoken by a funeral director who had never known Birely nor, if he had, would have approved of him. A few words and then without further ceremony Birely's casket was lowered into the ground next to the grave of his sister, Sammie. Only a handful of people attended: Max and Charlie Harper, the Damens, Emmylou Warren, and Kate Osborne. Lucinda was at the hospital with Pedric. Those were the human mourners, if one could call their solemn attendance a kind of mourning. The five cats sat at attention, exhibiting varied degrees of pity, sat concealed behind a headstone featuring the image of a praying angel with lifted wings. Six humans and five cats silently attending Birely Miller's last contact with the souls of this world. The day had turned heavy, with a wet, gray overcast that made the women's hair curl willfully, and made the cats lick their fur to try to dry it. What Joe Grey wondered, as he watched Emmylou drop a handful of dirt onto the casket, was, *Where's Birely's old uncle buried, old train robber Lee Fontana? Where did he end up, carrying with him the secret of that final robbery—escaping without restitution and most likely without remorse?*

But maybe now Fontana would make restitution of a kind more valuable than the U.S. courts demanded. Emmylou, like Kate and the Greenlaws, had decided to give some of her newfound wealth to CatFriends, their local rescue group that Ryan and Charlie and a raft of volunteers had helped to start. Money to pay for cat food and supplies, to pay Dr. Firetti, who so far had donated all his services and all the needed medications. There'd be money, too, to build a central shelter where volunteers could care for the abandoned animals that were brought to them. Joe thought about the starving cats the group had trapped when, at the first downturn in the economy, so many householders left their homes with back rent or mortgages overdue, and left their pets behind.

What would Lee Fontana think of this use of his stolen money? Maybe, from the stories Misto told of Fontana—if Joe could bring himself to believe Misto's tales—maybe the old train robber would like that choice just fine. If the old yellow cat *had* been Fontana's ghostly confidant as Misto liked to say, guiding Fontana safely through his self-inflicted troubles, then Fontana must have a warm place in his spirit for a cat, maybe he'd be pleased and amused by his unwitting gift to catdom.

VIC HAD FLED from Ryan badly shaken by the attack of the cats. Headed for open country, he had parked the Suzuki on the berm of the narrow dirt road, as far under a drooping willow tree as he could get it without tilting over into the drainage ditch; the willow was already shedding its small yellow leaves down onto the hood and, in the light evening breeze, its stringy branches dragged back and forth across the metal, scraping annoyingly. It was nearly dark inside the car, shaded by the tree and with the windows blocked by his makeshift curtains; bright-colored cashmere sweaters with their store tags attached hung down from the two lowered visors, and along the driver's side he'd secured a blue sweater into the crack of the rolled-up window. He sat sprawled in the back where he had pushed the clutter aside, no room to put the backseat up, the whole seat was in one piece, but at least the resultant platform was low, giving him some headroom. He sat bare to the waist, his bloodied shirt wadded up, the ripped tweed sport coat already discarded, resting ten miles back in the trash can of a FastMart where he'd stopped for a dry sandwich, some salve for the scratches, a bag of corn chips, and a Coke.

He'd parked, for that quick shopping trip, at the back of

the FastMart building among some scraggly trees. That area up along Molena Valley road was a mix of scattered fields, sad old houses and new ones, pastures with horses, scraggly woods, weedy unused land all mixed together. He'd got in and out of FastMart as quickly as he could, keeping his head down just a little and the collar of his ripped coat turned up. He'd bought a brown sweatshirt, too, off a rack by the refrigerator. There'd be a BOL out on him, with Birely lying dead back there and probably, by this time, Debbie Kraft hollering up a fuss that her old car'd been stolen.

Leaving FastMart after making his purchases, a café two doors down had smelled so good he'd been tempted to chance it, go on in there for a hot meal. But even as he paused, looking down that way thinking about scrambled eggs and potatoes and sausage, wondering if it was worth the risk, a pair of sheriff's cars pulled up right in front, couple of deputies got out, moved into the restaurant hardly looking around them. Mid-morning snack, he guessed. They didn't glance his way, didn't make the Suzuki or they'd have skipped their meal and come after him. As soon as they disappeared inside he'd hightailed it to the Suzuki and got on out of there. As he turned out onto the two-lane highway a cat ran across, he gunned the car but missed it. He'd like to cream every damn cat he saw, his back still stung like holy hell. He'd driven on watching the side roads, looking for a place to get out of sight, to stop and smear some of the salve on, see if that would help. He wasn't far from Molena Point, maybe only ten miles, he knew he should get on over the grade to Highway 68, head for Salinas and onto the faster freeway.

But then again, maybe not. Maybe not hit the freeway until full dark when the cops couldn't make him so easy. Maybe hole up until then close to the village where they wouldn't think to look for him. Lay low for a few hours and then move on. He could use some sleep, catch a couple hours before he headed for the 101, if he planned to drive all night. Up through Eureka, on up to Bremerton, he knew a guy up there he could stay with, place way back in the boonies. Dump the Suzuki, pick up some decent wheels.

Now, bending awkwardly, he smeared salve on his bare back, on the scratches and bite wounds. Damn friggin' cats jumping down on him like that, as vicious as that cat up at the wreck. He never had liked cats, sneaky and mean. The bloody wounds stung, but then in a few minutes the salve began to ease the pain and burning. And why would that cat *chase* him, there in the parking garage? Dark, ugly cat, just like the others. He'd never have seen it except for that kid shouting. He'd got one glimpse of the cat racing across the concrete right at him, piled in the car, slammed the door, and when he looked back the damn thing was gone. Shivering, he'd started the engine and peeled out of there, then slowed so as not to call attention to himself.

And then when that contractor woman got in his way blocking the Lincoln and them cats jumped him for no reason. Twice attacked by cats, and chased by another one. Spooky as hell, still made him sick to think about it, unnatural, bloodthirsty beasts. Pulling the brown sweatshirt on over his salve-smeared wounds, he lay down in the space he had cleared. The bed of the station wagon was hard as hell. He pulled an old, torn blanket over him that smelled of peanut butter and sweaty kids. He wondered if Debbie had ever had the backseat down all the time she'd owned the heap. The sun had set now, the car dim under the tree and under his jerry-rigged curtains. He lay there a long time, he didn't sleep until heavy darkness drew in around him.

32

IT WAS EARLY evening, nearly eight hours since Pedric's knee surgery. He sat up in bed, a blue cotton robe pulled over his skimpy hospital gown, his bandaged leg propped up on two pillows. The general anesthetic had worn off. The bandage around his head had been removed. The red scar across his forehead looked raw but clean, the four stitches standing out like four little fly legs, Kit thought. Bruises still marked his forehead and down his cheek, but his short gray hair was neatly trimmed and brushed, and he looked bright, happy to have his surgery over with. Kate sat on a built-in day-bed by the window, Lucinda sat in a folding metal chair beside Pedric's bed, holding his hand with her good, right hand, comfortable to be close to him.

The room was spacious and quiet, a great improvement from the crowded little cubicle in the noisy ER. The view through the wide wall of glass had sent Kit bolting to the windows, forgetting that a nurse or orderly might come barging in. She had returned only later to Pedric's amused embrace—he was mending, he was safe and happy and she loved him, but right now she wanted to be out there in the amazing garden that rose up the hill just beyond the glass.

The two huge windows were framed by heavy white pillars jutting out into the room, part of the superstructure of the strongly built hospital. The big garden beyond was softly lit, and was enclosed at some distance by the glass walls of the three-story hospital. Kit crouched on the wide sill, her nose to the glass, her heart lost to the garden, to its cascading waterfall that tumbled down beneath the trees and past the flowering shrubs. Bright plashes of water fell and were lost within the rough escarpment of granite blocks—giant, rough-cut stones piled one on another, towering high above her looking as natural as nature's own casual toss of rocky elements; the water fell down the stone in clear cascades, she wanted to dabble her paw in, to splash at the little pond below where the last rays of the sun reflected, she wanted to leap up the rocks, race up the little trees, she wanted to play out there in that small Eden.

The big windows were fixed in place, there was no way to open them. It would not be until later, as night fell, that Kit would discover, down beyond the end pillar, a narrow, hinged pane with a hinged screen and with handles that would open both. Now, Pedric watched her from his bed and watched the closed door, wary of a nurse's intrusion. Kit would find the opening later, he thought, smiling, find it sometime in the dark hours and would slip out there in a wild bid for freedom just as Alice had once finessed her way through the first locked door into Wonderland. Watching her, he and Lucinda exchanged an indulgent smile.

This was Lucinda's third journey out of the house since they'd arrived home, but she was pale still and felt weak. Yesterday's banking transactions had tired her, as had standing for even that short time at Birely's funeral. The aftermath of the wreck and attack, the theft of their car and the intrusion into their home, had left her feeling incredibly fragile and vulnerable, quite unlike herself. But now, with Pedric's surgery behind them, the torn meniscus in his right knee repaired, and with his head injuries healing, she was beginning to feel easier. Pedric's blood work showed normal levels of sugar, the swelling in his brain had subsided, and he would come home in the morning. The anticipation of having him home so lifted her spirits that when Max Harper and Charlie knocked at the door and peered in, Lucinda's smile was bright and she was filled with questions.

Both the Harpers were dressed in jeans, boots, frontier shirts, and smelled comfortably of horses. Maybe Max had taken off early, and they'd had a late-afternoon ride. Even before the tall couple stepped in, Kit had hidden herself in the carryall, not sure what Max would think of her there. She peered out for one look as Kate tucked an edge of the brocade down, hiding her from the police chief.

Charlie's curly red hair was tied back with a leather thong. Leaning over the bed, she hugged Pedric. "Glad the surgery's over with, and that it went so well."

Max grinned down at Pedric. "Glad all this mess about the car is pretty much over, too. We've impounded it at Clyde's place, locked up in one of the back shops. As soon as forensics finishes, Clyde's crew will clean it up and start work on the scratches and dents. Forensics will be going over your packages, too, for fingerprints and to see if any stolen items are mixed in with your own things." He looked at Lucinda. "Could you give us an inventory, and then come down later, to identify what's there? Make sure it's all yours, and maybe go through some of the packages?"

Lucinda nodded.

"Clyde thinks the blood stains should come out of the leather all right," Max said. "He hopes not to have to reupholster. Blood type matches Birley's blood in the wrecked pickup, and that on the sleeping bag up at Emmylou's place. Forensics has particles of paper from the old bills, from the cubbyhole beneath the back console where Ryan and Clyde found Emmylou's money."

There had, in the end, been no way for Emmylou to avoid reporting the stolen money, reporting at least part of it when forensics found part of a torn wrapper and two musty hundred-dollar bills that had slipped down among the packages. Emmylou had told Max the money was hers, that it had been left to her by Sammie with the house, and had given Max a copy of the will, leaving her, "All contents within the house or on the property," and she had told him about Sammie's letter. Some recluses were like that, Max had said, guy lived in poverty all his life, he died and was discovered to have been worth several million, usually with a handwritten will leaving it all to a favorite charity, Salvation Army or animal rescue or a church that had been kind to him.

Pedric said, "Birely Miller is dead, but no sign of the other man, of Vic Amson?"

"Not yet," Max said. "We have a BOL out on him. He's wanted for Birely's murder, for his attack on you two, for theft of your vehicle, and leaving the scene of the wreck. There are several old warrants for him, including a person of interest in a murder over in Fresno.

"Both Vic and Birely have records," Max said. "Though Birely's didn't amount to much, most of his offenses the result of overenthusiastic bad judgment. Going along with one pal or another, and then left holding the bag. Acting as lookout during a gas station robbery, and he's still sitting there watching for cops when the other guy slips away. By the time Birely realizes he's all alone, two sheriff's deputies are pulling in, to cuff him and book him. Maybe just born a loser," Max said with a shrug. "Poor guy just couldn't get it together."

"If Vic Amson escaped in Debbie Kraft's car," Lucinda said, "then was she involved with them?"

"Not sure, yet," Max said. "Except for what we know from the child." He smiled. "Debbie's little girl ratted her out."

"Vinnie?" Lucinda said, surprised.

"No, Tessa. The little, quiet one. Detective Garza stopped by the house, wanted Debbie to come down to the station to file a report on her missing car. She'd made enough fuss about it, called the department three times since she reported it stolen, wanting to know if we'd found it yet, demanding faster action. Said we'd have to furnish her a loaner, claimed it wasn't her fault the car was stolen," he said, smiling. "Said that was due to our failure in protecting her property.

"In fact," he said, "street patrol was about to haul her in, the day she reported her car missing. Brennan had been watching her, off and on, but he was reluctant to come down on her because of the kids, with their daddy already in prison."

"What did you tell her when she said you owed her a loaner?" Pedric asked, grinning.

"What I told her," Max said, "isn't recorded in the department memos."

Lucinda laughed. "But little Tessa, what did that shy, silent little child say? I can't imagine her speaking up and defying her mother."

"She said quite a lot. Debbie was reluctant to ask Dallas in, finally offered him a chair, in the kitchen. She was making up excuses why she couldn't come into the station, when Tessa came out of the bedroom, sniffling, bundled up in an old pair of oversized pajamas, maybe her sister's. She looked up at Dallas, and sniffled, and for some reason, she took to him. Came right to him, climbed up in his lap, snuggled right up to him. Maybe because her mother was being rude to him, maybe the kid didn't like that.

"She told Dallas her momma loaned that man her car, and that Debbie had made him put all the stolen clothes in there before he took it. Debbie tried to shut her up, said there were no stolen clothes, wanted to know where she got that idea, said, why would she have stolen clothes? She told Tessa she had it wrong, that it was the car that was stolen, not clothes. Said, 'You know that. You've got yourself all mixed up.'

"Tessa might be a quiet little thing," Max said, "but not this morning. This morning she had her back up. I guess when she wants to let you see it, she does have a mind of her own."

Maybe with Pan's coaching, Kit thought, listening unseen, her whiskers curved in a satisfied smile.

"When Tessa said her momma gave the man her car, she pointed away across the neighborhood. 'Drove down to *that* house,' she said, pointing straight in the direction of the gray house where we found the Lincoln. Dallas could see she wanted to say more, but Debbie pulled her off his lap and hauled her back into the bedroom."

From outside in the hall they could hear the clink of metal on metal as the dinner trays were delivered, and the smell of boiled beef and overcooked vegetables seeped in under the door.

"If they pick Victor up," Pedric said, "you have proof enough to hold him, proof he killed Birely?" Pedric rubbed gently at his knee, as if it were beginning to hurt now that the local anesthetic had worn off.

"We have Vic's fingerprints from the rubber-glove dispenser in the adjoining room," Max said. "Particles of cinnamon and sugar icing on the edge of the dispenser and on the floor under it. Sugar and cinnamon scattered across Birely's blanket, where Vic punched him in the belly. Vic might have been wearing gloves, but he didn't think to brush off his clothes, to get rid of the crumbs down his front.

"Dallas talked with the volunteers who work in the cafeteria. Two of the women remembered Amson, from our description. When Dallas took them the mug shots, once we'd run the prints and got photos, they gave us a positive ID. They said they don't serve anything there with cinnamon icing except for their cinnamon buns. They had a couple of stale ones from the day before, and forensics has those.

"And that fits in with the phone tip," Max said. "That's not admissible evidence in court, and we don't know who she is, but—"

"A phone call?" Kate said innocently. Maybe, she thought, if no one asked, Max would wonder why they didn't. Beside her, Lucinda and Pedric had stiffened only a little.

Max said, "The woman described Victor, said she saw him punch Birely. Said before he hit him, he was fiddling with the IV tube, bending it, that he had a syringe, looked as if he meant to pierce the tube, plunge the needle in. Said suddenly he dropped the needle as if something had changed his mind. Instead he pulled back his fist, landed Birely a real hard one in the stomach, and ran. She said the dials went flat, alarms went off, he passed the nurses yelling at them to help the patient, ran straight through the crowding nurses shouting for someone to help Birely, and not one of them thought to nail him."

It was just another anonymous call, Kit thought, *no different than any other, and we do have ID blocking, Pedric checks it every week to make sure it's working. Just another phantom tip*, she thought nervously, *even if I was still shaky and mad, after jumping Vic, and even if I did almost* yowl *into the phone! Well, not exactly a yowl.*

"And we have one witness," Max said, "who was in the parking garage, who saw Vic burst out through the glass doors, running. After she got home, she caught the murder on the local TV, and she called in. Said she and her kids were just going inside, into the ER to see her sister, when a man ran out, nearly ran over them. She described Vic, described Debbie's station wagon, saw him pile into it and take off. Dispatcher who took the call, she said the woman seemed to have more to say, but then she changed her mind. She was reluctant to leave her name and number, but Mabel talked her into it." Max shook his head. "People afraid to get involved. Can't say I blame them, sometimes."

On the windowsill, Kit breathed easier. She'd gone rigid, thinking that woman would have described the whole chase. She guessed the great cat god *was* watching, to stop her from mentioning the cat or her kids' excited shouts. *Maybe that upset her, to see an angry cat chasing a running man. Maybe she didn't want to talk about that and come out sounding like a nutcase,* Kit thought, smiling. And maybe the great cat god was smiling, too.

33

I<small>T WAS FULL</small> night when two hobos, dressed in dark clothes and bearing heavy backpacks, had come walking down the winding grade that cut through from Highway 68 down onto Molena Valley Road. As they turned right onto the shoulder of the dark two-lane, the light of a half-moon illuminated the surrounding bushes and trees as if ragged and ghostly figures were watching them in the night. Heading west along the dirt shoulder, moving in the direction of the ocean some twelve miles beyond, they watched for a deserted side road, somewhere to get off the highway and camp for the night, maybe a denser woods than these scraggly, stunted oaks, or maybe some deserted old house or barn where sheriff's deputies wouldn't come nosing around to hassle them.

They'd parted from the slat-sided farm truck they'd hitched a ride in, up at the top of the grade, the driver hauling crates of chickens, coming over from Salinas. Truck stunk real bad of caged chickens, the smell still clung to them—or maybe it was the dead chicken they carried, dangling by its feet. Riding in the back in the truck bed, they'd slid open the nearest crate, hauled out an old brown hen and wrung her scrawny neck, her squawks hidden by the rattle of the truck's old engine and loose body. Now, by the time they'd hoofed it down the grade, they had their dinner already bled, cleaned, and plucked.

The narrow road was dark as hell, no car lights streaming by, no houselights off to the sides, and none of them fancy overhead vapor lights out here in the boonies to pick them out moving along the blacktop. In their dark old clothes, they were part of the night itself, blending into the hill that rose steeply on their right. Half a mile down, they crossed the two-lane and stepped off into the shadows of the berm, moving along beneath another stand of scraggly trees. When they came on a battered station wagon sitting there on the berm, they stopped to look it over, watching for movement within.

Nothing stirred beyond the dark, partially covered windows. They approached warily, with a keen and predatory interest. The oddly shaped curtains blocked their view through the windshield and through the driver's window. They tried the doors but they were locked. Cupping their hands to peer into the back, they couldn't make out much more than a long, dark lump in the darkness, a bundle of some kind, but then they snickered and pressed their ears to the glass.

"Guy asleep in there, snoring. Dead to the world."

"Here, hold the chicken. Hell, don't lay it down, you

want gravel in our supper?" Slinging off his pack, the taller man reached down into it and fished out a long, heavy wire that he kept in the side pocket, a carefully re-cycled coat hanger fashioned for just such emergencies. Hauling a flashlight from his coat pocket, he shielded its light, moved to the driver's window, peered down where the beam led, and got to work.

DEEPLY ASLEEP IN the car, Vic's dreams carried him through scattered stirrings from a bumbling childhood, as his father moved them all from one small town to another, one sorry job to another, one miserable grammar school to another. His father was sometimes absent altogether, while he did a short stint in some two-bit jail, but mostly he was traveling, dragging the nine kids and wife behind him like cans tied to a stray dog. The dreams were always the same, of a sorry and muddled past without shape and without hope. Maybe it was the scuff of footsteps in the gravel outside the Suzuki or maybe the faint scrape of the coat hanger as it slid in through the crack in the window that stirred him, that sent his dreams careening down into the dark nightmare chasm where one twitches and moans and cries out, where one would try to pry himself awake again, if he'd *known* he was asleep.

He woke feeling hands tightening around his throat. This was not part of the dream, cold hands and rough, cold air sweeping in through the open car door, and the ripe stink of an unwashed body and unwashed clothes, and a bright light blazing in his eyes so he couldn't see.

"You got money, hand it over." The guy had his knee on the blanket, gouging into his ribs, leaning his body full over Vic, close and threatening.

"I got no money. If I had money, would I be sleeping in this heap?"

The other door opened, second guy flashed the beam over the mess of broken toys. "Where's your woman and kids?"

"I got no woman and kids. I borrowed the car." He had no weapon handy, either. He'd been asleep, for Christ's sake, peacefully minding his own business—and with what little money he had left, that that contractor woman hadn't found, tucked deep in his pants pocket. He should have hid it better before he went to sleep but he'd wanted it on him in case the cops showed up and he had to leave the car, make a run for it. He tried to sit up, tried to push the guy's clutching hands away from him, and it was then that he saw the knife. The guy with the flashlight had a switchblade in his other hand, the knife open and gleaming.

"Take the car if you want," Vic begged. He fished in his pocket for the keys then knew he shouldn't have done that, maybe the guy thought he had a weapon. The knife flashed in the beam, he felt it go into his throat, it went in so easy, like slicing butter. He felt nothing more for a minute, then pain exploded. He heard himself screaming and then he couldn't scream. He felt the blood bubbling up and he couldn't breathe . . .

Vic's own scream was the last sound he ever heard, the last sound he would ever make. He lay dead in the backseat of Debbie Kraft's battered Suzuki. Blood spurted for a minute more and then stopped, his heart no longer pumping. The bleeding subsided to a dribble like a faulty tap, and stopped. He lay in his own blood, his own bodily wastes seeping out as his killer picked up the dead chicken from the front seat, and fished in Vic's pocket for the car keys.

BEFORE ANYONE KNEW of Victor's death, the cats waited hopefully for the law to pick him up, for a sheriff or the CHP to spot the Suzuki and pull Vic over, cuff him, lock him behind bars, and transport him back to Molena Point for arraignment and to stand trial. None of the cats allowed that justice might go awry and that Vic might walk, cats are ever hopeful, they didn't want to think about failures of the U.S. justice system, they expected ultimate punishment for Amson. Maybe it was the cats' expectations, sparked by divine fate, that had prompted Victor's own peers to deal out his retribution, to provide his last judgment in this world, in a far more decisive manner than the law would have done.

But now, at this moment, Kit wasn't thinking of retribution. Having just heard the current police report on Amson, and sure he would soon be apprehended, she smiled with satisfaction but then set those thoughts aside as she sought a way from Pedric's hospital room out to the waterfall.

Max and Charlie Harper had just left, heading back to MPPD where a call had come in from a horse rancher up in the Molena Valley. His teenaged boy, out riding one of the yearling colts, had come on the Suzuki in the dark, the scent of death sharp to the colt's senses so the young horse would not approach the car. Curious, the boy remembered a TV newscaster's description of the Suzuki, and of Amson. He didn't pause to see if Amson was in there, he hurried his horse home and dialed 911. The county dispatcher had routed him through to the sheriff's office and then to MPPD. At once sheriff's deputies had moved in that direction, and now were searching again along the two-lane roads though they had driven that area the night Vic had fled. Kit prayed the sheriff would find Amson and treat him as he deserved. But once she'd wished the worst for him she'd dismissed him and turned her attention to the garden again and to slipping out into it.

Able to prowl the room now that the Harpers had left, she had quickly followed the thin draft of cooler air that teased her from the far end of the room. Padding down to look, she found the narrow window, half concealed beyond the last pillar. Eagerly she set about opening it.

The room lights had been turned low. Lucinda and Kate sat by Pedric's bed, the three of them deep in conversation as Kit slipped up onto the sill, finessed the hinged screen open with a soft paw, and pulled at the window handle. Yes, it flipped up. Pushing the glass out four inches, she was through and out into the night, into the damp and sweet-scented garden.

Beyond the small trees and scattered bushes the hospital building rose up on four sides, some windows dark, soft lights shining in others behind drawn shades. Did sick people prefer privacy over a glimpse of the more fascinating world? Only in Pedric's room were the shades still up, the room as bright as a lighted stage. Pedric in his bed,

Lucinda and Kate huddled close, the three of them lost
in conversation. She smiled at the little tableau, then spun
away, leaping up the rocky escarpment beside the waterfall. Pausing, she patted her paw in the falling water and
then danced away; she spun, she bounced up the rough
ledges to the very top where she crouched in shadow
among the highest crags then raced away again down the
rocks, ducking beneath cascades of falling water and out
the other side, wet and giddy.

She played among the falls for a long time but then
at last came down the escarpment again slowly, stepping
daintily now, dropping from one level down to the next,
quiet and thoughtful—wishing she were not alone. Where
the thinnest sheet of water slid down over a little rocky
cave, she slipped in through the clear curtain, into a small
and secret aerie; looking down into Pedric's room through
the fall of distorting water, feeling her fur grow damper,
she saw Pedric's door swing open.

In the square of brighter light she saw Ryan and Clyde
step inside to join them, they stood by Pedric's bed next
to Kate and Lucinda, Ryan talking excitedly. Clyde had
placed his backpack on the floor, she watched Joe Grey slip
out, heading straight for the windowsill. Leaping up, he
made a dark silhouette looking out into the night, marked
by his white chest and white paws. But another shadow
slipped out, too, and, nose to carpet, he moved across the
floor to the narrower window, where he slid through into
the garden and disappeared among the bushes. Watching
him, she drew back beneath the waterfall and remained
still.

He stood in the darkness of the bushes looking up the

little hill, taking in the wooded glade and the tall rocky escarpment and the bright, falling water. He looked intently at one part of the garden and then the next, scanning each, and lifting his nose to taste the air. Seeking her? Oh, she hoped he was.

At last he moved on, following her scent up the rough stones, up and up he went over the tumbled rocks and down again, leaping a fall of water where she had leaped but then he stopped, looking around.

Did he wonder if she was hiding and sulking, if she was still angry? The water plashing down before her sang softly; its sliding gleam distorted the garden and distorted Pan himself into a phantom image as he stood scenting out.

Suddenly he headed fast straight up the rocks to disappear above her. She listened but heard only falling water; she lay behind her watery curtain, her paws crossed, and then sat up nervously. Where had he gone? Had he given her up and turned away?

He burst in through the falling water, pounced on her like a lion capturing its prey, he cuffed her, boldly laughing. She struggled free and rolled him over and cuffed him good, too, and he let her. Battling and laughing, pushing each other out into the water, they were soon soaked.

"Let up," he said at last, but she didn't. "Let up! Listen! They found Amson."

She stopped battling him. "They got him? He's in jail?"

"No need." Pan smiled. "He's dead. Knife blade through his throat."

"Oh, my," she said. "Who did that? Oh, not Debbie?"

"Not Debbie, but they picked her up, *she's* in jail. Charlie called Ryan and Clyde, and we came over to tell Pedric and Lucinda."

"If Debbie's in jail, what about Tessa?"

"She's fine," Pan said. "She's more than fine, I'll get to that. On the way over, we stopped by Wilma's." Kit imagined the homey scene as they pulled up in front of Wilma's stone house, Pan and Joe galloping through Wilma's deep English garden to the carved front door.

COME IN BEFORE the fire," Wilma said, opening the door, "what can I get you? Coffee? A drink? A snack for you two tomcats?" She bent down to stroke Pan and Joe.

"Nothing," Ryan said. "We can't stay." Joe leaped to the couch beside Dulcie, thinking a small snack wouldn't take much time, but Ryan said, "We're on our way to tell Pedric, we thought you two would want to know."

"What?" Wilma said, pulling back her loose gray hair and tying her plaid robe tighter around her.

"They found Amson," Clyde said. "Sheriff's deputies found him out on Valley Road, dead in Debbie's car, his throat cut. Looks like he was robbed. No other fresh tire tracks on the dirt shoulder, maybe someone traveling on foot, maybe some homeless person. They found grocery sacks in the car full of cashmere sweaters, upscale costume jewelry, new handbags, all with the tags still in place, and all too bulky for a person on foot to carry away."

"They picked Debbie up at home," Ryan said. "Her prints match those on the store tags—from four upscale village shops, and even two small pieces from Melanie's, and their security's pretty tight."

"It'll do Debbie good to cool her heels in jail," Wilma said. "But what about the children?"

"Emmylou has them," Ryan said. "We took the girls up to her, helped her fix them some supper. Left both girls tucked up in Emmylou's bed, Emmylou making up a bed on the couch for herself. Every time Vinnie opened her mouth to sass her, Emmylou scolded her. By the time we left, the kid wasn't saying a word, she'd crawled into bed and curled up around her pillow, real quiet."

"They'll be all right with Emmylou," Wilma said, smiling. Though what the girls' future held, no one could say.

It was after the Damens left, that Wilma returned to the computer to read Dulcie's newest poem, and the lines made her very sad. But one doesn't choose a poem, the poem chooses the writer. Dulcie couldn't help that this one left them both filled with a dark mourning, a strange uneasy balance, tonight, to the sadness of Birely's unfocused life that was now ended, and to their satisfaction that Vic Amson would not torment and hurt anyone else.

> *A shadow in the somber stillness*
> *Sways serenely.*
> *The river in its roaring race*
> *With the waning, woeful wind*
> *Laughs loudly, luxuriously at the loser.*
>
> *A mockingbird, moved by the midnight moon,*
> *Trills tender notes*

To the shadow standing silently now
Before a ruined barbican and bail
Now dead, decayed
Only the devil left within its fallen ranks.

The shadow sways,
Slumps sadly to the dark and hoary ground.
Nothing left but emptiness.
No bird sings now
No castle stands
Where ran the laughing river.

Dulcie herself didn't know what to make of the poem. It just happened, a shadow of the lost Netherworld. Wilma put out the fire, stifling the cheery gas logs, and they tucked up in bed, Dulcie stretched out quietly on her own pillow. "What will happen to the children now? The law won't let Emmylou keep them, an older woman without a husband. And their aunt won't want them."

"If the court lets Debbie out on her own recog," Wilma said, "and then if she gets probation, maybe Emmylou would keep the girls during the day. Debbie will have to get a job, or try to, that will be a condition of her probation." Stroking Dulcie, Wilma smiled. "Tessa would have a little more love in her life, with Emmylou. And Pan would be there for her, too. Emmylou won't throw him out."

"Maybe," Dulcie said, "if Pan has his little girl back where he can be with her, maybe he won't long to travel so far away. He knows Tessa needs him."

"And Kit needs him," Wilma said. "What's that sigh about? What are you thinking?"

"Thinking how strange life is. Still thinking about that dark world where Pan wants to go, so different from our world—and thinking about that long-ago time in *our* world, where Misto once lived, that was so different from today. Two strange and different places," she said, "but each is only part of something bigger. So many centuries, so many chains of life, and each one unique and different. So much we don't know," she said, "and in the end, what's it all about?"

"It's about the *wonders*," Wilma said. "That's what it's about."

Dulcie looked at her, purring.

"Wonder, and joy," Wilma said. "No matter where you are in time or place, joy and wonder are what stand between you and the evil of the world. That, and love, are all we have against our own destruction."

AND AWAY IN the night, in the dark garden, there was wonder, too. Kit and Pan, coming out from beneath the waterfall, sat on a rock away from the mists, licking themselves dry. "Maybe," Pan said, looking around the garden, "maybe *this* world *is* pretty amazing, maybe what Joe Grey says is true."

"What does he say, that pedantic tomcat?"

"That the greatest adventure of all is right here in our world," Pan said, twitching the tip of his tail. "That the biggest thrill of all is to outsmart the bad guys right here, not go chasing off somewhere that's already destroyed and beyond help." He looked deeply at Kit, his amber eyes gleaming. "Maybe Joe's right that it's more fun to work the system right here, take down the bad guys right here. 'Hold the fort,' Joe says, 'and make our own world better.'"

"Maybe," Kit said. "But what if somewhere in the Netherworld, down among those dark caverns, some small portion of those lands did survive undamaged, as Kate thinks might have happened? What if there *is* some small country there that's still strong, some hidden village that managed to escape the dark?"

Pan said nothing. They sat thinking about that. Maybe it was the enchantment of the garden that made everything seem so different tonight, that made them come together in their thoughts, that helped the two resolve their conflict. Sitting close together looking around at the garden and down into Pedric's lighted hospital room watching their human friends, they no longer bristled at each other; they sat thinking about the amazing world around them, and about their roles in it. And when, at last, they returned through the narrow window, their ears were up and they were ready to move on, to trot boldly on into whatever amazements waited, there ahead of them.

SHIRLEY ROUSSEAU MURPHY

CAT STRIKING BACK

978-0-06-112400-6

With the help of two feral locals, Joe, Kit, and Dulcie must thwart a killer using the criminal's powerful fear of cats.

CAT PLAYING CUPID

978-0-06-112398-6

Joe and his friends, Dulcie and Kit, will need to use their powers of feline perception to bring justice to the small town of Molena Point . . . and save Valentine's Day!

CAT DECK THE HALLS

978-0-06-112396-2

A stranger lies dead beneath the village Christmas tree. As they care for the child who may be the shooter's next target, Joe, Dulcie, and Kit realize they're facing their most heartbreaking case yet.

CAT PAY THE DEVIL

978-0-06-057813-8

When Dulcie's human companion, Wilma, disappears, Dulcie and Joe are on the case.

CAT BREAKING FREE

978-0-06-057812-1

When felonious strangers start trapping cats, Joe, Dulcie and Kit know they are the only hope for their imprisoned brothers—and perhaps their whole village.